COMMON CRIMINALS

An East Bay Tale

By Ernie Koepf

ISBN: 978-1-66782-672-1 (print)
ISBN: 978-1-66782-673-8 (eBook)

BookBaby Publishing

Cover composition by Matt Regan.

For John Kennedy Toole and Donald E. Westlake,
who showed me how it is done.

Also, by Ernie Koepf

Opening Day

CONTENTS

CHAPTER 1

Young Criminals

Richmond 1966.

On a hot summer day, 5 young teenage boys sauntered out of the Whale Hardware Store with Cokes, rope, surgical tubing, wire and a 5-gallon Gerry can of gas. They pushed, shoved, laughed and squirted Coke amongst themselves as they headed down Harbor Boulevard to their hand-me-down rowboats that they had salvaged from the boatyard. After a group refurb effort, the boats were seaworthy and awaited the next adventure in the Richmond Canal. The largest teen of the group was stripped to the waist and of muscular build. He spoke to the group as they walked.

"I get the *Marauder,* that's my boat." Spoke the tall youth who went by the name of Joaquin.

"What? You always get the best one, it's not fair!" Answered a slim blonde boy called Zilm.

"We'll pound ya' Zilm, shut up." Answered an Asian kid missing a tooth who spoke from the back of the group. All of them were right around 14 years of age but showed different signs of physical maturity. The gap-tooth boy was a pudgy mop-top, the group referred to him by his nickname, Wrong Way. His real name was Eddie Wong.

"Eddie, you are always on Joaquin's side." The Zilm boy was whining, his primary defense in all situations.

Another lad in the group pounced on the whiner, got him in a half-nelson and gave him a Dutch-rub on the top of his close-cropped blond head. The attacker was Ricky Reeger, his actions were greeted with howls of approval. He let go.

"Okay, you win, I call the *Avenger* though, that's my boat." Zilm maneuvered into his fallback position. He intended to get something besides a Dutch rub out of this.

"You call shit Zilm. And that's what you get-and shoved in it." The black youth spoke in even and unemotional tones. Cassius was his name, they called him Cash. "Never seen a fool like you; always causing trouble."

"I don't cause trouble." Zilm seemed surprised, meek and defensive. The tall boy, Joaquin, stopped and turned to face the group as they reached the dock and the boats.

"Hey. Okay, look, here's the plan. Cash, Eddie and Reeger in the *Avenger* and Zilm and I in the *Marauder*. You guys go out first and we'll follow behind. Don't screw around and tip over, you guys got the best outboard and you *know* it will sink." Joaquin laid out instructions. The warning about the outboard was a reminder of a previous incident. Everyone nodded without a word and trudged down the ramp to the boats.

The boats were constructed of heavy plywood. They had a homemade look about them. Both were about 12 feet long with a seat across the middle and the stern. They also had a small seat in the bow. They were rowing skiffs, but a mast had been constructed in each and an outboard motor was fixed to the stern. A canvas drop-cloth-sail was stowed under the stern seat. Each boat had a wooden crate fixed to the forward floorboards for ship supplies. The *Marauder* and the *Avenger* were freshly painted, and most striking at first glance, was the row of shark's teeth at the waterline and at the bow. It was a menacing grin that both vessels sported proudly. The boys took their places and unshipped the oars, leaving the harbor in stealth, their motors silent.

Out in the Canal they went. There was no breeze yet and the water was glassy. They went by the shipyards, the marine rails and by the yachts. This was a working harbor, and they were on their guard for tug-boat wakes that could swamp them. Leaving the canal and the channel was out of the question and their destination was Brooks Island, located at the mid channel marker of the Richmond Harbor. Brooks Island was uninhabited and had once been owned by Bing Crosby who acquired it to shoot the ducks that landed there. It was largely a forgotten piece of real estate now, ever since Bing left the planet, much to the delight of the duck population. The boys loved it; it was their sanctuary. It was surrounded by very shallow water and was inaccessible by anything larger than a rowboat. The boys had never seen a single human on the Island outside of their group and knew the terrain well. It was big enough for any game or adventure that they could come up with and they spent the afternoon running and hiding over the beaches of the island, playing one of their favorite games, war; mock-killing, capturing, jailing and torturing your friends, all great fun. After a few hours of this, it was back to the boats and out into the channel seeking more adventure. An ideal afternoon.

The *Avenger* and the *Marauder* glided to a halt when Cash raised his hand and Eddie put his finger to his lips. Prey was in sight, spotted by the lead boat. Joaquin and Zilm coasted up to the motionless *Avenger* and side-tied boat-to-boat. Quietly, the mast went up on the *Marauder* and Joaquin and Zilm took positions: one in the bow and one in the stern. They worked with rope, wire and surgical tubing, fashioning a weapon of warfare. The *Avenger* propelled the two craft ahead at dead slow speed and all was going according to plan as they prepared in silence. They had waited for this opportunity for a month.

About mid-channel, abreast of the crane docks and across from the Muni dock, the *Avenger* stopped the silent vessels. The *Marauder,* still tied abreast, unfurled a length of surgical tubing suspended between its mast and its sternpost. The outboard motor on the *Avenger* ran at a quiet idle. Across the channel from the boys and tied to the Muni dock was the immaculate 45-footer named, the *Beaver*; home to the Sausalito Sea Scouts. They were on their monthly outing. Nobody aboard the *Beaver* took notice of the scruffy little skiffs in the channel and the Scouts went through their elaborate flag ceremony on the foredeck of the *Beaver*. Aboard the *Avenger,* a different ceremony was about to commence.

The lid of the wooden ships-stores crate was opened, an egg came out and was placed within the pouch that was a baseball cap tied between two lengths of tubing. The surgical tubing was stretched back across the boats to its furthest extension and held there, and as such, was a giant slingshot.

"Come about 90 degrees to starboard." Joaquin gave a quiet instruction to the helmsman.

"Roger." Was the reply and the helm answered with a turn of the outboard coming about to the required *3 o'clock position,* more commonly known as a broadside in naval warfare.

"All stop and hold position, prepare to fire on my command." Joaquin was focused. A few breathless moments passed as Reeger adjusted the angle of the tubing, pouch and egg to the proper elevation and held it.

"Ready to fire." Reeger reported quietly.

"Let 'er go!" And with that command having been shouted, a whoosh sound went across the rafted boats. The missile in the cap was launched and the egg took flight across the channel for about a five-count arc. No one spoke, all eyes were focused on the arc of the egg.

On board the *Beaver*, an officious, fat and uniformed middle-aged man instructed a group of twelve-year-old boys on the protocol of handling the flag.

"Jimmy; you settle down over there and now you boys pay attention! This is very important." Bill Brainard, formerly second lieutenant-3rd class, Navy-retired and now commodore of the *Beaver*, Sea Scout Squadron #372, cleared his throat, puffed his chest and addressed the little rag-tag regiment of adolescents assembled in two crooked lines. The boys had nicknames for this officious prick commanding the *Beaver*; El Supremo, BB Brain-fart, Brain-tard, Brain-Wreck, and other derogatory variations of Brainard.

"Our fathers and our fathers' fathers have handed down to us, no wait; have bequeathed to us a tradition! A tradition to be honored! A tradition to be respected! I am talking about the Flag, boys! The Flag is the symbol of this great country, this country that has given us all the wonderful things we enjoy today, things that did not come easy! You will respect these traditions by handling this Flag in the way it so deservedly, umm uhh, well, should be handled!"

He was doing great for a while but blew the ending. No matter, he had their attention, all puffed up like a toad and decked out in white ducks with gold buttons and spit-shined shoes. A portly figure at five-six tall, with one of those gold braided commodore hats that was 2 sizes too large for his head and was perched over his ears like a bucket.

That's when the first egg hit the *Beaver* full across the foredeck. It hit the flagpole and the overspray got the Commodore and his crew, marking them with little yellow stains and chunks of white shells. The egg really came apart well; all that the attacking boys had hoped it could be. A cheer went up across the channel and the boys were giddy and surprised at such success. Another egg came out of the box and into the pouch-cap. The tubing was drawn back to its full extension and held there.

"10 degrees to port, fire as you come to bear!" The command was given and Cash moved the little outboard slightly to the left. The second missile was launched and onboard the *Beaver*, fingers began to point across the channel as the second egg splattered amongst their ranks.

"Double and triple shot, fire at will!" Joaquin screamed and a general commotion of cheer and enthusiasm broke out amongst the little rag-tag navy under his command. It's a beautiful thing when such coordination bears such a splendid effect. The *Beaver* was in irons tied to the dock and receiving punishment, unable to move. The once spotless vessel received the merciless barrage of eggs, coming 2 and 3 at a time now. Scouts were falling in the yellow slime on deck; the only adult present was screaming like a banshee in language unbecoming to his rank.

"You little fuckers, I'll beat the shit out of you. I'll cut your balls off you little pussies! I'll beat you silly you little bastard-dickhead-motherfuckers!!" He swore until he was out of breath. The Sea Scouts had never heard such language come from the Commodore nor anyone else. Then, he too fell on his ass just in time to take a barrage across his torso which splattered into his eyes, blinding him and shutting him up.

"That's it, out of ammo, Captain." Reeger reported.

"Full speed ahead back to base!" Joaquin ordered the retreat.

"That was too beautiful! Did you see those Sea-Squirrels? They were screwed, glued and tatoo-ed!" Zilm was transcending into his manic state; misfortune in others, instead him, was always a source of mirth and joy.

"How 'bout that old fat bastard? We pasted his ass good!" Cash was animated with the recollection. Both boats had the throttle wide open, and they remained tied together, fleeing at about 7 knots up the channel.

"Damn straight! Scrambled his eggs!" Eddie Wong chimed in, glancing back at the focus of mayhem. He paused and then said again, "Uh-oh, the *Beaver* is moving out. It's away from the dock."

The *Beaver* was a surplus World War II submarine chaser. It had twin screws and was designed to go fast and launch torpedoes and depth charges at Japanese subs. It was in its prime in 1945. In the last twenty years, it hadn't been doing much since the surrender and all. But it had found a home; a rather tame existence, idling its engines in Sausalito for Squadron #372, where the Sea Scouts maintained the hull and machinery in anticipation of their weekend trips in the Bay or World War III, whichever came first. It did not matter much to them either way; they were ready. That polished hull and machinery was now swinging into action, and it was like a dream come true for the Scouts-the joy of an enemy engagement! Black smoke began to pour out its exhaust stacks as it built to attack-speed. Sirens were heard in the distance. The Battle of the Richmond Channel was on.

The boys of the *Marauder* and *Avenger* saw that events might turn against them, and their tone changed. Fear began to smother a previously giddy and triumphant countenance. Escape by any means was the single thought that they had in their adolescent heads. One clear head in group spoke to reason. It was Joaquin of course.

"Untie the boats, split up. Cash, you guys go ahead, me and Zilm will duck under the pier here. We'll meet at the ramp; tie the boats up under the dock. Then we beat-feet home." Joaquin laid it out and then cut the lines that held the boats together with his trusty buck knife while Eddie held the throttle tight to the pin, white knuckles on his hand.

The speeding little boats evacuated the mid-channel for the safety under the pilings of the docks. They were now in full flight; capture and consequences poisoned the once cheery squadron. They had about five minutes before it hit the fan.

Back aboard the *Beaver*, the crew worked the deck over with mops and buckets. The Commodore pushed the solid brass throttle forward. The linkage resisted as the engine ventured into territory unknown since 1945, responding with black smoke, twin screws churning the water of the channel into a perfect V-shaped wake behind the transom of the old craft. The Commodore forced the handle forward yet more and the engines responded with more RPM, smoke and a terrible vibration developed over the whole boat. This was ignored; pursuit was all and the engines were now screaming. The Commodore lost the first round, but he was convinced that the second round belonged to the *Beaver*. The skiffs were sighted in full flight and the *Beaver* was fast closing in on them. But the end zone was in sight for the boys and the five youths could sense a chance for escape. Maybe they would not end up in Juvie again if only luck would smile on them. When the ramp was dead ahead, they wasted no time evacuating.

"Under the docks! Tie em' up under the pilings! Let's get outta' here!" Joaquin's voice was crisp, and the boys put the boats under the dock and threw lines, securing the skiffs. They scrambled out and took nothing with them as they fled up the ramp and into the dusty parking lot where a solitary red Plymouth Valiant stood alone.

"There you ladies are. I been looking all over for you." The driver of the Valiant stood in the dirt, leaning over the roof. The little group of five escapees reached the Valiant, the back door opened without a word from the group and the five piled into the car.

"Get us outta' here Van. Right now!" Five versions of this command came from the new passengers. "Sea Scouts are after us!"

"What the hell ladies? Screwed the pooch again?" Van Zant, the sixth member of the gang had his Learners Permit and this was his mother's car. He was a year older than the rest but had been held back in 3rd grade. He looked like an adolescent Elvis Presley, complete with the sneer. Van Zant's loyal sidekick was in the front passenger seat. He was a gnome-like adolescent who had the look of an electro-shock survivor. It was Dirty Ernie. His eyes had the dull look of a farm animal, and he never changed his clothes or said much. Later in life, he did go on to receive real electro-shock therapy in a court-ordered attempt to cure his felonious habits.

"What are you guys up to?" Van Zant asked the group in the back seat.

"We pasted the Sea Scouts with eggs and now they're after us, go-Van-go!" Eddie said with excitement.

"Got 'em good too" Said Reeger.

"We better get outta' here now Van, this is serious." Joaquin spoke. But instead of leaving, Van Zant got out of the car and stepped over to the edge of the dock and shouted at the *Beaver.*

"Hey!! You little woosies!! I got 'em right here in the backseat of my car and you can't have 'em!! How you like those apples, Sea Squirts!" Van Zant had his arm held high in a one-finger salute to the intrepid *Beaver.* He started laughing and a profane chorus erupted from the back seat, versions of, 'Are you nuts Van Zant?'

The Commodores' twelve hysterical Scouts were jumping, shouting and pointing fingers toward the little red Valiant. The Commodore dropped the engine RPM's and reversed full throttle. The old boat shook, shuddered and trembled as it came to a halt in mid-channel. A flurry of activity began amongst his crew on the forward deck. The Commodore was now presiding from the bridge of the *Beaver* and ready for action. Momentarily, all was quiet until the command boomed over the ship's intercom.

"Action stations!"

Van Zant was the only one ashore who heard the sound coming from the deck of the *Beaver*. "*Whump-Whump-Whump*", and then again, "*Whump, Whump, Whump*".

Three one-gallon paint cans landed in front of the Valiant and broke open. Paint splattered the dock, three five-gallon cans of slop landed behind the car and made a helluva mess. Then, a five-gallon pail of kitchen garbage hit the roof of the car. A slop bucket from a latrine hit the trunk and nasty stuff oozed over the rear window and garbage littered the hood. Fear now gripped Van Zant as well and he jumped in the car and punched it in reverse. Missiles from the Beaver landed all around. The Beaver had been fatally underestimated: the depth charge launchers were now proving to be the deciding weapon in the battle, flinging nasty projectiles a great distance. The little Sea Scouts cheered as they scored hits. The Commodore was redeemed, now victorious, the enemy in retreat from battle. Sirens approached in the distance when the magic words were spoken.

"THE COPS ARE COMING!" That universally understood phrase of four words that held such promise. That was all Van Zant needed to hear; no more explanations were necessary. He floored it and gravel flew out the back. The little Valiant headed for the gate but first he wheeled the car around to the edge of the dock with a squeal of the brakes. He got out and started screaming at the Scouts.

"Suck sack you woosies!"

The battle was over, and the getaway car disappeared in a cloud of dust. The Valiant cleared the parking lot without touching the brakes, sped through the gate and wheeled out onto Cutting Boulevard, crossing Harbor Boulevard doing 60 mph. The boys washed the car and slipped it into the garage at Van Zant's house. The paint on the tires came off with paint thinner and the rest washed off. They decided to lay low for a few days and they watched a lot of daytime TV. They laughed their butts off every time Eddie did his Commodore imitation.

*   *   *

Richmond 2008.

*R*ichmond affords a view of the Bay Area and on a fall day the visual definitions of the surrounding cities are sharp and clear; the Transamerica Pyramid, Sutro Tower, Mt Tamalpais, the Bay Bridge, the Golden Gate, the foothills of the South and East Bay; all of these are clearly visible and are familiar icons that define the Bay Area panoramas in the clear winter air. There are other definitions that are sharp and clear; definitions that can be seen at any time of the year and they are the economic definitions. In Richmond today, the freeway goes right through the town and the road is either elevated or walled and that suits the auto drivers who use it just fine; stopping off for gas or cigarettes in Richmond today is, is well, for the most part, unthinkable for a non-resident. The drivers push right on through. They do not venture into the Iron Triangle because if they did, the neighborhoods might exceed their comfort zone. For the residents, it was just home.

The whole country and the whole world was in the grip of economic uncertainty. Anxiety was running high amongst those who were previously secure. The stock market had plunged, banks had failed, credit was no longer available. The politicians up for election scrambled for political cover as the pundits talked of 'recession' and 'depression'. But here in Richmond, the depression could have come and gone, and no one would have even known the difference. Just getting by was considered a monthly victory.

So, in economic ascension or decline in Richmond, children laughed, and school bells rang, people went to work if they had it, went to church if they believed, assembled on corners for gossip, made plans and entertained hope to one degree or another. Joy and sadness occurred regardless of the economic circumstances in which they found themselves. Certainly, no one was going to jump off a building because of money trouble – everybody would have been broken and flat on the sidewalk long ago if that were the case.

CHAPTER 2

Zilm Has A Bright Idea

The boys avoided the Sea Scouts and the cops that day but the one thing that could not be avoided was fate. Their date with destiny was already parked at the curb and was advancing up the walkway to meet them. Soon, it was gonna hit the fan and splatter all over them. After the umbrella of high school was gone, life without protection from their carefree high school days was upon them-real life. Today we see them together thirty years later, still hanging out, yet under different circumstances. The thirty years between then and now is a whole other era, if not several. But some things do not change, and people are in that category.

Richmond 2008.

"They got millions of dollars going through that place and all they can afford to pay me is $12.50 an hour? It's not right, I tell you! They give me 25 hours a week-classified as a temp worker which means no benefits-how am I supposed to live?" Frenchy asked.

"By your wits I guess." Zilm answered absent-mindedly.

"I guess, geez, there ought to be a law." Frenchy replied.

Robert Zilm had not yet made his mark in life and was still in the process of finding a career that suited him. Frenchy, aka Michele Marie Gigot, was similarly challenged. She had been living by her wits ever since leaving high school and bouncing around from one job to another, reinventing herself as circumstances required. This morning they were at coffee at the kitchen table, both with their laptops and searching for work.

"Wait a minute; did you say millions?" Zilm looked up from the screen at Frenchy.

"Yeah; believe that? It's either some Arab prince or Russian gangster flying in, in a helicopter with a suitcase of money, trading it for gems or art or some-such. And there I am taking home $250.00 a week?" Frenchy said while buttering her toast.

"So……. a suitcase full of cash or gems over in that Tower across the way?" Zilm questioned further.

"Yeah, that boss of mine, Chacon, he's a sleazy character and has all kind of things going through that place-all illegal, I'm sure. I think he launders money." Frenchy replied.

"Imagine that." Zilm mused quietly and to himself, thinking about the well-laundered five dollars he found in the clothes dryer yesterday. He snapped out of his daydream.

"He got a safe over there and everything?" Zilm asked.

"Oh yeah, more like a vault he walks into." Frenchy replied.

"Do tell." Said Robert Zilm.

*　*　*

"Rick, we can do this. I got it all scoped out and we even got Frenchy on the inside. But we need people; this is a big job with a lot of moving parts. That's why it's so beautiful, can't you see? We got the people, we got Frenchy. No one ever imagined this could happen and they got their guard down. That's when we step in; we can make the big score!" Zilm was making a case for a crime.

"But don't they have a guard?" Rick asked a simple question.

"Yes, but he's 25 stories below in the lobby guarding the elevators!" Zilm explained, always persuasive when dealing with Rick. Zilm often sought him out as an ally.

"I dunno, sounds risky Zilm." Rick was not sold.

"Van Zant is key; we got to get him in on this. But first we got to talk to Joaquin. If Joaquin says he's in-we can get Van. If Van and Joaquin are in-it's a go. Eddie, he's up for anything we got goin' on. Add me and Frenchy and you-that's a wrap-the old gang together again, we just can't miss!" Zilm lobbied his old pal.

"Can't hurt to look at it, I guess. "Rick replied.

"That's the spirit! We'll go over to Joaquin's tomorrow and run it by him." Zilm's enthusiasm was now peaking.

*   *   *

At Joaquin's house the following day Joaquin was not so sure of Zilm's plan.

"I'm not going to do it you moron." It was a clear statement, voiced matter-of-factly by Joaquin (pronounced "walk keen") Randal Rogers. "Zilm, you always have some crazy-ass idea about how to get rich quick."

"Why not? It's all right there for the taking, just like I laid it out. It's a little crazy, I know that. But who could be prepared for something like this? We can get away with it!" Robert Zilm pulled up a chair before the immovable position of Joaquin, sitting across the kitchen table.

"Zilm, what's the matter with you, anyway? You've never been quite right in the head. That's why they always beat the tar out of you." Joaquin said from his chair at the kitchen table, a location where all matters of importance were discussed since childhood.

Joaquin Randal Rogers was a welder and a biker, just like his mom had been. He lived in Richmond, CA all his life. He was 6'5' and 230, given to wearing heavy leather wrist guards and steel toed boots. His straight black hair was longish, and he wore a drooping mustache. When he had seen the picture of the bandito Joaquin Murrieta at 16, he liked the look. Now, all he lacked were the bandoleers of cartridges crisscrossing his chest and he could double in that same picture.

"There's nothing wrong with me." Zilm shot back. "I am workin' all the time and I'm still poor. That's how it's always been. And now, I don't wanna be poor anymore, it's that simple. How about Rick here? Two little dump trucks running around town-he's not going to ever get rich. Neither are you, Joaquin; welding fences and grates so thieves can't rob you blind?" Zilm was never at a loss for words or explanations, he had come by this talent early as a survival technique, a fast talker using it to dodge beatings since grade school.

"I know that Rick here wants a little more than a dump truck business, right Rick?" Zilm asked.

"Well, I'm doin okay, I guess." Rick said.

"Quick Dump? Really?" Zilm turned toward Reeger.

"Some people think it's funny." Reeger meekly replied.

"Maybe some people don't wanna be rich, Zilm. Ever think on that? Zilm, it's kinda nuts. Even for you." Joaquin stated apprehensively.

"Don't wanna be rich? Gimme a break! Everybody wants to be rich! It's like Easter, Christmas and the Fourth of July all in one! Look, I know we got a shot at this, Joaquin. You can't gimme two reasons why it won't work." Zilm was now downshifting into a more congenial personality range. But still a weasel.

"Are you delusional? I'll tell you why. First, we are not criminals. Two; we can't do it without Van Zant and he's a psycho and then you got a psycho in your life. Three; it's nuts. Four; we got lives, wives, girlfriends- we are not kids! It won't work!" Joaquin had the last word.

Zilm and Reeger didn't say a thing and Joaquin's words just hung there. Lunch was on the table in front of them and they stared at the bologna sandwiches and chips. Reeger took one chip in his hand and fed it to the dog, absent-mindedly, thinking mostly about Zilm, poverty and the name of his dump truck service. Zilm was right of course; Rick was almost poor most of the time, and he had to work all week to stay that way. All week long he dealt with drivers that quit, late-payments, customers pissed off, old machinery and dirt; the grind and the repetition of problems, all related to money. It was little wonder that he was intrigued with the notion of getting rich quick. He had always been more comfortable being a follower and if Joaquin would do it, he would do it. The little dog at Reegers' feet begged for another chip with his bug-eyes the size of a quarter. It was a pug-dog and it belonged to Mandy. He wasn't sure if he liked the odd little dog, so ugly that it was cute. It was a pest whenever food was around, that was for sure.

"Van Zant's a prick, all right. He's also a criminal, which we aren't-that's true. We do need a criminal in on this and he is it." Zilm replied.

"He is our homeboy, don't forget that." Reeger added through a mouthful of bologna sandwich, turning his attention to the tall pitcher of orange Kool-Aid on the table in front of him. He poured himself a tall glass then drew a picture of The Happy Face on the sweating pitcher.

Steve Van Zant was in question; he looked like Elvis with the build of a middleweight prize fighter since the age of 16. They had gone to school every day with him; played after school every day with him, had adventures with him. He had been one of the gang. But then, sometime during high school things began to change; Van Zant disappeared from the after-school games and started hanging around with an older crowd, tougher kids doing crazy stuff. He started smoking Marlboros in the bathroom. He sold firecrackers and cigarettes to the little kids. He got suspended and then expelled. He stole a car. Rumors were heard that he beat somebody up with a battery cable. He went to Juvie. He disappeared altogether for quite some time. He returned to the neighborhood with a scar across his forehead and a Corvette. The homeboys had all graduated without Van Zant.

"Have you talked to him lately? That might be wise." Joaquin spoke through a mouthful of Wonder bread.

"Yeah, I saw him down at Peets. I was cool." Answered Zilm.

"I bet you were cool, cooler than penguin shit." Joaquin answered. Reeger kicked at the little dog as he ate. The pug was aggressively begging for food.

"Hey, watch the dog Rick! She's family around here and don't kick that dog when Mandy's around, she'll rip you a new one." Joaquin cautioned. "What kinda guy kicks a little dog anyway? Jesus Christ Almighty, Rick." Joaquin said with disgust.

"What kind of dog is that anyway?" Reeger asked.

"It's a Pug" Joaquin answered.

"I thought Pugs were bigger than that." Reeger mused.

"Well, they aren't. They're all exactly that size and they only come in two colors." Joaquin didn't need this aggravation.

"Really. A pug-dog? Who knew?" Reeger ended with genuine enlightenment, staring down at the little animal who was staring at him with his bug-eyes.

The group sat around the Formica kitchen table in silence after finishing lunch. The little kitchen had a fresh coat of butter yellow paint and cheap ceramic knick-knacks. The refrigerator had a collection of magnets with pugs dressed in tutus, raincoats, sunglasses, hats, etc. A large poster, the words in French, naming all the spices and their usage adorned the wall space in the tiny kitchen.

Joaquin broke the silence. "What makes you think he'd get involved with this, Zilm? I hear he has straightened himself out, got himself a great gig running those cranes or tugs, or whatever he does."

Zilm smiled inside, happy that Joaquin was taking a little nibble of the bait. Soon, he hoped, he might have him hooked on the notion. He had to present it just right and he had practiced with these guys since childhood. Zilm knew that he was the smartest of the three in the room, that was his reality.

Reeger mumbled through a bite of sandwich, "Van Zant is a crazy bastard. One time we went to a car show in San Jose. We were partying at a tailgate, everybody was having fun, Van Zant was holding court with the girls from the show. They are lovin' his rap, and they are swimsuit models, totally bitchin babes. In rolls this guy in a 57 Impala convertible-all tricked out and sharp; a beautiful car customized to the dash knobs. When we go over to check it out, Van's not the center of attention anymore. He's standing alone at the tailgate with nobody to impress. He walks over to re-join the party, stops to admire the Impala. Van hitches up right next to the owner and starts bantering. He's getting along a little too good the way I see it. I'm across the white interior of the car looking at Van and the owner and something's not right. Van's being a little too nice. We all know Van's not nice and sweet, right? Not for no reason, he's got something up his sleeve. Van has that little gap in his front teeth, right? Every time the owner is not looking, Van swivels his head and squirts spit through his teeth, quick-like a snake. A little stream of spit lands on the car seat each time and nobody sees, except me. Van does this three or four times, I say nothing. The Impala-guy finally looks down at his car seat and gets wise to what's happening. Van's still all nice and sweet. The Impala-guy jumps back from the car and looks down at his seat covered with spit. Meanwhile, Van unzips his fly, flops out his big old pecker and turns his front pocket inside out."

"Ever see a one-eared elephant, hotshot?" Van Zant says to the Impala guy. Reeger paused his story a moment.

"See what I mean? A psycho." Joaquin replied mildly.

"That's beautiful." Zilm chortled evilly, "I love it, what happened next?'

"The girls scream, the Impala-guy swings at Van Zant and then the Van beats the livin' shit out of him with his dick still swingin' in the wind." Rick concluded.

"Pre-meditated mayhem and malice." Joaquin said mildly.

"Yeah, I saw something was coming. The Van got style points with the dick-trick." Rick flipped the last potato chip at the dog. He popped out a small dental appliance from the roof of his mouth and swished out his mouth with Kool-Aid. Joaquin was disgusted by this.

"Gee-zus! That's disgusting Rick. You gotta do that at the table? Go over to the sink and rinse your filthy mouth out! It's like a reverse-enema!" Joaquin pointed to the sink.

"Sorry. I'm gonna get implants soon and I won't have to wear this thing. Food gets stuck between my stay-plate and the roof of my mouth. Those implants cost 5 grand a piece." Reeger wrapped his two front teeth in a paper towel and set it down on the table while he went over to the sink.

"Lookin at your stay-plate covered with food makes me want to puke. Disgusting!" Joaquin said.

"Sorry." Rick said.

The group lapsed into silence again until Zilm broke it. "I look at this set-up every day. I know it will work. We got limited time; my jobs over and the goods will be gone. Now is the only time for this. Think about 9 million dollars or more split 4 ways; that's millions with an "M". That means better wheels, better house, no bills." Zilm turned his appeal directly toward Joaquin with the finish, "I'm telling you Joaquin, its respect and peace of mind in lots and lots of fat stacks of cash! We can live well for a long time!" Zilm pitched it. He was now on his feet and waving his arms for emphasis.

"I live pretty good, Zilm. I go to work; Mandy and I are comfortable. I can expect it might stay that way." Joaquin was maintaining his calm demeanor.

Joaquin had struck a sore point in Zilm's nerve center. This was exactly what Zilm was afraid of; whatever modest financial security he ever felt he knew it was temporary and he *did not* expect that it would stay that way. What sounded like an acceptable future to Joaquin was more like a prison sentence in financial limbo-land for him. He blurted out a heartfelt assessment.

"What do you got Joaquin? How many people got shot in this town last week? The Neighborhood Watch program is run by the SWAT team around here! And your job? How many fences and gates you gotta weld up every day at that shop before you can afford to go to Costco once a month? It's not even a union shop anymore! You got no health insurance; no pension and we make payments on everything we own that's bigger than a refrigerator! I just don't get what's all so good about this!" Zilm unloaded.

"Yeah, Rhonda went to the ER last month, with a fever, they did tests, they found nothing. They sent her home with a bill for over eleven grand. Believe that?" Rick chimed in.

"There you go." Zilm said.

"The problem with you, Zilm? You're just not a happy person inside." Joaquin stated this calmly, stepped through the living room and into the front yard. Reeger followed him. Zilm headed for the rear exit, leaving the kitchen to the little dog.

Rick spoke to Joaquin when he joined him in the front yard. "Maybe we should take a drive tomorrow and look at it Joaquin?"

"We could. We might actually think that we can do it; think that we are smart guys, bold as brass. We might think they are stupid marks-wide open and vulnerable." Joaquin answered.

"So, what's the problem? We can always talk about this kind of stuff; doesn't mean we have to do it. It's kinda fun." Rick ventured a little. Joaquin answered,

"It's risky no matter what it looks like. But the first decision you have to think about is this; do you want to be a criminal? It's not like TV; you don't get to change the channel when you don't like the show. Am I the only one here today that sees that? You know Rick, sometimes you're not so bright listening to that talk of Zilm. The problem as I see it is this; say it is the opportunity that Zilm says it is. And say Van Zant agrees to go in. And even, let's say it works. You're still not done; the problem is you're partners with Van Zant and he's capable of anything. What do you do when he's telling you a lie, big and bold? He *knows* that you *know* it's a lie, but to him, that doesn't matter. All that matters to him is winning any way he can. Now what do you do? You never thought this would happen, but surprise is a secret weapon. Now what? Do you back down? Go blind to the whole thing? Or are you gonna confront him, knowing it gets ugly from here on out?" Joaquin took a breath and continued.

"You know he's not right in the head, Rick. You know he's gotten away with stuff. You know he should probably still be in prison. Just because we don't say, doesn't mean we don't know. He can be charming if you're on the right side of him, but he's a one-eyed-jack." Joaquin laid it out.

"Zilm has got me thinking about the money I guess; just one pop, that's all, one job would put us all over. I'd run the business just like always, but those fat stacks.... they would smooth out the rough edges-for a long time. Let's go check it out and see what Zilm is talking about. It can't hurt." Reeger lobbied.

"Okay. We'll take a drive tomorrow-just for shits and giggles. Now put your front teeth back in; you look like you belong in the front row of a Willie Nelson concert."

Joaquin left Rick standing in the front yard, among Mandy's cement gnomes and oversized red-polka-dot mushrooms that were congregated and secure within a low chain link fence around the perimeter of the property, separating them from the sidewalk and a shabby street scene. Zilm had Joaquin thinking. Rick looked out at an abandoned mattress and an exhausted and torn easy chair.

You get used to where you live, you adapt, you make it okay, you get comfortable with it and ignore the bad stuff. But Zilm was right; where he lived was a mess and getting messier. There was a lot less of everything good to go around, less money, jobs and patience. There was a lot more of the bad stuff and drugs had ruined this neighborhood. Couple that with the fact that everyone pictured themselves as a bad ass now, and you got trouble. He wouldn't mind having a couple of acres in the country somewhere, with a shop, with a few trees. Maybe a new truck, too. Mandy wouldn't mind a few nice things; she had her own wish list. A one-pop deal, that's all. Zilm had sown the seeds of discontent and they were sprouting in fertile ground. Rick stepped back into the house to retrieve his teeth. Zilm met him in the living room.

"Well? What'd Joaquin say?" Zilm asked conspiratorially.

"He said you're a weasel and Van Zant's a psycho. But we are gonna take a look at the layout tomorrow." Rick answered the wiry blond-haired man.

Rick headed into the kitchen to get his two front teeth, wrapped in paper on the little yellow table. Zilm stood silently in the middle of the living room, pleased that he had won the first round. Then he heard a scream of terror and rushed into the kitchen.

"You little fat-furry-pig!" Rick was screaming at the pug-dog on top of the kitchen table.

Zilm saw the little beige and black animal chewing up the paper napkin that wrapped up Rick's two front teeth in his stay-plate. The pug had chewed up Rick's dental appliance, drawn to the mashed up potato chips stuck to it. Now, pink pieces of plastic were scattered about the tabletop, and among them were two artificial teeth that perfectly matched those in the gap-toothed, screaming and cursing mouth of Rick Reeger.

CHAPTER 3

Robert At Work

Robert Zilm walked into the employee break room at 7:55 AM and poured a cup of bad coffee into a cheap Styrofoam cup. He sat down at the 4x10 brown Formica table in the breakroom. He stared at the cup and then at the windowless wall. A large bulletin board was filled with workplace cautionary posters such as *minimum wage, report an accident, OSHA safe workplace, discrimination is illegal,* etc. Another wall held a faded orange print of a sailboat at sunset on a glassy sea and a calendar that was two months behind. Boredom was intentionally produced within minutes of sitting in this breakroom. Zilm was at the yard office of Allstate Electric where he had been an employee for a little over a year and this was his eighth different vocation since turning twenty-one years of age. He was starting this new career at a late age. So far, he didn't like it much, just as he had suspected all along. He took the job because it was a requirement to get the grant for the re-training program at the local JC and take yet another stab at settling his dissatisfaction with working for a living. He had lived on the grant money for a year; it ran out, and now, he was trained as an electrician, and here he was working for Allstate Electric, a high-ranking nightmare.

During that year of paid leisure, he had grown accustomed to certain things. He liked hanging out at Starbuck's and Peet's with his laptop. He liked hanging around people at leisure. He wondered how it was that they weren't working at 11AM? Instead, they were meeting a friend and chatting over a pastry and an expensive coffee drink. He would listen in and overhear certain things, whether real or imagined, things that he took as proof of affluence. Talk of world events, children at swim clubs, and urgent phone calls on cell phones and crisp conversations about meetings and projects and deadlines. They had $1000 Smartphones, they were busy, sought after and popular people with a need for constant contact with a central network of.... what? Similarly, privileged people? He could only imagine because in his network of phone calls, people usually didn't want to hear from him.

Zilm came from a religious household, *Latter-Day Saints.* So named 'Latter Day' because they came after the real saints and were thereafter looked upon suspiciously as a cult. Everyone who was LDS was an oddball in one way or another, or so the gen-pop assumed. The father was not particularly religious, but Zilm's mother was very, very religious. Cokes, coffee, alcohol and masturbation were forbidden in the house. The father ran a Chevron service station and he drank at work, confirming LDS family members as weirdos. Unlike gas stations today, at a *service station* people worked on cars, pumped gas, checked oil and washed windows. There was no snack station and mini mart within a brightly lit interior. There was a Tom's vending machine with 12 selections and a Coke machine. There was a place for the cash register in front of shelves of motor oil, anti-freeze and windshield wipers. The décor was shabby, dusty and the floors were not regularly cleaned. No one expected anything other than this in a service station. The station was a *one horse operation* and chances were good that Zilm's dad would pump your gas, adjust your carburetor mix and tender your payment personally. Not conscientious service, but one of necessity on the part of Mr. Zilm. The bad part was his drinking was on public display. This didn't make life any easier for little Robert Adolf in a small town.

In grade school and high school, little Robert was a straight A student. This fact only made a difficult life more so. He was persecuted. He was the butt of jokes. The stupid and tough kids beat him up. Zilm got used to it, accepted it, adapted to it, but never let on that he was not happy with the rough treatment, because after all, weirdos like he deserved to be persecuted; he would do the same had the shoe been on the other foot. Things got better for him in high school though, he found a gang of nerds to hang with who accepted him and the stupid kids were falling by the wayside, either working at PG and E, on the garbage truck or in the army. His straight A's meant something real now. He excelled in track and wrestling, and he began to shed the stigma of his younger days.

As he sat now in the break room of Allstate Electric, there was no thought of past persecutions- only of a future not to be spent *here*. He was going out on the Krystal Towers job again and he contemplated riding the construction elevator up to the 26th floor with his tool belt and bags, contemplating today's installation of wiring in the office high-rises, built right at the waterfront along the shore of SF Bay. Tower One was completed and occupied already and the second one nearly so. He would occasionally stare across into the adjacent building. The glassed-in offices across from him were like fishbowls inhabited by happy, well dressed and attractive people. His future, as he wished it, incorporated more people like this in his life. His immediate future, like today, did not even have one of these fortunate people among it. Today he would be talking and interacting with Buzz, Kevin, Murph and Godzilla, all working on the 26th floor with him. He was waiting for *the Buzzard,* as his co-worker was known, and Buzz was walking into the room now. They rode in the same elevator every day.

"Buzz Boy." Zilm acknowledged the entrance.

"Hey Fool." Was the returned acknowledgement. "You ready?"

"All set." Zilm replied.

."Lemme get a cup of this swill first. Why don't they buy good coffee, is that too much to ask? Something else besides this shit?" The Buzzard looked in his Styrofoam cup and scooped a handful of packaged creamers and sugars and put them in a large metal lunchbox. That lunch box had carted off a lot of Allstate inventory over the years and he wasn't called *The Buzzard* for nothing; he didn't leave a lot behind, picked it clean.

"They sweep that coffee off the floor and package it; I read that." Zilm said.

"*Godzilla* been through here yet?" The *Buzzard* asked about the boss as he absent-mindedly picked a floating particle out of his coffee.

"I dunno, I just got here. She's probably on the jobsite already. We're a little late maybe." Zilm replied.

Godzilla was the pet-name for the foreman that they answered to. Actually, she was the fore-woman that they answered to. She didn't take any bullshit; she did her job, knew the rules and knew she was in charge. Murphy had called her "God", Kevin added the "Zilla" part. Zilm didn't call her anything and they all called her Gabrila to her face because Gabrila Rosetti was her real name.

Zilm and the Buzzard walked out into the asphalt yard and got into the elevator, which resembled a cage. They arrived onto the jobsite and yarded their tools out of the elevator, walked through the safety gate of the primate cage and entered the jobsite on the 26th floor. Kevin and Murphy were there already, so was Godzilla, who turned to regard the entering pair.

"So nice of you to join us today, Mr. Buzzard" she greeted them sweetly. She had already formed the words of the greeting in her mind, along with the letter she was going to place in their file.

"Truck wouldn't start" Robert Zilm covered quickly.

"We got a lot to do today, Murphy will fill you in. Zilm. I need you to meet with the alarm people today, look over some drawings, get to know what's coming so you can tell us. I gotta be down on the ground all day. The auxiliary generators are in place, but it's all messed up down there." She spoke to Zilm, ignoring Buzz. She didn't like the Buzzard.

"I'm on it", Zilm replied to the rotund and intimidating figure in overalls and hardhat.

"Good" she replied and walked off.

Murphy and Kevin watched the two back pockets on the large retreating cheeks walking away. When she was safely away and out of earshot, they puckered up and made two kissing sounds, directed toward Zilm.

"You smacked it pretty good, Robert, well done." Kevin laughed.

"You got a little on your nose and it's brown now. It smells like shit, too." Murphy joined in with a laughing observation, pointing a finger.

"Ass kisser!" From the Buzzard.

Zilm walked away from their taunts. He was nobody's fool. His future wasn't with Godzilla and these clowns at Allstate Electric; fate held bigger things for him. His dreams were starting to take shape and they might soon lead him to a better status than a wire-puller. This Allstate period was just a step; the wheels of fate were turning. If all went according to plan, things might just work out, just the way he always wanted them to. He pondered this as he glanced across the way at the beautiful people in the glass tower directly across from him. He knew what they were up to over there, he knew who they were, Frenchy had filled him in. He knew why the helicopter came and went on the rooftop heliport, attended by men in black suits and earpieces. Robert Zilm had made it his business to know what went on over there. The more he found out, the more intriguing the whole thing became. Coincidence and fate had entered when his girlfriend started working there. From her he had found out that he was 200 feet away from the home of the Global Investment Corporation. Which by itself wasn't particularly interesting, but that changed when large sums of money, jewels, art, and other collectibles entered the conversation. He became fixated upon it when he read in the paper that some Sultan-dude of Brunei had purchased one of the largest colored diamond collections in the world from the Global Investment Corporation. It struck him as opportune when days before, an armored transport had arrived and supposedly delivered the precious stones to the Krystal Tower Number One, 200 feet away from Zilm. The Global Investment Corp had them and Zilm wanted them. He pondered the whole night when he went home. He got a notion that would not leave his mind. The notion burned, and in the center of this heat was an image of orderly banded stacks of 100-dollar bills, the weight, the color, the smell, the raw power of green indifferent cash.

Logically and step by step he tried to talk himself out of, or into, the notion of committing a crime. He grappled with the pros and cons of the caper, but he labored under a handicap. That handicap being that he thought himself, as always, the smartest guy in the room. Against logic, he outsmarted himself at every turn from beginning to end with reasons why he *could* do it; the set-up, the snatch, the fence- all night this went on until the sun came up. He called in sick, took his place in the café with his laptop, and he started getting serious in his research. He had convinced himself that this would be the perfect crime; the crime that would provide him with just the springboard he needed to get out of this unworthy lifestyle, in which he seemed to be rooted like a tree. But he could not do it alone because this was big. But then again, he had a ready answer for that; he could talk the gang into doing it! Yes, just the people he needed. All he had to do is talk Rick and Joaquin into it-just as he knew he could-because after all, he was smarter than they all, wasn't he? They just needed a good talking to, and he was just the guy to do it. He felt inspired, elevated, special, chosen and wholly prepared for this. But for now, he was still back on the 26th floor with the Buzzard, Murphy and Kevin.

"You goin' to lunch with us today, Ass Kisser? We're gonna get Chinese, $4.99 at the Jade Palace. You in?" Murphy asked Robert Zilm as he ambled over to get his belt and bags.

"No, I gotta see somebody at lunch." Was the short reply from Zilm.

Murphy looked quizzically at the Buzzard and spoke, "What's with him?"

"Lover Boy. He's got a squeeze over there." The Buzzard motioned toward the office in Glass Tower Number One. "I seen him over there chatting her up."

"Ass kisser anyway, I say." The Murph said.

"Yeah. Ass kisser." The Buzzard repeated.

* * *

At lunch break, Zilm took out a sandwich from his brown paper bag and offered it to Frenchy, an attractive woman but with the lines of a hard life beginning to appear on her face. She smelled like perfume and cigarettes. Her well coifed, sandy blond and streaked brown hair needed a dye job, the dark roots were beginning to show. She had a singular way about speaking; thoughts came out of her mouth in a rush.

"Thanks Bobby but I can't eat-too much on my mind-that job is getting too me I think-the security guard hits on me-my co-worker is a dyke-she hits on me-what is it Bobby? -what kinds of person do they take me for anyway?" Frenchy took a breath.

"It's just how people are, don't get excited. Want an orange?" Zilm asked.

"No-I thought we were going to a nice restaurant and get real food-not sit on a plastic chair outside-eating out of a paper bag-what kind of a cheap date am I Bobby? -I'm not feeling the love here." Frenchy lit up a smoke and drew deeply.

"We'll go out to dinner. No disrespect. Actually, I was wondering if I could walk you back to the office over in the Tower and see where you work." Zilm said.

"Why? It's a pit. Formica office furniture-crummy people who just want to get in your pants. I got one asshole in there already; I should want another? I'll tell them you're my boyfriend-then maybe they'll leave me alone for a day." Frenchy said.

"See? Everything works out." Zilm was satisfied that things were going his way. It was fate at work he thought as he began to peel an orange.

CHAPTER 4

Check It Out

J oaquin stepped through the front door with his second cup of coffee and sat on the front stairs of his one story, two bedroom stucco home, nestled among a row of similar homes on Market St in Richmond Ca. He was waiting for Reeger. On this particular morning he was outside on the stoop and reflecting on just what he and Reeger were gonna do today. He sat on the stairs in Levi's and a *Richmond Ramblers* T-shirt.

It was about 7: AM, the streets were empty, and the sky was slowly clearing from a light rain that fell in the night. Morning light fell on wet concrete, asphalt, painted wood, power poles and a few trees. It was quiet. In the distance, but within earshot, was the buzzing of rubber tires on a 6-lane freeway that ran through town, separating the gentrified residents from the non-gentrified residents. A bird sang enthusiastically across the street and stopped momentarily and then began again. The bird flew away and all became quiet once again. Everyone was still asleep on a Saturday morning, and many had only gone to sleep hours ago. The up-armored homes were modest, but most showed that the owners valued them. Bougainvillea, fresh paint, landscaping, cheap concrete statuary and patio furniture were all protected inside black iron fences, spiked at the top like medieval pike poles. The windows on the homes had grates to match. Joaquin didn't have the pike pole fence, just a chain link fence. He did have grates on the windows, recently added after a break-in that cost him his guns, stereo, and TV-all that two people could carry out in a hurry (and sell about as fast right down the street).

Joaquin took a swig of coffee and looked out over the neighborhood where he had lived for fifteen years. He looked past the abandoned car, the house with plywood windows and the Golden Seven Market that was converted to a barred fortress after numerous robberies. Funny, he thought, how a person gets used to things by degrees. Funny how you convince yourself it is not that bad. You find the good things hidden beneath the bad and focus on those first. You had to find a way to be happy where you were.

Mandy was still asleep. She was a nurse at Kaiser and had worked a night shift the previous evening. They just celebrated their 20th anniversary. Joaquin and Mandy went together all through high school and got married after graduation. She was an attractive woman and without children. She had brunette hair with chemical variations, was buxom and savvy. She plucked her normally thick eyebrows, then swept and tapered them up and back. The effect was dramatic, like that of a 1940's movie starlet. Her brown eyes were further accented with tattooed eyeliner. Men stared when she wasn't looking. She was a mentor to her younger gal pals at work. She also had a second job in which she was self-employed, offering in-home parties that featured sex toys, lingerie, soap and lotions in an organizational sales pyramid. The job was a network of women helping other women start businesses of their own, no men allowed. The gals in her group kicked down a percentage of their sales, but more importantly, they became friends and gabbed on the phone and e-mailed.

A black F-150 Ford pick-up turned the corner and stopped in front of Joaquin.

"Hey." Was the greeting, Rick Reeger had arrived.

He looked a bit athletic in his Levis and his black *Zildjian* T shirt, which signified to the world that he was drummer. His new basketball shoes were white with blue graphics and the wrap-around sunglasses completed the look. He was trim and wore his hair short. He had a couple of rock and roll tattoos around the biceps which gave him the hip look in the night club on Saturday and the bad ass look when he drove truck during the week. Despite the costume there was no swagger in Rick Reeger. He was easy going, passive in the company of his pals and Zilm was forever trying to put one over on him.

"Coffees in the kitchen, help yourself. Don't make a lot of noise, Mandy's asleep." Joaquin scooted slightly on the stairs to allow Rick enough space to walk by him and into the house.

"Nice day." Reeger said, taking the first stair.

"Clearing up." Was Joaquin's reply.

"Dog inside?" Reeger said as he passed.

"Howdy Doody got wooden balls?" Joaquin answered and added, "Don't worry, she's squared away."

"Has she eaten any more teeth this week, the little furry dick-dog." Rick asked with the reference to yesterday's incident.

"It's a girl-dog, name is Lilly" Joaquin corrected and reminded.

"Excuse me, I mean the little whore-dragon, then." Reeger said with disinterested annoyance.

Reeger returned and set himself down silently on the porch and sipped his coffee, looking absently out over the neighborhood. Without turning to look back at him, Joaquin spoke to Rick.

"What would be different if you had money, Rick?" Joaquin spoke out to the air in front of him.

"That's not the question that bothers me Joaquin, that's an easy answer. The question that bothers me is more like, *what would it be like in jail?*" Reeger replied.

Joaquin continued to speak to the air in front of him. "I got a big check once, $25,955.00. I stayed home from work the next day and just walked around the house. It felt good having money in the bank. I spent it all though, I don't know what happened, but it disappeared fast." Joaquin was almost wistful, like he was talking about a dog he had once.

Joaquin snapped out of his daydream. "Your car or mine?"

"Yours." Reeger said without hesitation.

Joaquin got up and walked around the corner to the back of the house. He reappeared rolling down the driveway in reverse, wearing sunglasses and a bandana in a red Buick convertible, 1956. It looked like a red and chrome boat; adorned with shiny chrome and you could see your reflection on any surface. It was beautiful, always kept in a little garage in the back yard alongside Joaquin's motorcycle. Rolling stock was important to Joaquin and driving around was more than getting from point A to point B; style mattered. As he backed down the narrow pathway to the street, he hit the button and the top folded down into the trunk, producing a slight smile of satisfaction at the corners of his mouth as it tucked itself away. Cool was the rule in the Buick. They loaded up, popped the clutch and laid a little patch of rubber in one short squeal. The automatic transmission had been replaced with a Hurst 5 speed for zip. They disappeared down the empty morning street.

They turned onto East 23rd Street and headed for the freeway that divided Richmond. The heavy Buick developed a rhythmic and cushioned up and down motion and the suspension had it floating along the concrete sections of the thoroughfare. They entered the FastTrak lane and merely touched the brakes as they sped through the toll plaza booth. In the distance was a view of the San Francisco skyline. Marin County opened straight ahead, and the Chevron Long Dock and Red Rock jumped out of the foreground on their left. Rick looked out the passenger side at Point Molate, the old whaling dock and the dilapidated Red Rock marina in ruins.

The morning clouds were parting over the Bay. Light from the east was shining on Marin County and the moon was setting over Mt. Tamalpais. On the immediate shore ahead, dramatic shafts of light came through the clouds and illuminated the starkly historic angles of San Quentin State Penitentiary. They approached the prison at 70 miles per hour over the bridge. They were both too smart to ignore the irony of the illuminated structure as they contemplated a crime, but they did anyway.

"You ever know anybody who was in there?" Rick asked.

"Yeah. The Greek." Joaquin answered.

"No shit, what was the Greek in there for?" Rick was surprised.

"I don't know, I didn't ask. You know how he gets; he gets all nutted up about stuff. He started to go all sideways when it came out that he was inside once, saying how it *saved his life*," Joaquin answered.

"Jail saving your life?" Joaquin questioned.

"Yeah, I guess that happens a lot. It happened when he was young, I do know that. The guy has money now. He must have done something right." Rick observed.

It seemed it took forever for the bridge to end, and when it did it only took them to a road outside the walls of San Quentin. They both got a good look at the place when the road came to a stop sign right at the front gate of San Quentin. They said nothing. The penal facility was silently haunting them now, like they were walking by the graveyard at night. San Quentin was a dirty collection of buildings in need of paint on the side that did not face the public. It appeared desolate and impenetrable. There was no sign of life. Rick and Joaquin watched it as they went by. There was a covered bus stop for released prisoners, also dirty and in need of paint. It had a sign on the little shingled roof, *San Quentin* it read, as if there might be a mistaking it for anything else but San Quentin. The architecture of the bus stop matched the prison in miniature. Rick broke the silence.

"There's no gettin' away from seeing it, I don't even want to look at it anymore. That is the most God-forsaken concrete structure and bus stop to match under the sun. We should have gone the other way down 880." Rick was almost moved to excitement.

"Makes ya think all right; if you ever end up in that place it's *schizen en hosen*- case closed." Joaquin uttered the only German words he knew; it was a favorite vulgar saying of his German boss. He punched the accelerator and loose rocks flew out underneath blue-white smoke, leaving San Q behind. He didn't let off the gas and the heavy car gently fishtailed before gaining speed and traction in front of converging cars, one honked and Joaquin gave him the bird. Joaquin tilted his head toward the rear-view mirror and adjusted his bandanna slightly downward toward his sunglasses.

They briefly traveled through Marin County before going through the tunnel and down the grade toward the famous orange bridge, both men commenting on the ships and boats below, pointedly ignoring Alcatraz and continuing into the city after negotiating a maze of tourist choked streets. They emerged on the freeway on the southern perimeter of the city. The Buick quickly stretched out on the open road and again began to float rhythmically at 75 mph.

"They sure built up that area south of Market St." Rick spoke.

"Yeah, the Peninsula too. South City used to be Italians, then Mexicans, now it's millennials and Genentech, Solartech, Technotech and BioTech, tech this and tech that. Mandy and I looked at a house down there, price was a little high. Glad we got what we got in Richmond. That was 15 years ago." Joaquin explained.

"Why'd you buy that place? It's a warzone down there. Why not on the hill? It's nicer." Rick asked.

"I don't know. It was easy and cheap. The neighborhood was okay. It was okay until the drug wars ruined everything." Joaquin said.

"True. Richmond wasn't bad back in the day" Rick conceded.

"Back in the day when people had jobs that paid enough to live on, you mean." Joaquin added.

They had all grown up and gone to school over in Point Richmond, where the old Victorians and brick buildings perched along the narrow and winding streets along the hillside that overlooked the train yards below. Eucalyptus trees afforded shade in the summer heat. A tunnel ran under the mountain to the old ferry terminal and to the beaches along the Bay. It was a different world apart from the train yards, the homes on the other side of the tracks. They fell silent again. Rick broke the silence.

"I never got into this side of the Bay, it seemed weird." Rick said without conviction as he stared off at a cluster of new houses.

"Oh, it's all right. There's not much going on down here on the Peninsula though. Except old suburbs and shopping malls." Joaquin answered disinterestedly.

They pulled off the freeway into the high-tech industrial park with manicured lawns and driveways studded with large palm trees. Glass fronted high-rises and fountains were around every corner. Overhead, jets climbed from the adjacent airport every three minutes. The buildings and park were built upon landfill atop a shallow bay. Rip-rap rocks formed the shoreline where morning joggers passed by the foot of two gleaming new high-rises, emblazoned with the logo *Krystal.Com.* These were the Krystal Towers that Zilm had directed them to. One of them had precise landscaping; neat rows of low hedge and bordered wide pedestrian walks toward the glass portico of the finished Tower Number One. Tower Number Two appeared finished on the outside, but a construction site fence was in the place around the base of the building. The construction materials therein denoted the place where Zilm and others wired the power, lights, alarms and other electrical systems required to finish the second twenty-six story building. From the East Bay to the Peninsula, they had entered another world: this one new and gleaming. Polished stainless and glass was evident everywhere in these corporate towers by the Bay. There was an eerie quality to the corporate acres that neither men could identify right off.

"It is weird here, see? I was right. What is it?" Rick observed.

"But why?" Joaquin honestly asked uncertainly.

They continued to wind around streets with cul de sacs and promenades and partitioned avenues, all the while looking up at the buildings and wondering why it all creeped them out. Construction still sprouted up in the park, aided by a massive crane that rose upon steel girded towers between the buildings. Then it hit them.

"There's nobody here. It's empty. That's why it's creepy." Joaquin stated.

"Everybody's home I guess, nobody lives around here, that's what's weird all right." Rick said.

"But it just might suit our purposes." Joaquin explained like Sherlock Holmes might explain to Watson.

The big red car came to a stop at the foot of the Krystal Towers. Light rain fell some miles out over the bay as they sat in the morning sunlight, a few drops fell on the convertible. A rainbow began to develop and formed a perfect arch that terminated at the newly constructed buildings before them.

"A pot of gold at the end of the rainbow? A sign from God?" Rick questioned.

"It's either prison, fame or fortune." Joaquin answered.

"Easy choice-that." Rick quipped, adding, "God isn't afraid of going to San Quentin, I bet."

"God isn't afraid of going anywhere, except, you know." Joaquin motioned downward with his finger.

Joaquin paused a moment and added, "So that's the high rise where Zilm works? The one on the right is finished and Zilm works in that other one next to it, the unfinished one?"

"I thought they were bigger than that." Reeger speculated, looking up at the huge tower.

Joaquin stopped to consider this observation by Rick for a second before he replied, "Rick. Tell me something: Is anything the size it's supposed to be?"

Rick gave his pal a quizzical look and replied "That's a really stupid question when you think about it, Joaquin. Everything is *exactly* the size it's supposed to be. It's a matter of perspective. For instance, we see thousands of stars at night, we think that's big. But do you know how many atoms it takes to make a human body?"

"No Rick; as a matter of fact, I do not. How many?" Joaquin replied by way of playing along.

"Yep, that's basically all there is to it. Like taking candy from a baby." Rick said.

"A big, fat, slobbering baby with sharp teeth." Joaquin answered.

"Yeah, more or less. That's him just sitting there pink and naked waiting for us." Rick said.

Joaquin was more cautious than skeptical about this. He was getting a sense that it was possible to put together a plan to pull it off. The more he thought about it, the more he pictured the crime, the more he was seduced; seduced mostly by the money but seduced also by the idea of pulling it off. Getting the old gang back together, the people he trusted, that appealed to him also; he would not do it with any others. Joaquin figured he knew he could do this because he had the balls, the brains, the people and now-the set-up; the circumstances were right. This was the picture he was getting.

'So how do we know when to break in?" Joaquin asked.

"Zilm's got Frenchy on the inside." Rick said.

"The French Fry." Joaquin was smiling.

"I think she's not a tweeker anymore." Rick leaned back from the table in the cushy booth. "That's Zilm's new girlfriend."

"Well, I'll be dipped. How did Zilm get hooked up with her?" Joaquin spoke as he slowly shook his head.

"Met her in Peets or online, I think. She put him on to the high-rise wiring-job too, while they were hanging out up on College Ave. Then later, they got to talking." Reeger responded.

"They were made for each other." Joaquin said.

"Just so you know Rick, I'm not planning on getting caught. No matter what." Joaquin said.

"No; getting caught would be bad." Rick concluded

CHAPTER 5

Getting Over

Mandy Rogers stared at her computer screen, reading the latest testimonial from one of her girls, one of the many consultants in her pyramid of salespeople in the wide-web world of Pleasure Parties International Inc. Although her nursing career was a good job, calling the shots in her own business was exciting and PP International offered that spark of excitement well known to the entrepreneurial mind-the hope of getting rich quick. People were making serious bank in PP International, and she had seen it, wanted it and convinced herself that it was a possibility for her. There was a set of *golden handcuffs,* as they were appropriately called by the successful entrepreneurs, just her size waiting for her. Mandy had the spare bedroom all set up as her office and mailing center for the packages of lubricants, gels, lingerie and marital aids that vibrated and wriggled around.

The *girls* were the members of her sales team whom she had recruited into the sales pyramid and some were her closest friends as well. They paid her a commission; consultants kicked down 5% of their sales action, who in turn raked 5% off their *down line,* thus, the pyramid was formed. The sky was the limit as far as they all were concerned. A strange spell was created by the success of others, it served as an example of what was possible for them. Which, in truth, it was possible, just unlikely. Self-employment was empowering and it felt good to be recognized within the group, and the paycheck helped. But it had a special charge; the fact that it was a company only open to women. Women had carved out an opportunity for financial and personal success that heretofore had been out of reach.

Last week, she had posed the annual Thanksgiving question to her group, 'What do you have to be thankful to Pleasure Parties for this year?', and the responses were loading up her inbox.

Dear Mandy,

What I am thankful the most for is the things I have learned about myself. I was brought up believing I would never amount to anything, that I was worthless. Knowing that I deserve my success, that I am not a bad person, that I can choose to overcome anything in my past and anything that comes my way in the future and that I don't have to be a victim of myself anymore is the most eye opening.

Finding that niche in life where I belong, no longer feeling like an outsider looking in, this is the part that the friendships and relationships of PP, INC has given me.

The financial aspect of course is wonderful…making more in one month than my husband does in two, having money in the bank, buying new furniture flat out and not on credit, being able to actually put away $3000 a month for our house, not worrying about my kid's future, planning on lots of family vacations, looking at that Navigator for next year…these are things I never thought possible in my life!

Relating back to that first paragraph, my biological dad made me feel all I would amount to be is a welfare mom! So being the polar opposite of that is something that I am thankful for!

Connie Lee Sandoval

And another…

Dear Mandy,

I have made lots of wonderful friends that I consider to be like family. I went from working 60 hours a week at a full-time job and missing all the important events in my children's lives, to working when I want and being there for EVERYTHING important to my children and myself.

I love my job. How many can truly say that? For the first time, I am in control of my future. It doesn't get any better than that!

Robyn Plummer.

Mandy stared at the screen and read within her cubicle, rimmed with a row of self-help paperbacks, pictures of her dog, mom and Joaquin on a Harley. She sipped her morning coffee. She heard the kitchen door open and close and knew by the footsteps that Joaquin had arrived and was now fiddling around in the kitchen with silverware and dishes. She continued with her reading.

Dear Mandy,

I'm thankful for you always working behind the scenes to help us accomplish our goals. I'm thankful for the personal growth that leadership requires and the tools I've been given to grow. I am thankful for TWO trips to Vegas in one year and my bonus check on the 10th of each month. I'm thankful for the fact that I went to Memphis Pleasure Power and visited Graceland with 75,000 other people to celebrate the Elvis Birthday. I'm thankful that my kids can get clothes when they need them from retail stores and not consignment shops. I'm thankful for my new floors bought and paid for and the new dishwasher we've done without for so long.

Paulette Foster.

Joaquin walked into the little office and wandered tentatively toward the cubicle, looking at pictures on the wall, purple vinyl sex toys, Double AA battery packs, catalogs and packages of other plastic things, boxed and ready to be shipped out. He approached the row of books and peered over into the desk area where his wife sat and read. He had been initially skeptical of this sex-toy business his wife was doing on the side. It seemed… too naughty and not cool. Besides that, what would his mother have said? The truth, he came to realize, was that money legitimatized almost everything. Especially a harmless business that hurt no one and helped everyone involved. There were constant e-mails, phone calls, zoom chats; it was a force to contend with, and Mandy was always chatting up some gal in a suburb in another part of the country. Joaquin told her once: "It's just another opportunity to gossip with girlfriends." To which Mandy replied, "Now you're starting to understand the world of women." She was smarter than him and most especially when it came to an understanding of the world of women, a world that Joaquin was enticed by and at the same time slightly frightened by. Joaquin wandered into the office area.

"Hi Hon, what's up?" Mandy asked without taking her eyes off the computer screen.

"We're going to rob a diamond broker." Joaquin answered and remained standing before her.

"That's nice." She replied, engrossed in her latest e-mail which read;

Dear Mandy,

Pleasure Parties has allowed me the financial flexibility to attend medical school and still pay my mortgage! In addition, I've met fabulous women and made lifelong friendships, plus, I've learned a lot about myself, working with others and running a business…need I go on? I am gearing up to start my next entrepreneurial adventure that will speak to the thousands out there that have been neglected, and even mocked, for all these years. For all those women who have spent countless hours of frustration and shame in dressing rooms trying to find just the

right fit. Next year, I will open the new online store- FatPants
International! Woohoo!

Tina Taylor

"I'm serious, we checked it out this morning. We're planning a heist."
Joaquin spoke.

Mandy finally looked up from her screen at her husband. She studied
him a moment before asking a question.

"Did Cash put you up to this? Is this part of some stunt to get me out of
the house? Like hiding Christmas presents?" A smile formed and her eyes
began to twinkle.

"No. It's real, I'm serious. We're going to do it. Zilm says it's an opportunity and he's got the inside track on it." Joaquin replied. "So, we're gonna
jump on it."

"Jump on it? More like jump *in* it, you think?" Mandy was chuckling.
Then she realized he was serious.

"You're serious. They actually put real people in real jails for this, Joaquin.
They do it every day Hon, really. And we get to see them on TV. Have you
ever seen those prison documentaries? I saw one last night about Supermax
facilities, guys were in solitary confinement for 17 years or more: a six by
eight room for 17 years! Four walls and a door with no windows. There was
a guy in Virginia doing 34 years with no chance of parole for committing
two robberies. I'm not trying to scare you, just tell you what is real. Don't you
think it's just another crazy idea from Zilm, maybe?" Mandy asked.

"It's not so crazy as it sounds. It's like this; there's this place on the
Peninsula where diamonds are kept for transfer to their new owners, real
high-end stuff. They're only there for a few days before they change hands.
Security is light, it's all ritzy and plush, all for show. We got someone on the
inside there and we think we got a way to get in and get away. Without getting
caught-clean. They'll never know what happened." Joaquin finished.

"Amazing. Delusional, I can't believe I'm hearing this." Mandy's words exited from her mouth through a slight smile, shaking her head slightly from side to side. An awkward silence descended into the room. Mandy broke it.

"So; it's not like you're robbing a bank? With guns and getaway cars and all? Because I've seen that movie too, and it never turns out good for the robbers, it always ends with a bad report for them." Mandy stated.

"Of course not, that'd be stupid." Joaquin was feeling a little better now, the ground he stood upon turning from sand to rock.

"Yeah, that's better; that would be stupid, it's better to steal diamonds, of course." Mandy replied and waited for a further explanation. When none was forwarded, she pressed.

"What if you get caught? Ever think about that?" she asked.

"The way Zilm has it figured, there's no chance of that. Zee-ro chance." Joaquin defended.

"Zilm; Why is it that every time a hare-brained scheme comes along, he figures into it? If his brains were dynamite, he couldn't blow his nose, I swear. He can just join the Aryan Brotherhood right now and be their poster-boy inside the San Quentin State Penitentiary." Mandy's tone was getting sharper. Joaquin knew he was in for it. Another silence and Mandy broke it.

"Joaquin." She said flatly, commanding his full attention.

"Yes." He replied.

"This isn't smart. This isn't what you do, you're not a criminal. This is like you coming home and announcing to me that you have decided to be an astronaut." She spoke in measured and controlled tones, deliberately trying to control her anger and bring this conversation back down to earth.

Joaquin jumped right in. "If I was smart, I wouldn't worry about money every month. I wouldn't live here if I was smart, we live in the Iron Triangle for Christ sakes, the homicide capital of the State! Maybe I'm just starting to open my eyes. Just starting to *get* smart. I look at this as a one-shot deal, a way to get over." He explained.

"Oh my God, you *are* serious." She stated

Joaquin had made up his mind yesterday after he and Reeger checked out the Towers. He was here to sell the idea to his mate, not ask for permission. So far, it was *no sale* from Mandy. He found his voice, low and rising to an even volume as he stood before her making his final attempt at a sensible, juicy rationalization.

"Look, we can do this, I know we can. Money won't ever be a problem after this." The room was silent for a few moments after he spoke.

"You don't have to do this. I make good money, you make decent money at your job, no? This is crazy talk and I'm not about to stand here and let you go to jail. What do I do after you're gone up the river? Ever think about that? This isn't smart, it's crazy! We got enough money, everybody has money problems, but they don't go out stealing, for God's sake." Mandy was starting to lose her temper.

"That's not it, Mandy, it's different than that. I want to take control-permanently. I'm not talking about robbing a 7-11 for rent money, this is a lifetime pop; I'm talking about *getting over,* a way out." Joaquin pleaded the case further.

"A way out of what?"

"Poverty that's like a low grade fever that does not go away. It's always money, this, money for that, money, money, money-I don't even want to think about it anymore. It's like I'm on this leash." Joaquin surprised himself, letting out an emotion he did not know he had.

Silence fell over the room after Joaquin dropped this. It was a conversation-stopper, for sure. Joaquin was out of words; after this, what else was there to say, he had surprised even himself? He had always thought himself a happy guy but the seeds of discontent had apparently found fertile soil.

"Who all is in this besides Zilm? The whole gang? She asked.

"Pretty much. Plus, one-Van Zant." He confessed and braced for the reaction.

"Van Zant! Why on earth him? He's not right in the head and you know this. He's an ex-felon-psycho. He can't be trusted and he's dangerous, Christ! Of all the people. Joaquin, you know better. Why even associate with him?" Mandy unloaded a barrage of disapproval, everything Joaquin expected from her. It was like she was pulling all the dishes out of the cupboard and letting them hit the floor, just like she did when he told her he joined the army to go to Vietnam.

"He has connections and certain skills required for this." Joaquin replied calmly.

"I really don't like this, and I really don't like it more now that I know *Van Zant's* involved. I will never understand men-you're all like children! You are not going to throw your life away with my blessing, if that's what you want. I don't even want to hear another word about this-that's how it is and that's how it stays!" Mandy laid down her pen on the desk and walked out of the room.

"I'm doing this." Joaquin yelled softly at her retreating back.

"Well don't tell me about it. I don't want to be an accomplice! Have fun in the Supermax pretty boy, don't drop the soap and watch out for those Nazis." Mandy replied and that was her final word as she exited into the hallway.

Joaquin looked around the empty room and mumbled to himself, "Goddamn rights she'll like the money as much as me." he mumbled to himself, "…talk to me like I'm common criminal?.................she'll see."

Mandy was quiet but her mind was making connections, connections that she heard daily from her girls. This realization illuminated a fact: people everywhere were under an economic stress and while some had accepted the fate, others sought opportunity to get ahead, albeit legal, but getting over to one degree or the other. They focused on a prize; they went for it powered by the driving force of hope. Hope begat motivation, and motivation found the ambitious person ready and willing. She had pages and pages of testimony on her screen right now that said the same thing over and over.

"How much money are we talking about here?" Mandy asked as she walked back into the room.

"Maybe as high as 9 million? I don't know exactly." Joaquin replied.

"Millions, you say?" Mandy asked.

"Right." Joaquin replied.

"Split 6 ways?"

"7 ways. Zilm's girlfriend works on the inside. She brought the deal to Zilm."

"You know her?" Mandy asked.

"Yeah, it's Frenchy."

Mandy laughed; she knew Frenchy. "Now there is a match made in heaven."

She stepped up in front of him and looked him in the eye. Mandy Rogers considered him for a moment before speaking. Then, in measured tones she spoke.

"Listen mister, I have my doubts about what's going on in your head right now." She remained right in his face as she spoke and stared him down.

"I just want to get over." Joaquin replied.

"One condition; you don't get caught no matter what. I don't want to spend the rest of my life like a widow-visiting you in jail and talking though a glass window on a phone. Okay?" She placed her hands up on his shoulders.

"Scouts Honor." He replied.

"You're going to have to deal with Van Zant eventually. He's not right in the head, never has been, you know that. You are letting a crazy person into your life." She added, "You don't even like him."

"Zilm says he different now, says he's changed." Joaquin lied; Van Zant had not changed one bit that he could see.

"I have one more condition, then." She stated, "You don't turn your back on Van Zant, ever. And you don't get yourself killed."

"That'll be the easy part." Joaquin reassured her.

"Which one, turning your back or getting killed?" She asked.

"Both. You'll see. We're gonna pull this off." Joaquin spoke with absolute assurance; he had convinced even himself.

* * *

Danielle Atwood revealed her striking figure when dressed in her silk pajamas, the silky garment hinted at every turn and curve of her well-formed athletic body. It left little to the imagination of the territory beneath the silk. Every nuanced curve of flesh and feminine form beneath suggested mysteries that beckoned to the chosen who were allowed the privilege of witness. She was tall, fit, jet black hair, divorced, kids raised and modestly wealthy by the pathway of divorce, charm, ambition and real estate. She had parlayed her engaging presence, manner and a perfect white smile into a comfortable sum by selling high end homes in the East Bay of San Francisco. She chauffeured her clients to homes that ranged into the millions in price, chatted them up, attended their every inquiry diligently and took her commissions upon sale of these stately homes. She was beautiful, single and independent in every way. She only had one habit that was out of character, she was a *player* and she was accustomed to getting what she wanted when she wanted it. On Saturday night she could be found in the latest hip and trendy nightclub. And on this Sunday morning, she looked back over her shoulder at the result of this. She reached to part the curtains of the French doors that opened onto the balcony from her bedroom and there he was-a handsome, curly-haired and sexy stranger in her bed. He stretched his athletic torso over the silk sheets, his chest, abdomen and arm muscles were well-defined and smooth, his face had a movie-star quality. They were no longer strangers, now being intimately acquainted in the carnal sense of the phrase. Last night, it seemed like such a good idea at the time and the girlfriends she was out with thought so too. This man was good looking, charming, and seemingly in possession of her ultimate aphrodisiac; money. Men like he deserved women like her, and vice-versa; the unconscious rationale that guided these decisions in the moment. They were like a matched breeding pair.

The curtains she opened this morning revealed a panorama that spanned 6 counties and included the most famous bridges in the world, the finest natural harbor in the world, a bay complete with islands, sailboats, and ships. The skyscrapers and bridges and the other creations marked the highly developed civilization. In other words, the whole of the SF Bay Area and beyond spread out before her as viewed from an East Bay hills perspective from an elevation of 1600 feet. The yellow morning light gave the room a warm and cheerful hue. It entered and warmed the room illuminating the handsome man in her bed whom she knew only as *Steve.* She studied the sleeping figure; he was muscular and approaching middle age with muscle tone intact. He had a $100 haircut, and his nails were manicured. He smelled nice and his manner had been assertive, pleasant and so persuasive. He gave her a ride home from her favorite tony nightspot in his red car, a car which was upscale as well. They laughed. She invited him in. They laughed some more over a nightcap and now, pleasantly she thought, he's still here. It all fit nicely into the movie in her head. One thing did not fit though, and it was almost a deal-breaker when she first looked at him; the jailhouse tattoo on his right forearm gave him a common and vulgar look, even though tattoos were trendy now. However, this one wasn't new; it was homemade and old, the colors were running and turning blue. It was a clown with a deranged look in his eyes.

The handsome man turned on his back and rubbed at his chest hairs as he opened his eyes. He saw her staring at him, smiling. He smiled back.

"Hey." He chuckled softly and rubbed the sleep from his eyes.

Danielle walked over and slid her silky self onto the comforter atop the bed. She snuggled her chin up to that place between his head, shoulder and neck and said softly,

"Morning handsome." She gave him a peck on the cheek under his ear. This is sexy she thought and closed her eyes and remained in there against him.

"I got lucky." He said.

"More than you know. The best may be yet to come." She replied, raising her head slightly for added emphasis.

"You mean it gets better than this?" He asked.

"That all depends on you." She replied somewhat coy and seductively and returned to her resting place upon his shoulder and closed her eyes again.

She opened her eyes and stared down his bare arms and torso, surveying and liking all that she saw before her until her eyes became fixed on that tattoo; the eyes and smile were off-putting; it had a look of evil and insanity. It's crude and grotesque she thought. It was not fresh and sporty looking like the fashionable young men of the day were wearing.

"Steve?" she asked tentatively, realizing she knew nothing about this man.

"Yeah babe?" he replied a little too familiar.

"What did you say your last name was?" she continued.

"Van Zant." He said flatly, adding, "And I didn't say, sweet *thang.*"

In all her well-chosen and extensive exposure to men in intimate liaisons, Danielle Attwood had never been referred to as *Sweet Thang.* She didn't like it, it sounded crude, vulgar and demeaning. It was a street name and made her feel common somehow. She was Danielle Atwood, self-made and elegant. Who was he to refer to her like she was a street walker? But she didn't say anything.

CHAPTER 6

To Boldly Go

In school or around the neighborhood, Zilm couldn't get a girlfriend to save his life. It was not ever easy for him. And he was not a bad looking guy. Blue eyes, blond squared off flat top, trim physique, Aryan features. But his attempts at courting always involved some inspired trickery that mostly failed. The guys used to taunt him.

"Zilm, you couldn't get laid in a whorehouse with a twenty dollar bill hangin' outta each pocket!" And it was true. His amorous entreaties were mostly DOA. Zilm had a shot once, but fate had cut him off at the knees. In eighth grade he was making positive inroads with the in-crowd and they invited him to go on a picnic to Mill Creek. Zilm was elated; all the cool girls with breasts and everything would be there and all the cool guys too. This was the pinnacle of his adolescent social life so far. Then, they dropped the bomb: they were going skinny-dipping. Naked? Naked girls? That is when the anxiety set in.

"Last one in is a rotten dirt-bag!" Jenny Mazzanti was the coolest girl, and she began to leave a trail of clothes from the car to the water. Bob was barely out of the backseat as he watched her pert little butt sashay into the pond water.

"C'mon in, the water's fine." Jenny screamed and the carload followed suit and joined her. Zilm took his shoes off, then his shirt and pants. He stuck a toe into the pond.

"Don't be chicken Bobby! Get in the water!" Jenny screamed. All feminine eyes were now on him by the edge of the water in his tighty-whities. He snaked off his shorts.

Zilm stripped down and immediately got a 4.5 inch, pre-pubescent boner as he watched the naked teen girls frolic in the water before him. He dove in headfirst, hoping to hide the appendage, or at best to persuade his erotic enthusiasm to go away. It did not. After a half hour he was alone in the water and four naked girls were now laying in the sun on the bank before him in a teasing and tantalizing array of nubile beauty. The boner still had not yet gone down.

"Bob, help us inflate this raft!" Tommy Miller, the coolest guy in school and a sophomore, was inviting Bob to join the cool guys. They were pulling a giant raft out of the car trunk. Zilm obliged the call.

He walked out the water in full view of the girls with a little boner and they tittered and giggled. The spirit-crunching humility bore down upon him, defeating him on all levels but one, his lonely boner. He barely had pubic hair and it was so light blond in color it was near invisible. The boner ached and made his skin so tight he felt as if his eyelids wouldn't close.

"Put that little thing away!" Came a shout from a frolicking naked girl.

All heads turned toward the mid-section of Zilm and his growingly famous *Boner at Mill Creek*. It got a good laugh from the male crowd. But Zilm could not put it away because it would not come down; an all-day boner and he had it like a third leg sticking out of the middle of his torso like a tree branch. Throughout the course of the next four hours, it got caught on branches, got too close to the fire, poked Bud Ackerley in the shoulder and served as a towel rack.

For the next four years of high school, every time a girl giggled or tittered when he was within earshot, he was sure it was about the now famous *Boner at Mill Creek Incident.*

It left permanent scars on his psyche but soon after high school Zilm found out all he had to do was stretch out his romantic horizons to places no

Point Richmond man had ever gone before- Robert A. Zilm launched his new offensive on the unwitting inhabitants of the distant galaxy of............ ... dun-dun-da-dah'....... Cyber space!

He was an overnight sensation as a cyber-space Casanova. Internet dating was a glorious field of opportunity for those who might boldly go there. His ego, on a starvation diet since an early age, grew with every response to his witty online letters as he charmed the damsels of the lonely planet Earth. He was double and triple-timing the women until they dumped him. Nevertheless, the guy's still poked fun at him, nicknaming his cyber-playgrounds *Snatch.com* and *LizardLife.com*. But their taunts no longer bothered Robert Adolf Zilm, because he knew he was a cyber-stud and now *he* was getting *action*.

His new girlfriend was Michele Marie Gigot, who later became known affectionately as "Frenchy." She was a high-function tweeker. Not some fallen angel type or bag-lady-in-training, but a working, housed, well-heeled and socially active tweeker. When Zilm first hooked up and went out on a date, he learned nothing about who she was because she talked non-stop for 8 hours about nothing. He had a few questions, but they would have to go unanswered, he could not get a word in with a shoehorn. It took 2 hours just to understand what she did for a living and what her "clients" were seeking, she danced all around the answer to that question. Frenchy didn't just speak conversationally, she gushed like a magnum of uncorked champagne for hours on end. Zilm finally pinned her down to a solid answer he could understand when she confided at last.

"I'm a domestic groomer and my clients love me-here, listen to the messages they leave me on my cell phone-they can't do without me-these are busy, professional people who appreciate beauty and style-I make their life attractive-their home sings with joy when I leave-they recommend me to professors and doctors-and the children-oh my-the children are the best-I look at their room and I look into their little souls and I match the two-I look at the dining room table-I look for an hour and then it hits me-I move the salt shaker to the left of the bud vase-just 1.5 inches and it all comes together, the room begins to sing-a brilliant union of soul, space and harmony-Oh my God-Oh my God-I love my job!"

She caught a breath. It went like this all through their first dinner date. She just talked all the way up the stairs into Zilm's apartment, grabbed a bottle of Jack off the top of the refrigerator, poured a few fingers in a plastic tumbler by the sink, drank it and ripped open her shirt to reveal a flimsy little camisole. Her little brown nipples were calling to Robert, and they raced each other to bed.

Now, you might think it would be over the morning after, but Robert fell under the spell of Frenchy. He found her entertaining, especially in bed and upon this rock, success or failure was measured. He had dated plenty of others, but they were dull in comparison. He didn't have a lot in common with normal people with normal and conventional jobs. In Frenchy, he seemed to have found his type; who knew his type would turn out to be someone who was slightly neurotic and fringy?

On the second date it was revealed that domestic groomer was code for housecleaner. More was revealed later or should say "leaked" as the relationship went on. Michele Gigot was a firm believer in *not* revealing a lot of herself on the first date, with the exception of flesh, which was *always* entirely revealed on her first date. As time went on, Zilm also learned that she was also a life coach, spirit guide, psychic healer, massage technician, small-time con, hairdresser, office temp, tarot card interpreter, sexual educator, aromatherapist, palmist, consultant on everything, and dancer. She was full of surprises. She found Zilm far more interesting than her former boyfriend, her boss, Beto Chacon. Her boss turned out to be a rich cheapskate who put money before anything else. He was bi, boring, self-centered, in love with his good looks, good clothes, cars and his home in a tony Los Gatos neighborhood. Marie Gigot was a trophy, a conquest, nothing more. Frenchy thought that was okay for a while, but she lost interest in proportion to her level of respect for this guy.

It was a Friday noon and Zilm was picking up Ms. Gigot (as she liked to be addressed) from her office job as receptionist at the Global Investment Corporation, located in the Krystal Tower #1, a short distance across from the Krystal Tower #2. The Krystal Tower #2 building was unfinished, and this is where Zilm pulled wire with his co-workers, Murph and the Buzzard, all day. Robert Zilm waited out front, parked in the street in his little convertible. Frenchy burst out the rotary glass doors and gave him a wave, all 107 pounds of pure energy topped with blonde and streaky hair. Zilm was still trying to guess her age. He put it somewhere south of 45, but it may have been deep into the northern latitudes of the roaring forties. She told him she was 41, so that meant she was older than that. In any event, the clock was running, and her youth had entered an elegant and subtle sudden death overtime. Stated indelicately, she had been *rode hard and put away wet*. Meth is so unkind to women.

"We gotta swing by the pound, it's just down the road-I got a photo of the cat I want. Please? Okay fine. You just wait in the car, and I won't be a minute-It's down at Coyote Point and they close in 1 hour-I got a box for the cat and I swear it won't go poo-poo or pee-pee on you or the car, please?"

Zilm nodded, "Poo-poo would be bad."

"You are the best Bobby-I could just eat you up-what am I saying? -I *am* gonna eat you up later. Just what are we doing later? The Topper? -I need a drink: every swingin' dick in there is houndoggin' my ass all day, even the rug-muncher. Guess what I saw today? Okay I'll tell ya-I swear I saw a rock today that could choke a horse-15 carats! -You know what carats are Bobby? Not the vegetable kind-The diamond kind-You know how big that is, do ya?" She stopped and took out a little pipe and a little Ronson butane torch, loaded the pipe with weed laced with a white powdery toxicity and sucked on it. She continued.

"*It's biiiiiiig ahzzz a fuhhhkin houhhhse, that's how big.*" She said with her breath held in. Her face turned red, and she exhaled. "That's how big it is Bobby. Want some?"

"No. How long is that rock going to be in there?" Zilm asked

"It's gone, sold to some Prince today. There's a big deal next week, though, -9 million I heard 'em talk about- a collection or some such, some kind of diamonds..." She was shifting gears and getting ready to unleash a barrage of verbiage. Zilm cut her off.

"Find out when: I want to know." Zilm was intent.

"*Ooooooookaaaay. You wanna know when, allriiiiiiiiiight.*" She inhaled again.

"Just find out." Zilm said. They commenced with their business, driving towards the SPCA. Frenchy was now chemically energized.

"Oh, Bobby it's the cutest thing- Just the most ordinary little common kitty cat you ever saw-I mean you can't swing a cat without hitting one of these fuzzballs." She giggled at her *swing a cat* joke.

"I had one of these little pussies bagged up in Martinez and ready to go out the door once-one of these SPCA *Pet Nazis* got me-knew me by name for Christ sakes-remembered me from a time before and she said I couldn't have it! -the bitch! She said they had to be careful of the homes the pets went out to-said they were doing background checks-can you imagine that? For a rotten little cat going to the gas chamber?! -a background check! Somebody ought to check the background of those *Pet-Nazis*. They should thank me for giving it a home before they kill it, for Christ sake!

Frenchy filled the pipe with weed again and sprinkled a little white dust on top.

"Too bad." Zilm commented, lost in thought driving down the Bayshore freeway, not listening to the attractive drugged lunatic in the passenger seat and currently wondering how big 15 carats was, he'd have to Google that.

They pulled the little car into the parking lot of the Peninsula Humane Society. He waited in the car and the French Fry got out and swished up to the front door. She knew they were all lesbians in this place and she was suited up and ready to flirt with them.

"Heeeeeeeeey there". Frenchy cooed. She recognized the two green-uni-formed figures shaped like short and stubby water-heaters, eyeing her with suspicion. Behind the desk was a collection of women waiting to check the credentials of the pet-adoring public. This was the first line of pet adoption defense, once past this, Marie knew she had it made.

"Back again?" Sternly said and not an auspicious beginning.

"Oh, I just felt so bad-my little Smidgeons got run over-I don't know what to do-can I have another cat? Here I am I guess, back for another cat." She pitched her story.

The head volunteer eyed her suspiciously but stated politely.

"Well, you'll have to fill out these forms again before I can even *let* you go back to the viewing wall. Then, the fees must be paid if you can find a replacement for your flat-cat." There was something a little off about the emphasis on the word *flat*.

Frenchy sucked it up and made nice. "Oh, I don't think I can ever replace Smidgeons-but I need a playmate for little Herbie-they were so close-He just *drooooooooops* around the house looking for Smidgeons-imagine how sad." She stopped and gauged the reaction.

"You're right. I *can't* imagine." The SPCA ladies weren't buying it, but they also didn't know what her angle was. They just assumed that maybe she was a crazy cat-lady, harboring a houseful of cats.

"Fill these out and Margene will take you back when you're done." Said SPCA lady. Across the lobby, Margene gave Frenchy a stern look. The papers came across the desk, and some were yellow, some were blue, and some were green. There were 5 forms in all. Michele Marie Gigot held the record for returning filled-out forms; 124 seconds flat. She pushed the multi-colored pile back to the SPCA lady and smiled at Margene.

In the back viewing room, The French-Fry was home free. She could now walk with her photograph in hand and look at the cats up for adoption. She wasn't here for Herbert-there was no Herbert; she was here for the reward from a forlorn family in Piedmont, trying to replace their lost kitty. Michele Gigot had pulled off a flyer from a telephone pole, promising a $500 dollar reward. This was one of her scams, returning look-alike pets for the reward, offered from a grief-stricken family who was ready to pony-up the cold cash. Michelle Marie Gigot eyed the mongrels in the cages before her. She had been successfully running this con about twice a month lately. It had amazed her how so many cats looked the same, you just had to know where to find them. And it was equally amazing how much reward a family will pay. That cat's picture might end up on a telephone pole like a child on a milk carton. Frenchy was there to provide relief to the forlorn family and pick up a hefty reward for herself in the process. She stuffed one of the mongrel kitties up for adoption in her box, went to the front, paid her fee and left.

Zilm was listening to Rush Limbaugh and thinking about hillbilly heroin. He was just waiting for Frenchy, who eventually arrived with a flourish and threw the box in the back seat. A frightened howl came out of it.

"Match?" Zilm asked.

"Close enough. Let's get out of here-we got some work to do-I got the winning ticket in the box and I'm gonna cash it in-I need a drink-Let's go to Tony's pronto when we're done-I think they are on to me in there-I gotta let that place cool off-that *bitch* is gonna do something rash if I show my face in there again-I hate this Peninsula!-God! This is work-Got a smoke? -God!" Frenchy burst like a dam.

Over the bridge they went and back into safe territory, to the East Bay where life was sensible. It was a relatively quiet drive, Michele Marie was practicing her lines in her head, looking occasionally at the kitty-picture on the flyer. Zilm punched the address into his GPS display and followed the directions on the map to a house in Piedmont. He cheerfully made a pronouncement upon arrival.

"Showtime!" Zilm remained in the car, Frenchy was a solo act, supporting roles need stay behind.

Inside the stately Brown Shingle, the Steinberg family, Bob, Alice and little five-year old Sarah, had assembled in the living room anticipating the arrival of their pet cat. Bob was especially glad the cat had been found, there hadn't been peace in the house for two weeks since its absence. In fact, there hadn't been a piece of any kind to be had, he anxiously anticipated one, possibly even tonight. The doorbell rang, Sarah started jumping up and down and Bob opened the door.

"Come in, Come in. Welcome to the Steinberg house. We are so delighted to see you" Bob Steinberg eyed Marie approvingly and held his gaze upon her pert little nipples under the flimsy silk blouse.

Michele Marie Gigot was no fool; she had this act down pat. She dressed for it, presented the animal, got the cash (emphasis on cash), and got the hell out. She tried to keep the ransom exchange to less than five minutes and she always had a driver waiting outside.

"Here's your little baby! Found him down on Grand Ave behind the Thai restaurant. Imagine the little dickens down there feasting on coconut prawns out of the dumpster!" She had rehearsed this on the way over.

"Mommy! Mommy! Let me see!" Sarah grabbed the box and opened it like a Christmas present. A skinny black and white cat wobbled out and ran right under the couch and stayed. The child followed as far as she could go and stopped when her little shoulders got stuck underneath the heavy piece of furniture.

"The little thing is so happy to be home! Say, I'm running late and must get to work. Any more questions?" Michelle Gigot anxiously asked, fearing she would be discovered any second.

Alice Steinberg had her doubts about this woman, something wasn't right about her, she couldn't say just what and she definitely didn't like her attire. Also, she hadn't had a chance to examine the cat yet, which seemed like something obligatory. $500 was a lot of money to just hand over to a shady-looking stranger. She spoke up.

"Oh nonsense, I've got coffee all made, I'll get us all a cup." And off she went into the kitchen, past little Sarah who had managed to get a hold on the back leg of the cat hiding under the couch. She pulled her by the back legs, out backwards as the cat sunk claws into everything it could, trying to maintain a safe position under the couch.

Michele Marie knew something was up, just knew it. This Steinberg bitch was on to her. Panic began to set in, but she squelched it; plan B was going to have to go into effect, she slipped her hand into her pocket and hit the SEND button on her cell phone. A moment later the phone rang in the Steinberg home. It was Zilm impersonating a fireman on the other end of the line.

"Sir, this is the Piedmont Fire Department, Engine Co 235? Sir, we have an emergency evacuation of Highland Ave, blocks 200 to 600. Sir, could you evacuate all your family immediately? Get your family to a safe place out of the area. You may return to your residence after a notification of the 'ALL CLEAR' signal. Sir, there is a gas leak; this is urgent, risk of explosion is high. Repair crews are not allowed in until the residents are evacuated. Thank you, sir." The voice halted.

"Oh yes, well thank you very much. This is so sudden. How long before we can return"? Bob Steinberg, on the other end of the line, was stunned.

"That all depends, sir. Repairs will not commence until the evacuation of the neighborhood is complete. No smoking, sparks or open flame, sir." Zilm was getting into it; it was getting good to him, he could be a fireman, he could see that now.

"Of course, of course, thank you very much." Bob Steinberg replied and hung up the phone.

"Honey! There's a gas leak in the neighborhood and we have to evacuate *right now!* There could be an explosion! Turn off the burner on the stove! The Fire Department just phoned!" He yelled into the kitchen.

Frenchy interjected, "This is terrible, Bob, but at least the kitty is back. Looks like WE ALL must be going now. And I do mean *right now.* If you don't mind, may I have the reward please and I will evacuate as ordered." She smiled sweetly. Bob took out his wallet and peeled off the bills just in time for his wife to see the cash enter the suspicious woman's hands.

"Well thanks, gotta evacuate, gotta go." Michele Marie headed for the door. She exited and didn't look back at the open door behind her. But she heard the child's little voice whining back inside, saying:

"Mommy, Smidgeon's got two butt holes now!" The little girl was staring straight at the back of the kitty under the couch, obviously a female. She had a death grip on its little back legs.

Frenchy was down the steps in a flash. "Oh shoot-darn-drive Bobby! Let's go-I got the dough-the little girl was getting wise to me-the mom hated me from the git-go, thank god the dad was a stooge-got a smoke? Friggen-hell!" Marie fumbled through her purse for drug paraphernalia.

"Well, I knew something was up as soon I got the emergency call. I expected it, actually." Zilm turned toward her in the passenger seat and continued "Why don't you just bag the little kitties in front of their house, wait for the flyers to show up and return the *right* kitty?"

"Robert! That is the most disgusting idea I have ever heard-what kind of person do you take me for. It's cruel, it's criminal, its, its…cat-napping!" Marie protested.

"Just a thought, that's all." Zilm defended mildly.

"Well, I'll think about it. God I was dying for a smoke in there-that wife-bitch was on to me-I knew it the minute she looked at me-the walls were closing in so I hit the panic button just before the kid started to squeal. The lost cat was a *friggin* male! -the flyer didn't say anything about that, did it? Who knew? Did the flyer *say* that? Christ sakes, I gave 'em back a female cat!" Marie ended her rant and fumbled with the junk in her purse as Zilm cruised down the leafy lanes of Piedmont, headed for the Topper Club.

"There must be an easier way to make a buck for God's sake, Robert." Michelle Marie Gigot confided.

"There just might be." Zilm replied.

CHAPTER 7

The Gangs All Here

The Topper Club was owned and presided over by the bartender, Tony Harrington. Tony was Irish with a slight brogue, was in his late sixties, short white hair and a pocked large nose centered in a pink face. His manner was a little gruff until you caught on. He was also a wry comedian, but often, the joke might just be on you. He liked the young ladies who considered him to be a funny and a dirty old man. The regulars all knew what was meant when Tony was referred to as the *thirteenth step*. In his bar, a twelve-step program was just another annoying fixture of modern life and getting a drink from Tony could be considered the difficult *thirteenth* step when he was distracted with chatting up a young lass. You might best get his attention by calling him on his cell phone to ask for your drink. That had happened, and the story was told famously over and over. His humor was dry, and he was a quick study when it came to people. He was an expert at assessing human behavior and had broken his assessment of the species into four categories; *like'em- punks-drunks-*and *phonies-*yet being a phony didn't exclude you from the two former categories. He was the one responsible for nicknaming Michele Marie the *French Fry* and she was one of his favorite phonies. His real name was Padeen, but only his mother could use that name. Rick's band, *The Spacebuds*, played there every Saturday for the last ten years and it was the gang's clubhouse. In fact, Tony had a round table in the back just for them.

Van Zant was sitting at the bar when Zilm and Frenchy walked in. Van Zant seemed to be having a jolly time, bantering with everyone who walked by. He saw them enter from his spot on the corner stool.

"Zilm!" he greeted, "Get your nappy-ass over here and let me buy you a drink little buddy!"

Zilm and Frenchy walked over, and Frenchy remained silent. She had two modes-silent and wide-open rapping. She nodded hello to Van Zant and kept on going to the jukebox. Van was one of those men she did not flirt with, ever.

"Tell me Zilm," said Van Zant, releasing Robert from a hug "Why is it that I just want to break your glasses and take your lunch money every time I squeeze you, huh? Can you tell me that?"

"I don't wear glasses anymore, Van, I got that Lasik operation a long time ago." said Zilm straightening his shirt out from the mauling.

"Now that's it right there, Bob; *you don't wear glasses anymore*, self-improvement Bob. That's one of the things I like about you Bob; you get the award for *Most Improved*."

"He doesn't need lunch money anymore either." Tony interjected from behind the plank. He didn't like Van Zant, especially when he was taunting customers and friends. In Tony's filing system, Van Zant was at the top of the list of *punks*, never did like him from the git-go.

"Oh, I know that Tony, shoot, Bob and I got all of that straight a long time ago, right Bob?" Van Zant gave Tony a wink and was grinning and pleased with himself. "Just having some fun with the old Zilch-man."

Zilm remained standing and motioned to a table, Frenchy was already playing bumper pool in the back against some college kids. Van Zant got up from the stool and they both walked over to the back table just as Cash and Eddie walked in followed by Joaquin and Reeger. Tony exclaimed a greeting from behind the bar.

"Joaquin me boy! You're not dead, I thought you were dead; I haven't seen you for so long." The old bartender kidded. He liked Joaquin.

"No, no. Just working, Tony, you know nose to the grindstone, Mandy cracks the whip. You good? Same old-same old in here, huh?" Joaquin was once a regular.

"Oh yeah, everything's fine around here, fit as a fiddle." Tony answered.

"Great, I'll be in more regular, we'll catch up later," Joaquin stated and kept walking toward the table in the back.

"Well, all the *big names* are here now." Van Zant grinned with sarcasm, looking toward Joaquin's entrance.

"Screw you, Van. Don't start no trouble and there won't be any." Joaquin pulled back a chair and Reeger took one alongside him.

"We're all friends here, *Wah-keen*, the past is in the past; like dirty water under that old bridge-history!" Van Zant replied, making a point to accentuate Joaquin's name.

Joaquin looked at him, finally deciding it was not worth it to get pissed off. They had discussed the plan many times this week with Van. Joaquin was still having a hard time warming up to this guy but realized the necessity of his inclusion in the caper. He would get over his distaste and distrust he concluded.

"Yep, like water under the bridge, Van." Joaquin settled.

Eddie and Cash walked in, Cassius Kingston and Eddie Wong. Cash wore an Italian silk suit and shiny shoes and wore lots of gold accessories from his pawn shop Downtown. Eddie by contrast, had a grease-stained Ferrari pit-crew T-shirt, dungarees and slip-on tennis shoes that were also stained with motor oil. The two made for the table and sat down without a word. Cash slipped his jacket onto the back of the chair and addressed Van Zant.

"Whassup Stevie V?" Cash said.

"Six-ten and even." Van replied in a congenial manner.

Eddie Wong spoke, "So Zilm: Everything still okay at the Towers? Plan A still in effect?"

Zilm thought for a moment before replying. "No change. Just waiting for word from the inside." Zilm gave a slight nod toward Frenchy, busy running the table on the hapless young English-majors in the back.

Eddie turned to Joaquin, "What do you think Joaquin?"

"Looks do-able, just like Zilm said. I got all the equipment we need. It's crazy. It's bold as brass, but that's why it works. Van says *no problem* on his end. That's the best part-the *why* we don't get caught-the getaway. I spent another day just driving around that whole peninsula over there, Bay-side and Coast-side. Roads in and out are good if we need them." Joaquin replied.

"We won't." Zilm jumped in.

Cash jumped in, off topic. "Back in the day we go over to the beach fishing. My dad loved fishing. We go over for the fireworks on the Fourth of July. You ever watch fireworks in the fog? Ain't nuthin' but a pink and green glow! Everything was all wet. They got all that natural beauty going on, but I got all tired on that natural beauty right away. All those trees and grass and water and shit? They just make me feel sleepy!"

Reeger added in "They get that Sunlight Attention Disorder from the fog. They call it S.-A.-D. That's a homonym."

"It's not a homonym, you moron, it's an acronym." Zilm corrected. "And it stands for Seasonal Adjustment Disorder, S.-A.-D."

"You're both S-A-D." Eddie cracked.

"Whatever." Zilm gave Eddie the stink-eye.

Eddie continued. "Everything cool on your end Stevie V?"

"Piece of cake. Just get me in, I'm golden. It's a Liebherr 300C, A child could run it. I could run those while I sleep." Van Zant answered. "It's got a 360 swing and a 150-meter reach."

"How 'bout it Zilm? When we gonna do this thing?" Eddie spoke.

"Frenchy says there are goodies coming soon and I told her to get me the details, she'll know a 'coupla days in advance, I think. Rumor is 9 million in colored diamonds is the next transaction. I'll be watching the action from over on Tower #2 as well." Zilm said.

Cash jumped in. "Now with these colored stones, it depends on the color and clarity. A carat is just the measure of weight-how big the thing is, you know. Some stuff worth a little and some worth a lot, like I say, depends."

"I think it's a collection, very valuable." Zilm said.

"You said 9 million Zilm, right?" Eddie piped up.

"It could fetch a lot, depending on the deal I can make. There will be enough to go around, believe that." Cash Kingston was cool and always underplayed his hand. He had money and he didn't get it by being a loud-mouthed fool. His money had come through the back door of his pawn shop down on Broadway.

Joaquin had a question. "So, you get these rocks, Cash. Then what?

"Well, like I say, it depends. Not the easiest thing. Got to make a good deal. Everybody knows' they stolen. Maybe it's a famous collection-then what? You got to be careful, find the right people, it might take a while. There's cons and cops and suckers of all kinda description. You know how it is-word will get around. Some greedy mo-fos will try to steal the things like they be at some garage sale; pay pennies on the dollar to me like I was some kinda crackhead. We don't panic-we ain't nervous-we don't say 'nuthin. Those kindsa people don't even get to know who we are. We gotta wait for the right client, you feel me?" Cash was king, just like the saying goes.

"And we just wait it out? How long does that go on?" Joaquin questioned.

"We wait; gotta wait for the right buyer and gotta wait for the heat to cool off too. I don't know how long, but usual, the longer the wait, the better the deal. Long as everybody stay cool, we be fine." Cash looked around the silent table.

The seated men were looking around the table now, staring briefly into the eyes of each of their new partners. These grown men had long standing relationships with each other that stretched back to grammar school. But they all knew that was a long time ago and seated at the table now, they were not the same people as those of long-ago, a lot had happened over the years. Also, and this was the most unsettling knowledge, a lot had *not* happened; some weren't that close anymore, specifically, Van Zant. Where once there had been a tight-knit and interdependent group as adolescents, as adults they had separate lives and different agendas. Time and events had placed a question mark over their solidarity. Trust that was once a given was often unproven in adult life. That trust was about to undergo the biggest test. *Money: dumb, greasy and green*, that almighty motivator that had the power to conjure nefarious behaviors for personal gain. This was the underlying subtext as they searched the faces around the table for any hint of lying eyes.

"How do I know I'm not gonna get fucked?" Eddie Wong asked in an in-eloquent and vulgar phrase.

Reeger started chuckling at Eddie's blunt reaction, "Really." Reeger paused before he continued. "But it's the truth; trust is something I don't really trust."

Zilm jumped in with his opinion. "You got not choice, Rick, it's part of the deal. We are not exactly strangers. If I didn't trust you all, I wouldn't have brought it to you in the first place. What's a matter with you guys anyway? C'mon; trust is the last thing we gotta worry about. Right?"

That question floated in silence among the group like the turd floated in the punchbowl. A double-cross was ugly, but too important to not notice as a possibility.

"Right." Van Zant looked around the table and continued. "Right-on Bobby. How 'bout it, Joaquin?".

"I didn't even trust you back in the day, Steve, you know that." Joaquin stated flatly without looking at him.

"We were just kids; kid stuff, that's all." Van Zant replied.

Zilm piped in, "You don't ever know you're going to get screwed until it's too late, I know that much." Years of experience had forged that truth in the mind of Zilm. He had been cheated, bullied, and belittled by the people right here at this table when they were kids. "We gotta pull together on this, guys, it's worth a little trust; this could be a lifetime pop." Zilm exhorted to the group.

"I trust you guys, no problem with that. Columbus took a chance, that worked out." Eddie concluded.

"Yeah, he discovered America, how good is that?" Rick added.

"Actually, he discovered Puerto Rico and got sent back to Spain in chains after torturing and murdering all the natives." Zilm clarified the Columbus issue.

"Are you some kind of a smarty-pants-communist now, Zilm? You're talkin about *Columbus and America* here. Love it or leave it." Van Zant said.

"It's only the truth." Zilm calmly replied.

CHAPTER 8

Morality Issues

Joaquin was riding his motorcycle down I-880 on Sunday morning, negotiating light traffic and daydreaming his way down to the Broadway exit. His destination was the Cash Kingston Pawn Shop, and he had these 15 minutes of scooter time for thinking. Sunday morning always felt different, and he knew why. He slipped into a daydream while listening to the rhythmic pulse of the Sportster.

In his daydream he was in church with his mom on a Sunday, he was little. The music of a choir resonated against the rising arched walls around him. He felt smaller than his twelve years of age, dwarfed in the pews that surrounded him. He and his mom walked together down the center aisle and took a pew ten rows back from the front. The polished wood was slippery, cold and hard beneath his corduroys. The kneeler before him was oak and it hurt his knobby little knees. He was here because he was supposed to be here. This is where you were obligated to be on Sunday mornings. He was Catholic. His mother and society both wanted religion for him lest his morals go astray. Such were the underpinnings of his obligation on a Sunday. This morality seemed to last throughout the week, held in place by guilt and fear. The teachings in catechism clashed badly with the reality of daily life. It was hard for his twelve-year-old mind to process and reconcile Catholicism. He didn't even want to *know* of the behaviors of the Apostles, much less live by them. But, with the help of the concept of sin and fear, he was able to make some sense of reward and punishment. The bad part was he didn't come out looking too good; somehow, he always seemed to be on the wrong side of judgment day issues. By the age of twelve, he was convinced that masturbating twice daily had earned him a long hitch in purgatory at best, eternal damnation at worst. But that was okay, it was worth it.

He liked the music in church, but he could do without the rest. The paintings and statues with Jesus looking heavenward with dreamy eyes that said, *"I wish I were somewhere else but here"* were attended by unisex cherubs. The cherubs gazed adoringly at the horribly suffering man and Little Joaquin found it all rather confusing and scary. Why didn't they help him? Graphically depicted square spikes driven into bleeding human flesh-and somehow this was Little Joaquin's fault? Jesus died for *his* sins? Who asked him to do that, anyway? No child should be exposed to that level of unwarranted guilt. The ceremony itself was in gobble-dee gook language that he didn't have a chance of understanding and the ritual of Sunday mass in his 12 year old mind just became a see-be-seen event, societal rather than ecclesiastical. It was also the only *family activity* going on at the time and the best part of the ritual was a trip to the bakery after church. He urged that they waste no time chatting on the church front steps after mass for three reasons; The warm bread, the focaccia and the donuts were awaiting them. His mother didn't mix well with the church crowd anyway. She gave birth to little Joaquin at 17 years of age while she was still riding on the back of motorcycles. This was well known in the little town. Back when she was riding, doctors, lawyers and bankers didn't ride scooters as they do today and you most likely were some variety of a screw-up, anti-social deviate or both if you were associated with motorcycle gangs with colorful names such as Hells Angels, Gypsy Jokers, Cannibals, etc. Although this all happened long ago and was mostly forgotten, it had the effect of abbreviating socializing in polite company on the church steps. Joaquin was happy to just say *'Hi'* to classmates and make his getaway for the goodies at the bakery. This was *his* earthly reward for suffering the threat of purgatory and giving his Sunday morning to God. The lingering bad thought about heaven was, as all Catholics boys knew, you have to *die* to know what it was like to be there. *Die,* really? And what if you didn't like it, floating around on a cloud all day singing hymns? He supposed it was better than the alternative, but not by much. That was just the chance he had to take. The music, the mystery, the ornaments; the magic worked for a while but then it collapsed like the Twin Towers in his teen-hood (as so many things often do) so he left it all behind: Donuts, Guilt and Morality: The Good, The Bad and The Ugly-this was *his* Holy Trinity.

He cruised to the Broadway exit, pulled off the freeway and onto a surface street. He powered out of the first traffic stop. Cruising through Chinatown, it was an anthill of activity and the pink Dim Sum boxes people carried seemed to be a theme. After a few blocks out of that neighborhood, it got quiet downtown. Cash would be alone on Sundays in his shop and Joaquin cruised to a stop in front, pulled off his helmet and gloves and rapped on the door and got buzzed in. His ears were assaulted by Grover Washington at volume 10 and bells tinkled over the door as he walked in. Cash was there behind the glass barrier with a jeweler's loupe in one eye examining the stone in a ring. He turned down the volume.

"Hey man, how you doin'? Let me put this stuff away." He greeted Joaquin with a fist bump and walked past him to the front door, locked it and pulled down a shade.

"I'm good Cash, but, like I said over the phone, I just need to talk. About yesterday, mostly." Joaquin stated.

"Well, come on into the back room. We can talk about anything you want man, and we can talk *about* yesterday-or any other day." Cash opened a door into a sanctuary of oiled wood, books, a UC Berkely diploma in a blue and gold frame, pictures of his wife, children, basketball awards, politicians, and a signed picture of Barrack Obama.

"Nice place you got back here; this is all right Cassius. Is that the President?" Joaquin entered, looking around at the photos and stuff.

"Oh yeah. Signed it hisself. The brother talked about *change for America*. I didn't know at the time he was talkin 'bout *small change*; seems that be about all we *ever* get, if they gives us something at all. I had something a little longer and a little greener in mind, myself. But that's okay, least he's the right color. We got our own economic stimulus package in mind, right?" Cash gave a laugh and another fist bump and continued. "So, what's this visit all about? What's on your mind bro?" Cash asked from his chair behind the desk.

"I guess I was wondering, since it's not exactly my line of work, so I'm just wondering. You guys are the only ones I would even think about as partners to pull this job off; except one. That's kinda why I'm here, I guess." Joaquin hesitated and his statement trailed off.

"Van Zant, I know. Ain't no different for me; don't trust him, don't want to. We all go way back; we know what the score is with the guy. Hell, you be the third phone call I got since yesterday. It's the same story, "What about Van Zant?" That be what everybody wants to know." Cash answered.

"Really? Well, I guess I don't feel so bad then." Joaquin replied.

"Feel bad? What that shit all about? You don't have doubts about the Van, you ain't right!" Cash exclaimed.

"What's he been up to all these years? He just shows up. Just like that?" Joaquin asked.

"Jail, one thing. He beat a guy good. Then he a union man when he got out, tugs and crane operator, good money and he know his shit.

"Who vouches for him? You?" Joaquin asked.

"I don't vouch for nobody but myself. They say a leopard can't change his spots, but I know that prison can change a man, I know that. We need his skill set for this so he's in." Cash said.

"Well, I don't trust him." Joaquin said.

"Don't trust him nor any *mofo* who be with him." Cash framed the situation from his perspective and continued, "But for the sort of thing we got in mind, guys like Van Zant be what we need. He's a criminal; I worry about straight guys like you."

"What you mean by that? You can trust me! If I say I got your back, I mean it!" Joaquin took offense.

"Slow down, man, that ain't what I mean at all. See, guys like you are always decent and do the right thing. Straight guys like you got this kinda

moral compass in your head and the needle always point to the right thing
to do. This here plan hits a *Boy Scout* like you all wrong. Reeger, Zilm; they
Boy Scouts too. Eddie, he's just a dope smok'in fool in a tin foil hat." Cash
spelled out his line of reasoning and continued further. "See, stand-up guys
like you can't trust what it is you intend to pull off when it's a crime, you got
mo-ral-ity issues, brotha." Cash emphasized each syllable in morality.

"See, you know the difference between right and wrong. Van is different. He don't have as many moving parts inside his head in the *mo-ral-ity*
department, not much can go sideways in a pinch cuz it ain't there to begin
with! Right and wrong is different for him; *right* is when he wins and *wrong* is
when he loses. He don't have that compass, he don't have that blue handicap
sticker." Cash paused and began again.

"You sayin' doin the right thing is a handicap?" Joaquin said.

"It can be. If you a criminal." Cash replied, it got quiet, and he continued
the explanation.

"See, this be more like a business deal to him, ain't no questions 'bout
right and wrong; I know he'll screw me for money; it's good business, I be
comfortable know'in that. But I got my eye out, see? I way ready for that *see-
narr-eeoo,* and if it starts to go down, if it starts to get weird, man, the weird
can get *goin,* believe dat." Cash paused for a moment and continued again.

"Look around here: I got broken dreams hang'in all over them walls
out there, a story to go with everything. I'd rather have a thief come in here
and hock something than some poor old man hocks his gold retirement
watch-*any day.* 'Cause with the thief, it not be a complicated thing, it not
be emotional; there be no *mo-ral-ity* issues." Cash maintained eye contact

"I get it." Joaquin said. Cash dumped on him like an avalanche. Somehow,
Joaquin felt a little dirtier with the realization that he was in a business deal
with the Van now. He would just have to deal with that.

"Personally? I don't think you got to worry 'bout no double-cross.
Nobody want to screw this up, too much at stake, be 'nough to go 'round;

you know it, I know it and the Van know it." The assurances continued from the big man behind the desk.

"You're right, we're solid. The gangs tight. Just like Canal St. back in the day, 'cept it's serious-like. I got nuthin' to worry about. Nobody's that big a fool to start trouble." Joaquin was coming around slowly.

"There you go man, be cool with it. We ain't no bunch of altar boys, we done scary shit, we seen scary shit. This just be a *bigger* scary thing, brother. 'Member that *'cool is the rule'* my man. Do this right and we gonna get so far over we ain't ever gonna even be able to see our way back!" Cash finished his piece of advice.

"Oh yeah, cool as a penguin at the pole." Joaquin ended.

"Cooler than penguin shit, my man. Now let's go down Chinatown and get some Dim Sum, crack a fortune cookie, set your mind at ease with some *Chine-nee* food." Cash was race conscious: it was a learned survival skill.

CHAPTER 9

Everybody's Doing It

The only bad part about street fighting was the soreness for a few days afterwards. That's how Steve Van Zant looked at it. The main thing for him was to come out better than the other guy and without any serious injury. He did a lot of fighting in jail, but no fighting ever since he got out. When he was young, he could take it; nowadays a fight was accompanied by the reminder that he was getting older; a twisted knee, a kink in his back, a sore shoulder, like that. None of this was even noticed back in the day but he noticed it right now as he waited for Danielle to arrive at the Club 22 across the Bay.

Previously, it had been a perfectly normal morning for him; up early, on his bike and down to Peet's Coffee. In the weekend street scene in the borough of Montclair up in the hills of Oakland, there was always a musician or two at the Farmers Market and the German baker turned out strudel to die for. Always pleasant, Oakland was sunny and warm, and he liked that.

He cruised down the street toward the popular coffee spot. He came in a little hot on his Trek 920 because the front brake was disconnected, but not like it was a problem, it just made for a long gliding stop. Perfectly gauged, his glide path came to an end just touching the back tire of a parked Ducati 650 motorcycle. He swung a leg over and looked for a place to chain his bike. It was crowded on the sidewalk with people buzzing about getting caffeinated. All was well until a little voice from the bench was heard.

"What are you doing hitting my fucking motorcycle." Came a voice with a thick Eastern European accent from the crowd.

Van Zant looked about; the voice emanated from a man who looked to be about thirty, small beady eyes like a pig and a shaved head that showed advanced pattern baldness. He was dressed in a trendy motorcycle getup consisting of a multi-colored black and yellow leather jacket with shoulder pads and matching pants, a color-coordinated helmet rested on the seat of the cycle. In this getup, he appeared like a five foot tall yellow jacket. His shit-kicker boots, of course, were standard issue for his outfit. Yuppie motorcycle riders hung-out in Montclair on weekend mornings, taking up space on the Peets bench. Most of them were tax accountants, lawyers, doctors, retirees or professionals of some sort and they looked totally ridiculous in their head-to-toe motorcycle uniform, especially in the Oakland heat. Van Zant wondered why they couldn't ride in T shirts, vests and a Nazi helmet like any self-respecting outlaw biker in the August sunshine. Now he had to deal with this vulgar punk. He had an appointment in 5 minutes to get his hair cut for a date tonight, a date that he was particularly looking forward to.

"What are you talking about?" Van Zant asked slowly and deliberately in as non-threatening a voice as he could muster. This did not de-fuse the situation: motor-punk wasted no time to go on the offensive, sensing weakness.

"You hit my motorcycle, that's what. You come speeding in here like madman. You hit my motorcycle!" he spoke in rising tones.

Clearly agitated with this trespass against his $14,000 motorcycle, motor-punk could not let this slide. He had decided to make an issue out of it. Van Zant had learned to suffer fools, but it had its limits. This fool registered just above the limit and into the red zone. But the Van had grown more tolerant with age. He just calmly replied.

"Keep it friendly, friend. Don't be vulgar and profane on such a nice day, in front of all these nice women and children. This isn't the place for this." Van was still hoping to defuse the little hot-blooded piroshki.

"What? What are you saying?" He rose from the bench and advanced toward the Van. Maybe there was a language barrier or something, a misunderstanding perhaps, because the problem began to escalate in earnest when he kept coming and repeated what was becoming his mantra.

"You hit my motorcycle! You hit my motorcycle! You ride in here like maniac! You hit my motorcycle!" Clearly, excitement was his chosen emotional state now and going back to being civil seemed unlikely.

Van Zant looked down at the motorcycle. A moment had arrived. He could shine it on; pretend that he didn't care, assuring himself that he was above this motor-punk, or whatever he thought he was in his leather get-up. Most likely he was a normal guy just acting out in this motorcycle suit, kind of like little Max when he put on his wolf pajamas in the book *Where the Wild Things Are*. Mad, Mad, Max had come to Peets Coffee; just bad luck that Van happened to be there.

Van didn't want to pretend it was okay anymore. He had tried to make nice. He didn't want to be punked, he was not to be intimidated. The more he gave in, the more abuses he got. It was stupid. Stepping back had not worked. The punk failed every benchmark of the attitude test and was forcing the issue. The only option left for Van was something akin to cowardice and he just was not wired that way. He came up in the jailhouse where he learned about cowardice the hard way; bullies can smell fear and they like the smell, fear is what they sought. To *not* fear them was to respect them. Being *civilized* dictated that the thing to do when confronted was for both parties to back off in the hopes that it would just cool down sooner or later. But for the motorcycle punk this morning, he mistook civilized behavior to be fear and he soon found out that he had picked on the wrong person. For Van Zant, the moment of decision had arrived.

"Screw you *and* your motorcycle." Van pushed him back about three feet with two palms to the chest and he stood there waiting for the inevitable.

The motor-punk went berserk and struck out at Van Zant, but in an odd and an ineffective way. First, he gave this Bruce Lee kick toward the groin and missed, then he kick-boxed two more misses. Van Zant stepped back. This guy had been watching too many Japanese gangster movies, apparently.

Events had conspired against a peaceful bike ride, and it had turned into a Bruce Lee movie instead.

The motor-punk threw himself at Van Zant and knocked him down and there they both were-rolling around on the pavement in front of Peets, wrestling in the street. Everyone on the sidewalk was screaming to stop. Van Zant was wearing walking shorts and he was getting a terrible road rash on his knees as he rolled on the asphalt. He eventually got to the top of the squirmy leather mass below him. Twenty voices on the sidewalk were hollering to stop: men, women, children, oldsters. Dogs were barking, all were in a chorus of disapproval, it was bad. Van Zant got his shoulders square on the squirming motorcycle punk and rose to his toes in the classic wrestlers T position-all his weight on the upper torso of the guy. He outstretched both arms to show the crowd he was quitting, hoping to appease their disapproval (what more could he do!) Still, the Russian guy held on to Van Zant in a headlock and struggled to get out from underneath. He finally quit when the jeering crowd prevailed, urging them to stop. Van Zant rose to jeers of disapproval from this sidewalk jury as he dusted himself off.

"Why am I the bad guy?" He asked them all aloud, knees bloodied and palms up on outstretched arms. It was like a scene from Gladiator.

His peaceful Sunday bike ride for coffee was ruined. He got on his bike to leave under death threats from the motor-punk.

"Next time I see you, I kill you!" Came the threats leveled at his back.

"Oh Jesus, give it a rest, hotshot. Next time I see you it will probably be behind a desk at Turbo-Tax." Van flashed on the perfect simplicity of the Old West movies and how scores were settled. There were no skinned knees in Boot Hill.

Later that night, sporting a $100 haircut, he waited at Club 22 with a lingering odor of Ben Gay and Tiffany for Men. His knees hurt like a bastard and looked like raspberries under his sharkskin slacks. No more Mr. Nice Guy, he thought. He should have known better- just hit him hard right away and put him down, be done with it.

"Everybody wants to be a badass nowadays, what's up with that?" he pondered aloud to himself as he waited.

Danielle walked through the doorway like she was on Project Runway. The Van was up and over in a flash, taking her hand and giving her a three-second hug. He led her to the table and complimented her on being a total knockout and poured her a glass of wine.

"You're looking good enough to eat." Van said with a wink. "How was your day, gorgeous?" he asked.

"I think I sold a house in Piedmont, 3.2." she replied with a degree of reserved joy, adding, "I'm rich, let's celebrate"

"You mean 3.2 million dollars?" asked Van.

"That's what I mean." She confirmed with a broad smile. The owner was asking 3 mil."

"That's a lot of scratch." Van remarked.

"And he offered all cash. I mean real *green* cash." Danielle answered with obvious admiration for the magic that cash could conjure.

"Holy cow. That *is* a lot of scratch. Where'd he get that kinda cabbage?" Van Zant asked.

"Crime of course. Perfectly legal, white collar crime; offshore accounts, tax fraud, stock options, futures trading, all perfectly legal. Legalized crime, everybody's doing it." She replied in a worldly-wise way.

Van Zant thought about this for a moment, thought about going to jail for stealing a $23 bottle of vodka when he was twenty years old. Thought about the guys on the inside, the crimes they committed. Possession of pot, second and third offense. Three strikes and they were *in* for life.

"Wow, $3.2 million cash money all in one place at the same time. Is it like stacks of $100 bills? Does it fit in a briefcase? Are they new and crispy or just wrinkled and regular?" The thought fascinated Van.

"How was your day?" Danielle asked, changing the subject.

Oh boy, anything but the truth. He couldn't tell Danielle he had been fighting in the street this morning. That was the fastest way to get dumped by a girl like her. Fighting would identify him as lower class; he would get thrown right out of her rich-girl club, but pronto, game over. Blue collar violence made her crowd uneasy and unsure, throwing a monkey wrench into their sensibilities. They had no defense against it. They engaged in a more subtle sort of violence and for higher stakes. They didn't bat an eye over the prospect of ruining the financial lives of thousands and some even admired the cunning required to scam on such a scale. Van Zant admired those scams too, but in an upfront and honest sociopathic manner. No, today's brawling in the street was for the stupid and the brutish in the mind of Danielle and was only acceptable in movies as a form of entertainment. Inasmuch, nothing had changed much since ancient Rome. Whether it be in movies or in the Colosseum, that was a nice, safe place for that sort of behavior to stay, only as entertainment. Van Zant opted to steer clear of what could turn out to be a major snag in the flow of their relationship. So, he did what came naturally to him, he lied.

"Fine. Got a haircut, looked at a motorcycle, went for a bike ride. Nice day." Van replied, still unable to get his mind off the 3.2 million cash.

"Do you ever work?" she asked.

"That's not a nice thing to say, Sweet *Thang*." replied the Van.

"Well, honestly, I hardly know a thing about you and, well, you seem to have money but never go to work on that boat, or whatever it is. You could be a criminal for all I know." Danielle took a turn down a new street with this suspicion."

"Would that be so bad? Seems as if maybe you took $3.2 million dollars from a criminal just today?" Van replied.

"That's different." Was all she said.

"Well, truth is I work 3 on and 4 off on a tug. Maritime construction mostly, I'm a crane operator and I never seen 3.2 in my life. Anything else?" Van replied.

"I was just curious; not like I'm writing a book or anything. Usually people meet, get to know one another-get to know things about one another and, you know, get closer, that's all." Danielle was a bit defensive.

"Or sometimes they don't get closer the more they find out. Maybe I like the mystery part to last a little while longer and maybe, just maybe, the front end is the best part. See, maybe I find out more that I *don't* like than stuff that I do?" Van Zant stated and continued.

"Look Danielle; I can get close enough to you without knowing that you had a lousy childhood, marriage or father. And if you tell me how much money you have, I just start thinking what's in it for me, so don't go there." Van Zant finished.

Danielle looked across the table at her new friend and thought to herself that this man might be a little dangerous; he certainly was a handful. She wouldn't be able to control him-he was too independent, a little wild. There was not much room for wild in her world. Still, all things considered, she was interested and very attracted to him. He made her feel a little edgy and adventurous. There was scant little straightforward honesty in her world and he was refreshing. And he was very, very sexy.

"I have a lot of money." She piped up, as if this was her hole card.

"I told you not to tell me that, Toots." said Van.

"Why can't I tell you that? Because you do not? Because you wish you had it too? Maybe you had the lousy poverty-stricken childhood and do not want to talk about it? You're a big boy now so put on your big-boy pants; you can handle it." She said this with a little more edge than she wanted.

Van Zant considered this for a moment and thought, *"We're going to play Show and Tell? Is that it?"* Laughter started small and grew large and ended with a statement.

"That's it! You got me pegged, I had a lousy, poverty-stricken childhood! The childhood left but the poverty stuck around! You found me out!" Van Zant said chuckling.

"Well, it's never too late to have a happy childhood." Danielle informed as a matter of fact. She had read that on the back cover of one of her self-help paperbacks.

"And that's just what I am doing." Van Zant shot back. "And what I intend to keep on doing."

"Let's order, I'm perfectly starving." Danielle stated.

"You are perfectly a lot of things." Van ended with the cryptic compliment, adding, "And I am delighted to hear of your good fortune regarding your money." He raised his glass to a toast. Danielle thought the toast was to her, but the Van was toasting the little green stacks of Piedmont money.

CHAPTER 10

Animal Planet

Frenchy sat in the living room and scanned the classified ads of the local paper from Benicia. She wasn't looking for consumer goods; she was mostly interested in the *Pets Column*. Fortunately for her, pets have a bad habit of losing themselves, much to the dismay of distraught owners who become willing to do anything to get them back. Right now, she was looking at an ad that offered a $1000 reward.

"Bobby, we gotta go up to Benicia this week-we gotta cat job-a grand in reward money, woo-hoo." She announced to the other room where Zilm was sitting with the guys; Joaquin, Reeger, Cash, Van Zant and Eddie. They all heard Frenchy and cracked up.

"Yeah Bobby, we gotta go to Benicia. We gotta jack-up some rich white-folks for pet-ransom money." Mocked Cash.

"I think it's a pretty good scam, myself. It's got *po-ten-tial* Zilm. But you're coming at it from the wrong angle. You gotta just *kidnap* the little furry poop-machine in the first place, then get the reward." Van Zant opined.

"That be like robb'in widows and orphans, Van; downright mean." Cash said.

"That's part of the beauty; it's like taking candy from a baby." replied the Van real smooth and without missing a beat.

"We'll have to think on that, right Bobby?" Frenchy said.

"You bet French." Zilm replied.

Joaquin squirmed a bit in his chair, finally saying, "Hey Frenchy? What's going on with Global?"

"Next week. They got a big deal coming in." Came the reply from a pre-occupied Frenchy. She was text messaging.

Joaquin looked at Zilm with his palms up, he appealed for more information. "What's up with this girl Zilm? We're gonna heist millions next week and she worries about the reward for a God damn lost cat?"

"She's a whackadoodle. What can I say?" Zilm nodded and continued.

"They got stuff in and out of that place two times a week. I hacked into their data base and there is a big deal this week on the 20th. Saudi prince is flying in to pick up 54 precious stones bought at auction. That oily sandbox is getting rid of dollars and getting gold, stones, collectables, art, antiques, real estate, you name it-they can buy it, they're awash in dough. They usually do a wire transfer but this time they will arrive by chopper, on the roof with a briefcase full of cash." Zilm explained.

"Cash? Do they carry guns?" asked Reeger.

"No; they got phasers on stun, stupid-of course, they got guns! Big ones that make big holes! Is the Pope Catholic-does Howdy Doody have wooden balls, fool?" Eddie cracked.

"I just thought I'd ask." Reeger said mildly.

"Frenchy confirms it's couriers by helicopter during the day when it's not a wire transfer." Zilm spoke and continued again.

"Then they go home with the loot. That's where we step in; they go home *without* the loot, because the night before, we arrive and bag it." Said Zilm, looking around to each of the faces, "I jam the security system with a bypass, and we are in and out with the goods. The getaway is the best part."

"I like the break-in. It's old-school." said Eddie.

"I like splitting up the take." said Cash.

"I like getting away clean." said Joaquin.

"Man, I tell you what. I be a *goddamned expert* on what it be I *don't* like; I got all kind of experience in that department. But this? What I like? Only one thing: the fat stacks." Cash said.

"Amen brother." from Van.

The group moved out the back door into the yard to discuss the details. Eddie and Van Zant lit up a fat one because Mandy did not allow smoking in the house. The plan was in place; Zilm had the security; Frenchy had the shipment date; Eddie had the transportation; Van Zant was set to go to work; Joaquin was the squad leader and had gone over and over the details during the week before. It was just a matter of time now. Frenchy burst out the back door, excited and waving the Benicia newspaper.

"Bobby-it's like Animal Planet up there! It's like *Lost* meets *Animal Planet*- that's what it is! -Animals are running around up there-families with cash are looking for them. We gotta go check this out-I added it up-there's $5000 worth of lost animals on the street up there right now! We could swing into Vallejo too; they're losing pets there left and right!

"Vallejo?" That's Injun country. Meth, motorcycles and molesters. They eat you up Frenchy." said Cash.

"Isn't that where they caught that Zodiac dude, that serial killer?" asked Rick.

"That's right. He worked at the hardware store; he was a real solid citizen in Vallejo." said Cash.

"You dudes be a bunch of *boo-szhee* racists. Bet you never even been there." Eddie said.

"Never been, doubt if I will." Said Cash.

"We'll go check it out, French. We might make an honest buck there." said Zilm.

"Oh, goodie Bobby-I got a good feeling about Benicia!" Frenchy was excited.

"An honest buck?" asked Joaquin.

"We're just returning pets for money." explained Zilm.

"Compared to molesting and murder it is honest." Said Eddie. "Hey, it's the new Animal Planet for criminals!" The light bulb in his head lit up.

"Hey! That's a good idea. A TV show; kind of an *Animal-Bounty-Hunter* show. I can see it now-*The Real Dog Bounty Hunter*. Zilm could get a blond mullet and wear a vest and wrap-around sunglasses."

"Yeah, you could do turtles and snakes too, it would be great!" said Rick, intrigued by the idea.

"Turtles? Friggin' turtles? What kinda show is that? Who cares about a lost turtle? *Turtle Hunter?* Get real, you're messing up my show already with your turtles, for Christ sakes." Said Eddie. He was already planning the first season, adding thoughtfully, "I'll give ya the snakes though, they gotta be big ones."

"No tweekers on Animal Planet, Frenchy, it's a family show." said Van Zant.

"I'm not a tweeker!" said the French Fry.

"Right, I forgot-you quit." Van shot Joaquin a glance and rolled his eyes.

Reeger checked his watch and announced his departure to the group. This was met by mutual grumblings of commitments to be elsewhere, and the meeting broke up. They had been having these meetings with increasing regularity, they could recite the plan in their sleep. They had contemplated and planned the biggest thing they would ever do in their life, an event with the most permanent, life-changing and far reaching consequences, but now they all had better things to do than talk about it some more. Rick headed for his truck and was down the road to his mom's house, intending to meet his weekly lunch date with his mom and her companion, Maria.

Rick looked after his mom. He treated her with the consideration and attentions one would expect from a dutiful son and in return, she treated him like he was still fifteen years old. She felt it her duty to remind him that his hair was getting a little too long, to wear a coat, and that he was not married yet. And that band of his? She still couldn't understand why they didn't play any Benny Goodman stuff because all the kids were dancing to that now. She lived independently in her home, assisted by her live-in companion Maria, who called her *mother,* and was always a willing recipient of her mother's directions. Maria was a simple and loving soul. The fact that she didn't speak or understand much English helped immensely as Maria patiently received her instructions. Maria could have been sharper than she let on, though. Rick walked in the door of his mother's neatly kept suburban home. All three televisions were going, two on Sunday golf and one on the Spanish soap opera channel, all were rather loud.

"Hi Maria." Rick greeted her as he opened the front door.

"Halo Ricardo. You wanta coffee? Some brebos? Su mother is inna offeese." Maria said.

"That's okay Maria, nothing for me." Rick walked to a tiny little room with a desk, a bookshelf, a computer, a fat cat and his mom in an electric scooter playing Hearts on her computer.

"I saved this for ya." His mom held a newspaper clipping out for his inspection as she continued with her Hearts game. It was an article on a Benny Goodman retrospective concert.

"I told ya." She spoke.

"Oh yeah, his music's coming back." A weak reply.

"I thought I'd take you to The Hilltop restaurant today. We haven't been there in a while. They have corn beef today, you like that." She informed him.

"That's true." Rick liked corn beef a lot when he was a child, then, when he learned that it was injected with salt and chemicals with giant needles, the desire melted away like Velveeta cheese.

"How's the computer working?" Changing the subject, Rick asked. The computer was always up to some confusing thing, usually due to fat fingers on the keyboard.

"Oh, this darn thing, I can't figure it out, it's goofy. Now I can't print greeting cards, it was working fine yesterday, I must have hit something." She replied.

"Greeting cards? Can't you buy Hallmark cards like everybody else does online?" Rick asked.

"Everybody prints them out now. You're behind the times." She was hip. She was 95-years-old and not by accident did she live this long.

"I suppose. You're certainly with it, mom, printing cards." Rick said.

"When you gonna get married? Your brother got married a long time ago." She spoke.

"Actually, he got married *3 times* a long time ago." Rick corrected.

"Well, third times the charm, I guess. Hope he learned something. How's business?" She inquired.

"Good. I started a new thing-junk. I pick up people's junk now." Rick said.

"You mean you're a junkman now!?" She placed her hands in front of her mouth, and stared at him, horrified at this news.

"It's not like you think-there's money in it now, Mom. It's not like before. You'd be surprised how much crap people collect. Excuse my language. They never throw anything away, they just buy, buy, buy and it all turns to crap." Rick explained casually. "Then they pile it in the garage or basement so they can buy some more crap. You can't even walk through it."

"That's called hoarding, I love that TV show-*Hoarders*-I watch it every week." She spoke.

"Well, I watch it every day and get paid for it now." Rick concluded.

"My smart son; if you would have stayed in school you could have been anything." A familiar line of thought was expressed.

* * *

"Oh, Bobby look! Over there!" Frenchy and Zilm were cruising through the nighttime streets of Benicia, hunting small game. Frenchy was on to a scrawny little kitty, all alone on the nighttime street. Zilm's interest in this activity was solely for the benefit of Frenchy, he had his doubts as to it's potential for profit. He rolled the car to a silent stop and set the bait on the sidewalk. They both watched and waited from the front seat of the car. The little gray cat cautiously approached the tin of tuna fish.

"Do you think she knows we're here?'" Frenchy whispered.

"Yes." Zilm replied.

"Just wait and swing the net down after she's been eating a while." Zilm told Frenchy as she sat poised in the passenger seat with the window rolled down and a fishing-net raised over the car roof, at the ready.

"Are you sure this will work, Bobby?" She asked quietly.

"No." Zilm said.

The little cat was wary, as cats usually are when eating or drinking. They had centuries of DNA info that told them: *"This was when you get it in the neck."* Frenchy was quick to swat the net down, but not quick enough. The little beast gave a yowl and ran into the bushes to hide, the net held the tuna fish can secure, nothing more.

"I missed him, Bobby! Not so sure this is going to work. Let's set those traps in the trunk and come back tomorrow and see what we got." Frenchy was whining.

"Okay." Zilm was easy, he just wanted to humor Frenchie's big idea, he didn't think it would go anywhere right from the start. He got out and opened the trunk that held several Hav-a-Hart traps. The first trap he set right there on the sidewalk. The next two they put by the dumpsters behind restaurants. That was enough for one night and it was back to Richmond. They returned the next night and collected one 'possum and two very pissed-off trash pandas. Zilm stared at the black and white masked mammals in the traps, considering their predicament, and in the end, he didn't even empty the traps and put them back in the car: he just left them right where they sat. So much for cat-napping.

"Bobby, I had no idea this would be hard. In fact, I thought it would be easy." Frenchy was somewhat contrite and surprised.

"We'll try crime, I think that's easier." Zilm said.

"I hope so."

CHAPTER 11

The Wrong Way

"Check this out: on one of the moons of Saturn? They found these clouds around the poles. But hey, these things are *gee-o-metric*! They're like tetra hadrons or something like that, five sided! Perfectly five-sided shapes thousands of miles long! I mean that's crazy! And the Air Force knows about it but-they're not telling anyone."

"Then how'd *you* know about it?" Reeger asked calmly.

"I saw it on the Science Channel, man. They're keeping it a secret, studying it and they aren't saying anything about it. They might have found the source of all life, the *Cree-a-tor*!"

"What's he doing on Saturn?" Reeger asked, poking at an ant moving across the counter.

"He's not on Saturn; he's on one of those moons *around* Saturn!" Eddie exclaimed.

"Oh yeah, right, I forgot" Rick was mildly disinterested.

Rick Reeger had come in to get one of the dump trucks fixed. He was at Eddie Wong's shop, Wong Way Motors. As always when at Eddie's, the first step was to go to the counter and listen to the latest conspiracy rap. Eddie was paying attention to world events very closely and wanted to share his knowledge with willing listeners. The Twin Towers conspiracy-sharing had lasted for months but now it dropped into second place behind the Saturn phenomena (you didn't even dare bring up Cheney and the Pentagon unless you had an afternoon to kill , because Eddie had *all* the dirt on them).

"I think the Air Force has got space probes sending back information or something. They got pictures! Look at this." Eddie produced a grainy print-out he got off the Internet. Sure enough, there they were, just like he said: giant five sided clouds around the poles of a planet except they looked to be photo-shopped. This was the third time Rick had stood there looking at them because Eddie kept them on the counter for ready-reference for weeks.

"Sumbitch, look at that." Rick mused, squishing the ant on the picture of a tetrahedron when Eddie looked the other way.

"Man, we don't know what goes on up there, look at those square rings-they're perfectly shaped! How can that shit happen without something making it that way?" Eddie handled the evidence like a proud father, giving it a little flick with the back of his middle finger.

"You sure those rings are a thousand miles long? Cause I thought they might look bigger than that." Rick held the paper up to his face for examination.

"Don't start with that whacko *'bigger than that'* stuff. Tell me what's wrong with the truck?" Eddie downshifted into reality.

"Well, I don't really know, but it's getting worse. A very bad vibration coming from the front when I go over 40 MPH. Sometimes it's not there though." Rick explained.

"Is it there when the truck is loaded or not loaded?" Eddie asked like a physician.

"Now that I think about it, it only does it when it's empty." Rick replied after a moment of thought.

"Ball joints. Front ball joints. Bring it in this morning and I'll order parts. Have it out the door by 5 tomorrow." Eddie stated.

"You're a frickin' genius little buddy, thanks." said Rick.

Eddie *was* a mechanical genius. He was always right-on about the mechanical questions that entered his shop. He worked with one employee, Gus. He was not a good businessman (notice *Wong Way Motors* for a name of a repair shop) and had no desire to expand his shop or get lots of customers. From all outward appearances, his shop was a place for him to hold court and share his worldview with anybody who would listen. He was very reasonably priced and offered no automotive accessories for sale. His business started out as an old garage that he rented to cherry out an MG for himself and one for a friend. Then people started leaving off cars and then he would fix them. Then motorcycles came. But when he started working on Ferraris, Jags and Beamers, his reputation spread, and chronic unemployment was in the rearview mirror. After he bought the building, he was set. One got the feeling that Eddie could've been a lot of things if he applied himself, but what he really liked was smoking a lot of pot.

Eddie put down the phone and announced that parts would be in before noon. Rick was getting a Coke out of the antiquated machine in the corner. He snapped the top and walked over to Eddie and spoke.

"You down with Van Zant?" Rick asked.

"I wouldn't piss on his head if his hair was on fire. I wouldn't trust him farther than I can throw him. If you put him through a virus scan-he'd break the machine." Said the little Asian man with the Prince Valiant haircut.

"I hear ya, bro'. How'd *we* hook back up with *him?*" Rick wondered.

"Short answer? Zilm; Zilm's been hanging out up in the hills, Montclair or some such. He goes for coffee one day and there's Van Zant in a silk shirt and $300 sunglasses-a real cool breeze now-hanging with the Gucci crowd up in the hills. They don't know he near beat some poor bastard to death with a battery cable or went to prison, I bet that never comes up at Peets." Eddie said, paused and then resumed.

"So anyway, Zilm hits it off with Van Zant up in Peets Coffee. After they're all *New Best Friends*, it comes out that Zilm is still a zero, but a zero with big ideas. He brags about Frenchy being on the inside and all the loot she sees at work. They're the ones that put this plan together, but they can't do it alone because it's too big. That's where we come into the picture." Eddie explained.

Rick replied, "Yeah, me and Joaquin went over there, it is big job, but not as............"

"Don't say it! I know: *it's not as big as you thought*, right?" Eddie interrupted.

"You think so too?" Rick asked innocently.

"The pay-off is big, that's what counts." Eddie answered.

"Yeah well, me and Joaquin think it's do-able. Joaquin doesn't trust Van Zant either, by-the-way." Rick confided.

"Stevie V doesn't scare me. Remember that Kurt Vonnegut book, what was it, the one with Montana what's-her-name?" Eddie paused on the question.

"I don't know, I don't read too much." Rick replied.

"Wildhack!" Eddie exclaimed and continued, "Slaughterhouse Five, that's the book. Well, I'm like Paul Lazzaro in that book. Van Zant knows he can't mess with me! He knows if he does, someday somewhere, Eddie Wong will even the score. He'll never see it coming; but they're I'll be to settle an old score because Eddie Wong never forgets!" Eddie finished on a high note.

"They say it takes more energy to hate than to forget." Rick observed.

"I got a lot of energy." Eddie said.

"Maybe you gotta get *permission;* that's mixed up in there somewhere. I don't know." Rick mused to himself in confusion.

"Forgive, forget; I say get even!" Eddie forwarded with relish and added.

"I'm just telling ya-nobody crosses Eddie Wong and gets away with it!" said Eddie calming himself and releasing the consuming effect of Paul Lazarro.

"You're a bad-ass." Rick's reply was mild, and he continued. "Van Zant does seem different. The more I hang out with him the more he seems normal."

Eddie answered a question from Gus, who emerged from the mechanics bay, and Rick looked for the recycle bin for his Coke can while checking his watch. He stepped outside and made a call.

"Just go over there and do what they say." Rick spoke into the receiver.

"Then bring another truck, that's all." Rick.

"That's not your job." Rick.

"They gotta do that before you can haul it away." Rick spoke and hung up.

When he returned, Eddie was leafing through a stack of real estate magazines on the counter. "What was that all about?"

"She wants us to haul away a homeless guy's tent and his junk-all over her yard." Rick answered.

"So? Do it." Eddie said.

"He's sleeping inside the tent with his dog." Rick said.

"That is a problem then." Eddie continued with the magazines.

"Gonna buy a house?" Rick asked, pointing a finger at the magazine.

"Country property. When the shit comes down, I'm just gonna electrify the fence and let the dogs out." Eddie said without looking up.

Rick looked down at the glossy full color page that advertised a 200 acre parcel, buildings, road, pool and more. He could read the price; $500,000 dollars.

"That's a lot of money." Rick speculated.

"You think that's a lot? I'll tell you what a lot is, cuz, and half a mil it ain't. A 700 billion bank bail-out, that's a lot. The Middle East War cost? About 3 trillion so far and that's a lot more. And just so you know, a stack of $1000 bills an inch high is a million; a stack of those 350 feet high is a billion; and a stack of a billion dollars 65 *miles* high is a trillion! And that my *bigger than that* friend is the definition of a lot!" Eddie was all excited.

Rick pondered that and asked, "How high is Mount Everest?"

"Mount Everest? About a mile high, I think?" Eddie responded.

"Well, if you had a trillion dollars it would be 125 Mount Everest's in a row. That would be like the Himalayas of cash, just think about it." Rick said.

Eddie considered this for a moment and could not find an appropriate response. There was something odd about Rick, it had something to do with size. Finally, he spoke.

"You wanna go fishing? I'm gonna take the boat out this afternoon, I think they're getting some halibut down off the Berkeley Pier." Eddie said.

"Yeah, that sounds good. How big is the boat?" Rick replied.

CHAPTER 12

I'm Down With Roger

The time had come, and the game was afoot, Frenchy said the transaction was set for tomorrow. Joaquin watched a set of red and green lights approach in the far distance from his boat as he crossed the open waters of the South Bay at night. The lights were approaching slowly and that was a good sign; fast approaching vessels might be Homeland Security and they were a cause for alarm. Fortunately, the Homeland Security boats seldom strayed into the South Bay, the terrorists they sought only frequented the cosmopolitan waterfront. Although they had never encountered a terrorist, if they ever did, Homeland Security figured it would surely be in an area with Starbucks close by. This worked out well for the crew because that way they could just patrol from the Sausalito Starbucks to the Marina Green Starbucks to the Jack London Square Starbucks, the Starbucks Triangle of marine lore.

The thing for sure was this: Starbucks was safe from terrorist attack. These bright orange rigid inflatables were always going fast and if you saw one, the other was somewhere nearby. They always traveled in pairs, and they always were heavily armed with .50 caliber machine guns mounted on the bow. Bad medicine for terrorists or any other variety of miscreant.

Joaquin threw on his heavy backpack and Rick and Eddie motored alongside in Eddie's boat. Joaquin's boat was anchored, and he was about to leave it to join his cohorts in crime in Eddie's boat, inauspiciously named the Wong Way. Before he jumped aboard, he yelled over to Rick.

"Rick: You guys got any fish? Did you catch any?" Joaquin asked.

"No. Eddie was sick." Rick replied.

"I would have been fine if you would have brought those saltines like I told you!" Eddie protested.

"You smoked a reefer. That made you sick." Rick stated.

"Don't be smoking dope tonight, Eddie, please." Joaquin warned more than a plea. "Take these two halibut aboard; I caught them while I waited. It will at least look like you were fishing." Joaquin handed the little halibuts over to Rick and then he followed. Once Joaquin was aboard, the three of them all together now, Eddie put the boat in gear, and they headed toward the distant lights of the South San Francisco shoreline.

"I got 12:30 AM. Check your watches. We are on that shoreline there at 12:45AM." Joaquin said, citing down his pointed arm.

Eddie and Rick checked their watches and mumbled an inaudible acknowledgement.

"Okay, new rule: when I say something or ask you something? You acknowledge by giving me a *Roger.*" said Joaquin.

"What's a Roger?" Asked Eddie.

"Who's a Roger?" Asked Rick

"How about a Jolly Roger?" Eddie cracked adding, "I like the green apple ones."

"Okay seriously-like your life depended on it. I need to know that I am heard and understood when I speak and you do that by un-mistakenly acknowledging and answering back, *Roger.* Capiche? Joaquin pressed it.

"Roger it is. Roger-Dodger." Rick answered.

"I'm down with Roger" Eddie chimed in.

They bided their time in silence, waiting to motor toward the shimmering shoreline with its massive towers silhouetted against the jumble of ambient light from South City. Everything in the shadow of these towers was as black as strong coffee, save for the lonely pathway lights that marked the perimeter of the industrial park. This was where Cash would soon be found in a security guard unform. It soon would be the destination of the Wong Way and its occupants in a rendezvous. Somewhere within those towers there lurked a janitor, a security station, a guard in the lobby and a lazy guard patrolling by vehicle. Also arriving in the park would be the rest of the East Bay invaders on a mission of economic recovery; the fast track version in the time-tested version known as crime.

*   *   *

Van Zant and Zilm sat at the bar in the South City Denny's, nursing drinks at the bar and killing time. Everyone was on a synchronized time schedule, and they had a few minutes to kill before they rendezvoused across the freeway in the industrial park. A pretty young girl in a black spaghetti strap dress, tattoos and combat boots served them at the bar. Van Zant turned to Zilm and spoke.

"You know what I don't get? What's with all these pretty young girls getting tattoos all over their body? I mean what is the idea? It's not beautiful. Some of them look like they have a tropical jungle disease. And what about those Ubangi plates in the earlobes?" Steve Van Zant wondered.

"That's only for the guys, the earlobe plates, the girls don't get those." Zilm corrected.

"They might as well. It looks like hell-no matter what gender sticks 'em in their ears." Van Zant replied, checking his voice so the little girl didn't hear him.

"I don't like it much either, but they do. They are trendy and hip now. If they want to look stupid, that's their business." Zilm said and added,

"It's all about sex of course. Everything is, now that I think about it, I mean, if you look at it right." Zilm stumbled upon his own realization.

Van Zant nodded at this and said, "The bad part is, when they get fat, they look like a psychedelic beach ball." Van Zant shook his head with this observation.

"That's not very nice. They call that body-shaming nowadays. Ever consider you are behind the times?" Zilm observed.

"Behind the times? Zilm, I don't care much about being *behind* the times. I don't care whether you come out non-binary, LGBTQ, resident spirit or what-the-f*ck. I'm not say'in they ain't real, but to me they're just a bunch of your snowflake bullshit. I live in my own times."

"That's kinda philosophical Steve. Smart for a dinosaur." Zilm replied.

"As far as I'm concerned, philosophical is what you get when you don't get what you want." Van Zant shot back.

"No really. They say you cannot put your toe in the same river twice: the water is here, then it's not here and then it's gone forever, just like time. I think some ancient Greek guy said that. That's an example of your own times, Steve, gone." Zilm explained.

"But you *can* put your foot in your mouth all of the time, Zilm. You've proven that." Van chuckled.

"We can learn a lot from those old Greeks." Zilm commented, ignoring the insult.

"Didn't those ancient Greek guys bugger each other? They were way ahead of the times, eh Zilm?" Van Zant replied with a chuckle.

There was a silence between the two men for a few moments as the tattooed bartender came down toward them. She rinsed a few glasses and left, then Zilm spoke.

"You've got a tattoo Van, why'd you get it?" Zilm asked.

"Oh shit, that's different. Dirty Ernie and I were on a tear, drinking, scaring hitchhikers, rousting hippies, only this time we got carried away." Van Zant started and then Zilm interrupted.

"I heard about that. Pretty sick stuff." Zilm offered a brief opinion.

"Well, that moron Ernie goes and whips out a pistol and scares the shit out of everybody at this hippie-house. This girl in the kitchen goes fly'in out the backdoor and calls the cops and before you know it, we're running from the law! We got caught and the charges were assault, B and E, kidnapping, robbery, parole violations, the works-so I got this tattoo." Van Zant responded.

"An insane clown?" Zilm stated flatly.

"Crazy shit that night. Pretty cool huh?" Van Zant asked and continued, "It sort of marked the event, like a milestone."

"I don't get it; a milestone in stupidity and cruelty?" said Zilm.

"No, think about it; evil just for the hell of it, all in fun and crazy, living right on the edge. Never been to the edge Zilm?" Van Zant replied.

"It must have been a popular tatt in jail." Zilm said, ignoring the question.

"Jail wasn't so bad; I made a lot of friends in jail. Three hots and a cot. Boring for sure, but you can get anything you want." Van Zant replied.

Yeah, except *out*." Zilm responded dryly.

"True dat. Okay Zilch-show time, let's hit the road." Joaquin abruptly left his stool and said good-bye to the tattooed girl behind the bar. "See you later down at the beach sweetie."

"What?" she said.

*   *   *

The industrial park of the Towers looked to be abandoned for the weekend. Van Zant drove the little Honda through curvy streets lined with expansive parking lots, all empty. He checked his watch; it was 12:15 AM. Two high-rise buildings side by side emerged from the complex and rose into the night sky. The pair directed themselves toward this destination with criminal intent. The little handheld radios in their shirt pockets received a transmission, a voice.

"Hello, all stations, this be *Supersize*." Came the crackling voice of Cash. Everybody had a code name now.

"*Water Dog One*, check." It was Joaquin.

"*Water Dog two*, check." It was Eddie.

"*Water dog three*, check." Rick looked at his pals in the boat.

"*Sparky*, check." Zilm checked in.

"*UPS*, check." Van Zant checked in. He was in the darkened section of a parking lot adjacent to Krystal Tower #2. Zilm and Van Zant had both exited the vehicle after Denny's and parted ways. In a short amount of time, Van Zant arrived at the security fence of the construction site of Tower #2. He clipped the links in a section of a chain link fence, folded it back like a limp dishtowel and entered the site. He immediately walked to the base of the tower crane, took off his pack, opened it and pulled out a few *Halvah* candy bars, ate them, and climbed up the 200 feet to the control booth at the top of the tower. Meanwhile nearby, Zilm disappeared into the bushes and the darkness on the side of Tower #1. Cash, in another area close by, parked his fake security vehicle and began patrolling on foot along the pathway adjacent the water in his fake security guard uniform.

Van Zant climbed, and all was familiar for him. This was a Liebherr Tower Crane, a 300C to be exact and it was common to building sites around the world. It was big; it rose 241 feet from the concrete foundation, and it was able to serve in the construction of both high-rises. It was anchored to the completed high-rise and set on a concrete foundation to serve both sites. It was constructed of a series of eleven 20-foot sections raising it to its full height. At the top of the tower was the gantry, carriage, counterweights, motor and operation control station. Although quite tall, the extraordinary feature of these cranes was the gantry. The gantry extended outward from the top of the tower allowing the crane its enormous reach. On this gantry was a track that enabled the cargo hook to travel outward 202 feet to the end of the horizontal arm, extending it horizontally almost as far as the tower rose vertically from the ground. The gantry rotated 360 degrees to serve the entire construction site. The immensely powerful DC motor was able to lift 11,500 lbs. at a speed of 560 feet per minute in third gear. Simply stated, it was able to lift a Cadillac Escalade from the street to the top of the building in 20 seconds, and unless you were right on top of the motor, it was silent. Van Zant began his climb to the top via an exceedingly long series of ladders.

*   *   *

Zilm skulked through the landscaping to a nondescript and recessed service door that led into the foundation of Tower #1, the completed and occupied structure where he worked everyday. He appeared official in his Allstate Electric jumper. He had the key to the control room and had visited it many times before, but he drilled out the lockset, giving it the appearance of a break-in so that it did not look too much like an inside job. The room was bright with fluorescent lighting which illuminated the electrical panels, gauges, circuit breakers and a complex diagram of the floors in the building. The room was aglow with LED lights and graphs in multiple panels behind glass. All this was surrounded by a series of computer terminals and keyboards. It was a work of technological art that Zilm had helped construct. He admired it for its thoroughness, so perfect and without a wasted milli ampere or space on the boards. It was the epitome of efficiency, and it could be compared to the nervous system of the human body, transmitting information from all regions to a centralized location where the information was processed, noted and stored. He was proud to be in the presence of such an organization of sensors, circuits, lights, and computer processors set to the purpose of electronic security, all of it centralized in this room; the security brain of both buildings and Zilm was here to blow it all to smithereens. Knowing exactly where to look, it took Zilm about 35 seconds to solder a little jump wire that bypassed the security system in suite 2600 on the 26th floor, home and location of the Global Investment Co.

The system was different from the human nervous system in some significant ways of course. First, a high school dropout could master it and second, it reacted badly with water. Armed with this knowledge, Zilm proceeded with his plans with evil satisfaction. He carefully removed from his tool satchel the components necessary for the construction of a timer and a battery-operated water mister. The water mister was shaped like a giant green frog, and it emitted a pressurized vapor from the top of his head, designed to cool all within a 5-foot radius in a hot patio in Arizona at ten second intervals. He saw it in the garden section of a SkyMall catalog, his favorite shopping magazine. The magazine also offered a selection of garden timers (what a wonderful and useful magazine it was!). He also set about to attach a little black box to a double A battery pack, twisting the wires together to a secondary timer. At the insistence of Joaquin, who did not like the frog idea, claiming it was stupid, explosive charges were placed. Joaquin had firsthand experience with C-4 plastic explosive in Nam, that was his disruptor of choice. Zilm attached a hunk of this to the main electrical breakers which brought service from the street. Zilm liked the frog, he knew it would do the trick. He thought that it added a certain style element to the task, a signature as it were. He removed the covers that protected the circuits and placed the frog in the center of the room, set the two timers and sat back to admire his completed work. The door, window, interior and motion sensors of suite 2600 would continually report the information that all was well within the offices of the trading company while they stole everything of value the gang could carry off. Time was a factor before everything went shithouse; mayhem was a shorted out milli amp away. He made a mental note that he should have become a criminal much earlier in life. Then he pictured Van Zant, criminals, and jailhouse tattoos and thought otherwise. Zilm left the room and stood outside the jimmied door and reached for his radio, adjusted the volume, and spoke.

"*Sparky* to *Water Dog*." Zilm spoke.

"*Water Dog One,* over." Joaquin.

"The green light is on." Zilm announced on his radio and hot-footed it to the shoreline to join the rest of the gang.

"Roger." Joaquin motioned toward the shore to Eddie and spoke. "Let's go slow Eddie, let's go see Cash and Zilm."

*   *   *

Cash checked his watch and put down the clipboard, it was time; it was 12:20AM. The route he had rehearsed took about 10 minutes and should terminate at just the right moment in just the right place. He removed a small penlight from his shirt pocket and fingered the leather tab that secured the Taser holster strapped to his leg. He had never used a Taser, but it held a certain fascination ever since he saw a guy in a video plead, *'Don't Tase me 'bro'*, just before he *did* get tased by the cops and fell quivering on the ground. He hoped no other security guard would see him walking around, but it was a chance he had to take. He had his story ready; he was a supervisor conducting a *'ready-alert'* survey. He wasn't too worried about being discovered because he knew that the *real* guard was not exactly vigilant, dozing in his patrol vehicle. The 2nd guard never left the lobby of Tower #1, guarding the elevator doors and trying to stay awake with little success. An employee in the lobby serviced his addiction to internet porn into the wee hours of the morning, glued to a screen.

Cash took out his little laser pen and aimed it at the control booth at the top of the gantry and three bursts of red light danced on the windows of the booth. It was answered by three bursts that hit him in the chest with red dots of light. Looking around, he continued to patrol along the waterfront promenade and as he strolled, three more red dots bounced of his chest in rapid fashion, only this time they came from somewhere out in the direction of the Bay. He reached for his radio and spoke.

"*Supersize* to *Water Dog One.*" Cash.

"*Waterdog* back." Joaquin gave the reply.

"*UPS* is in motion." Cash replied.

"*UPS* in motion-check." Van confirmed.

"Roger out." Joaquin gave the final answer in the silence of the Bay, over the distant roar of rubber-on-asphalt from the Bayshore freeway in the distance.

Joaquin, Eddie and Rick watched through the darkness as they approached the shoreline in the Wong Way. At first it was hard to see but the crane gantry was rotating, and the hook was descending. Joaquin turned to Eddie and Rick and told them he spotted it.

"Get ready to hook up, I got it spotted. Estimate the hook will be at the shoreline in one minute." Joaquin said.

"Roger *Waterdog One.*" Eddie replied.

The little craft throttled up slightly and then after ten seconds adjusted the throttles back a bit in an attempt at perfect timing. Rick and Joaquin cinched on their packs and stood by the rail in the ready position. As the boat approached the rip-rapped shoreline, Rick and Joaquin moved to the bow and Eddie set them gently off on the rocks and then backed away into the darkness of the night. The timing *was* perfect. Cash and Zilm were also waiting there and so was the hook from the Liebherr 300 tower crane. All four men snapped into the cable with D-hooks attached to their harnesses and Van Zant gave them the ride of their life up, away and into the darkness of the night. Rick had to close his eyes; it was too scary for him as they ascended the 240 feet in 20 seconds or less. The best part was that Van Zant was simultaneously rotating the gantry; the hook would land the illustrious foursome, gear and all, above the balcony of suite #2600 of Krystal Tower #2, home of the Global Investment Corporation.

"*UPS*-on time!" Van Zant was in a good mood.

"Roger-dodger-codger!" Eddie was getting into it, and reached for a blunt in his shirt pocket, now alone in the Wong Way offshore of the Towers.

"I am *soooo* down with this Roger-shit." He mumbled as he torched the stubby cigarette. He inhaled the rich and skunky smoke.

CHAPTER 13

Release The Flying Monkeys

Rick opened one eye as he flew through the night. He had closed his two eyes earlier in the ascent, but now he had to see what went with this feeling in his stomach and the sound of the air rushing by his ears. He opened one eye into a squint and then the other until they both were wide open. It was something to see all right; all the Bay and the eastern shoreline lay before him as he ascended towards the heavens and dangled like a helpless worm on a hook. His harness suspended him from a point in the small of the back, attached to the cargo hook of the crane, leaving his arms and legs free in flight. It was pretty comfortable, but it had Rick dangling face out and down toward the ground. The butterflies in his stomach were in near-riot, he really wished he hadn't taken a hit off Eddie's joint. Rick was getting flashes of scenes from the Wizard of Oz and right now he imagined he was a flying monkey. Then, he pictured the four of them landing atop the witches' tower trying to rescue Dorothy in fear of those grotesque monkeys. 'Hoe-ree-oo -Hee-ooooh-roe' went over and over through his mind. This imagined vision was interrupted by the sound of Joaquin's voice.

"Rick? You okay?" Joaquin asked.

"Yeah, I'm good." Rick replied.

"Get ready, we're slowing down, we're coming in for a landing. You were singing the Flying Monkey song." Joaquin informed.

"I was? I mean, yeah, I was. I like that movie." Rick fell silent.

"Yeah, you *was*." Joaquin stated and then a little louder he continued.

"Everybody listen-up: Don't unsnap until I say." Joaquin issued the command, referring to their individual carabiner snaps that attached them to the cable and hook. That was answered by a chorus of 'Roger' from the group of flyers.

Van Zant slowed the cable and focused on the tip of the crane gantry which was getting very close to Tower #2. He needed to position the gang just right; on the edge of the building so that he they could lower onto the balcony of the 26th floor below. Scraping them off the hook on the side of the building in the process was the danger and adding to that danger was the fact that it was dark out there where they dangled. Van was going to have to rely on Joaquin to issue certain commands when they were in place. The electric motor and gearbox were quiet, and all Van could hear were greased cables and pulleys in motion. The control booth had an array of safety gear such as extinguishers, rope, carbine snaps, first aid kits, eyewash, radio gear and a rope ladder. The ladder cautioned that it was only 60 feet long. Steve Van Zant eyed this warning and he thought to himself that it was a bit short of what was required in a real emergency. He eyed the dangling foursome out in the distant darkness. They looked like they were in position, but he awaited the signal from Joaquin just the same. He was just creeping the gantry over as slow as it would rotate when he finally heard the radio and Joaquin say:

"All stop *UPS!* Lower away."

Van Zant lowered away as slow as the crane would go in first gear. He set the brake on the gantry, locking it into place. This was the most difficult part for him in the caper. It was impossible to practice the move, so he was by the seat of his pants and winging it.

"Stop!" Joaquin showed a hint of fear in the command.

The Flying Monkeys were 250 feet above sea level, gently rocking to and fro. Some pointed toward Oakland, some toward San Jose and some toward San Francisco, all of them were dangling almost directly above the balcony of the 26th floor. Joaquin spoke.

"I'll go down first. The rest come after me. When I hit the deck, you come down. Ready set? Here I go." Joaquin lowered himself with his 3/8 braided line, aiming for the balcony deck. The problem at hand was that he was off to the side of the balcony ledge, he had to get over a few feet. He kicked off the ledge and started his swing until the arc swung him five feet and he could drop square on the balcony deck, but he missed and instead he teetered on the railing, sitting on his butt, looking out and looking down. He let himself fall backwards and landed on his heavy backpack. He was on the deck.

"Okay, *Waterdog* on the deck. C'mon down and I'll pull you in."

They had practiced this out at Pt Castro under the Richmond Bridge. Rick had gotten so good at it they called him Spiderman. Cash never quite reached a proficient level. They called him Gumby.

Rick, Zilm and Cash dropped in on Joaquin on the balcony. When they arrived *on* the balcony, Zilm wasted no time getting into his tool bag and over to the large glass door. He pushed the diamond bit mandrel into the glass, and it began to bore, the four inch hole saw entered the glass behind the pilot. Diamond saws are very effective cutting tools, and it wasn't long before the cylinder cut through the 5/16-inch glass. No alarm sounded as expected and Zilm reached in and lifted the latch on the sliding glass door, pulled out the security brace from the bottom with his homemade hook and opened it as easily as one opens the patio door. Frenchy had taken pictures of the glass barrier and interior with her cell phone and Zilm made a mock-up to practice on at home. His best time was four seconds flat for entry and he almost beat that time now. Zilm again was establishing his mettle as a Jack-of-all-Trades and promising career criminal. Once in, he made a beeline for an electric panel in the closet and opened it.

"*Sparky* to the panel." He reported.

Joaquin removed his pack and hooked up his little 3 gallon air bottle of Argon gas to a machine about the size of a microwave oven and Rick plugged in the power cord. Zilm and Cash examined the locks on the door, then drew rectangles around them with a Magic Marker so Joaquin didn't have to figure out where to cut or waste air., because without Argon gas, there would be no robbery.

"You sure that be the right place, Zilm? Looks a bit too far over to me." Cash asked.

"Well, I was sure until you said something, geez-louise." Zilm said with agitation. "Get out the tape measure."

"Measure twice, cut once." Cash repeated that old chestnut, drawing tape out from the edge of the door. The marker was correct.

"See? I told ya this is the spot!" Zilm said as Joaquin looked on with the torch.

"Cut away my man. Do your duty." Cash quipped to Joaquin.

The machine Joaquin was holding was a plasma cutter, a portable version of the one he used in the welding shop at work. When first brought to the attention of the group it was greeted by the group as one might treat the introduction of a sci-fi ray gun, which it was. Joaquin was incredulous at the reaction because he used one every day, it was as common as dirt. Rick and Cash took him at his word, Eddie pretended that he knew all about them, but Zilm went online when he got home. He was quite surprised with what he found:

"In the early 1960's engineers made a new discovery. They figured out that they could boost temperatures by speeding up the flow of gas and shrinking the release hole. The new system could reach higher temperatures than any other commercial welder. In fact, at these higher temperatures the tool no longer acted as a welder. Instead, it worked like a saw, cutting through tough metals like a knife through butter."

"What?" Like a knife through butter?" Zilm liked that part. "This is just what the doctor ordered-cuts through metal like a knife through butter, do tell more." He read on.

"A plasma cutter can pass through metals with little or no resistance thanks to the unique properties of plasma. There are four states of matter in the world:

solids, liquids, gases and plasma. Super-heating the gases to extremely high temperatures create fast moving electrons that collide with other electrons and ions releasing vast amounts of energy. This energy is what gives plasma its unique status and unbelievable cutting power.... the reaction creates a stream of directed plasma approximately 30,000 degrees Fahrenheit and moving at 20,000 feet per second when configured in the cutter. The plasma cuter is one of the most interesting tools of the 20th century. Using basic principles of physics to harness the fourth state of matter, the plasma cutter performs with nearly magical results."

"Magical?" It was just getting better and better. Zilm and his confidence swelled, he read on and his eyes almost left their sockets with amazement when he came to this:

"Locksmiths use plasma cutters to bore into safes and vaults when customers have been locked out."

"Every criminal in the world needs to see this, Professor Google I love you!" Zilm exclaimed aloud that night.

Back at the crime scene with the magical cutter, Zilm first had to alter the electrical service by rewiring two 110 volt circuits in series, doubling the juice to 220 volts. Joaquin touched the trigger and a little blue arc surrounded by a jet of argon gas jumped from the tip of the gun.

Zilm looked on with satisfaction as the blue arc penetrated the metal with a clean cut. Rick and Cash held up a flash curtain to conceal the cutting, Zilm set up the radio gear monitoring the local police, fire and the security frequencies used by the guard service in the industrial park. Joaquin steadied the torch in his right hand and applied its magic along the proscribed lines on the door.

His torch hissed softly, and a small blue arc disappeared into the steel of the door around the lockset. Zilm was amazed, it really worked just like Professor Google said. In a steady motion along the lines, Joaquin sliced off a rectangular chunk of the door, lock and latch mechanism. A perfect chunk of lock and door fell into the safe room with a soft thud. Rick bumped against the door with his foot, and it swung wide open.

"In we go boys." Joaquin took out the little LED flashlight and looked around. There was a safe on the other side of the room.

"Oh dear. Now what? Frenchy didn't mention there was another safe, did she?" Rick asked.

"We'll cut it open, that's what. Get the torch and I'll peel the Goddamned thing like a banana." Joaquin stated as he studied the vault door.

Rick went over and picked up the plasma machine and its companion gas bottle. He set it down inside the room as far as the cord would allow. Then he took the nozzle and handed it to Joaquin. It was three feet shy; the cord was too short. Zilm and Joaquin looked and each other.

"I thought it was longer than that." Rick said.

"Of course, you did you idiot." Joaquin was getting edgy; the pressure was on.

"You startin' to drive us crazy with your '*bigger than that*' shit, Mr. Quick-Dumper-Rick." Cash said.

Zilm was already making an extension cord. He had a length of suitable gauge wire and was headed off to the panel to wire it up.

"This'll take two minutes; I'm on it." Zilm told the pair as he left the safe room. He walked by Cash, who was standing guard, listening to the police radio.

High above the break-in, Van Zant relaxed in the comfy chair of the crane booth, snacking on imported Cost Plus candy, confident that the gang was at work below and all was well. Below Van Zant on the 26th floor, Zilm reentered the safe-site and moved the plasma cutter six more feet, within reach of the interior safe.

"Try that." He said indicating the cutter to Joaquin. "We're running about 22 minutes behind schedule now." Joaquin didn't hear him because he was already at the safe with the cutter, which was emitting the little hissing noise as it cut the metal.

Cash was monitoring the radio frequencies closely. He heard the county dispatch frequency indicate Krystal Towers, so he opened up the squelch and listened closely. He didn't have to wait too long before the woman's voice came on again.

"Reported vehicle in lot, broken window, apparent theft. Report from Advance Security, they are on scene, over." The dispatcher said.

"580 to 20, out." was the reply from the patrolman.

Cash addressed the gang, "They found the truck in the lot with a broken window, believe that shit? Criminals are off the chain over here."

"Punks and thieves. What's next?" Rick commented with disgust.

Joaquin and Zilm heard the alert, but they had bigger fish to fry than a burglarized vehicle. They had just cut through the door and were looking inside at a safe. On the shelves were little boxes. Some were just ornamental and looked like antiques, some were plain tin boxes. They opened the antique ones first and the contents were surprising, because they had no contents. They did not like that.

"This better work Zilm, I swear. If Frenchy messed this up, she's dead. I'm sorry, she's just dead." Joaquin said. A very serious glitch had appeared.

"And I'll be the one who kills her." Zilm replied as he began opening the plain tin boxes.

"Wait a minute." Zilm spoke, "We hit paydirt pardner." He handed the opened box to Rick. The box was not big, and it was ordinary, like a box for your important papers at home. It was about 9 inches wide and 12 inches long, perhaps 6 inches deep. Upon opening it, it revealed several layers of colored stones of various small sizes: The prized colored diamond collection had been found in an ordinary tin box. Zilm handed the box to Rick for inspection while he gathered up his tools in his bag.

"Take the box Rick. Check 'em out. We are 25 minutes behind schedule, we gotta pack up and go." Zilm said to Rick.

"Wow, they're beautiful, but I thought they would be bigger than this." Rick said.

"We're out of time, here. We're in overtime." Zilm said and took out his radio and continued.

"*UPS*, packing it up. Package *see-cure*." Zilm suppressed his giddiness.

"Roger, standing by." Van Zant replied.

Twenty-six floors below the criminal gang, Ahkmoud Azzerzin unwrapped his favorite candy bar and took a break from his Phoenix University online course. He was studying to get his master's degree in the Science of the Administration of Justice and Security. It was too dull and tedious to endure for more than an hour at a time and he needed a break, so he turned to his usual diversion. In a mesmerized state, he surfed the worldwide web of naked women, while unbeknownst to him, a little green frog silently emitted a watery mist over electrical circuits in the basement below. The little droplets ran off the counters and onto the floor. An increasingly dense layer of moisture found every nook and cranny on the circuit boards. Ahkmoud thought he detected a slight flicker of the lobby lights. He looked up from the *Arabian Hooker Hotties* site on the screen before him, looked around, and got up to stretch his legs. He rubbed his eyes and watched for more electric anomalies. At first there was nothing and then they flickered again and this time he was sure of an electrical malfunction. Now vigilant, he began to scan the array of video screens before him, switching from one section of the building to another. All screens showed the same tomb-like nothingness, not even a janitor moving around. He switched from floor to floor viewing one still room after another. Then the lights went out on several of the floors. Then, a few more. He rapidly began scanning the remaining camera locations that had light, aware of an increasingly serious problem. One of those locations he scanned was the central electrical room in the basement. Looking closer, he zoomed the lens and saw the unmistakable grin of a giant frog sitting amongst the computer terminals. It was just grinning at him and misting the room from the top of its head. It was green and yellow, and its frog-grin was exaggerated like the Cheshire Cat and stretched across an over-wide frog face. It looked wet and happy. Then, the lights went out all over the complex. The guard reached for his radio.

"Power failure! I'm going to the control room." Security One said and exited the lobby. Ahkmoud follwed. Ahkmoud headed for the door and out of the lobby. The little radio replied.

"Check. I'm in lot 26." Security Two answered into his little radio.

Security Two was rudely awakened from his nap. He had parked his truck where no one would see it. Now, he had to do something.

"Security Two standing by." He wiped the sleep from his eyes.

*   *   *

Cash commented as he looked down at the street. "Uh-oh, it's starting to hit the fan downstairs. Flashing blue and red lights everywhere."

"We are now exactly 36 minutes behind schedule." Zilm reported.

Joaquin was packing up the cutter and closing his pack. He considered leaving the plasma torch behind, but that might turn out bad, so he cinched it tight to his waist. Zilm was already out on the balcony.

"We're done here; c'mon lets' go." Zilm spoke. He was nervous now.

"Activate *UPS*." Joaquin spoke into the radio. The whole gang awaited on the balcony, ready. Joaquin was the last one out and the last one to snap into the hook.

"*UPS*-deliver." And with that command, the hook began to rapidly raise the four flying monkeys off the balcony.

Eddie had been listening from his place offshore in the darkness. Anticipating the next action, he was idling the boat back towards the shoreline after he heard his name on the radio.

"*Waterdog Two*, package in motion." Van Zant announced.

"Roger-dodger-codger." Eddie replied, mocking one of his favorite movies 'Airplane,' with stoned nuance. With idle time on his hands, Eddie most always rolled a fattie and this time was no exception to the rule.

Van Zant did not appreciate that stoned-silliness from Eddie one bit as he focused on the dimly dangling group, seen on the end of the gantry. One false move and they would be broken up like poultry parts against the building.

"I'll kick that fucker's ass up to his shoulders if he's smokin dope out there." Van Zant mumbled silently.

Van began to rotate the gantry away from the building and out over the water. Slowly at first, he began to lower the group into the darkness below. Eddie and the boat appeared along the shoreline, and it looked as if the drop was going to be a well-timed conjuncture from air to sea. He kept the cable speed steady at five feet per second and gauged that in 40 seconds, the little dangling gang should be dropping in just above Eddie in the Wong Way. The plan was for Van to escape after the flying monkey guys, releasing himself from a descending hook when he was just above the boat, dropping in just like the others had done before him.

"All stop *UPS*." Joaquin spoke into the radio. It was time to drop in on Eddie, waiting in the boat just below them.

"Unsnap and lower away, slowly. We don't want to tip the boat over." Joaquin spoke to the dangling group who affixed their ropes.

Eddie was twenty feet below them and, like they had done before on the balcony, they all dropped down using their ropes. This time they landed in the boat in various positions. Except Rick. He now was being helped aboard the boat by Eddie-he had landed in the water. Joaquin spoke into the radio.

"Okay *UPS*. All done here and safely aboard. C'mon down."

Van Zant had his harness on, and he was ready. He would be snapping into the hook for the final trip down, hook descending toward the water. He would unsnap at the right moment and join the gang on the boat. At least that was the plan until the power went out everywhere. Tower One went completely black. Tower Two went completely black and unfortunately, the Liebherr 300C Tower Crane ceased to spool.

"What is going on now?" Van Zant mumbled to himself, twiddling knobs and throwing switches to no effect.

"Hey; I'm stuck up here!" Van Zant said into the handheld radio.

*   *   *

Ahkmoud Azzerzin had his game face on as he walked down the ramp to the electrical room. He was ready to mace, cuff or whatever for a bad-ass take-down, proving that he was not a pushover and a security force to contend with. He reviewed the three-point stance and decided he would go for the wrist-lock, cuffing and then spraying. He approached the metal door of the utility room cautiously; creeping along and staring at the door, ready to meet menace with menace in equal measure. But instead, a small explosion knocked the door off its hinges, and it flew through the air and gave Ahkmoud an unexpected body-blow that knocked him on his butt. He was stunned, it was dark and dust clouds blurred his vision. He could not find his radio, flashlight *or* mace. His eyes were not only blurred with dust, but he was blinded by the flash and now brilliant red spots floated across his field of vision. His ears rung within the muffled chamber of his head, blocking all external sound. He pushed the door off his chest. He sat up. This was not how he expected it to go. In the distance he could hear a siren. He was in no shape to talk to or assist the police. They did not respect security cops to begin with and his frazzled, dazed and dusty appearance would be everything they expected. He was now a legend of security cop incompetence. He should have gone to MIT like the rest of his brothers and got his degree.

CHAPTER 14

The Chips Are Down

Joaquin watched his friends, and the little box of diamonds disappear into the darkness of the Bay. They had split up; Joaquin in the previously anchored up Zodiac, waiting for Van Zant to come down from the crane, and the rest of the gang escaping and off to the Estuary. The return route had been discussed and the southern entrance to the Oakland side was thought to be the safest, through the backside of the Estuary. Two heavily armed rigid inflatables were the threat to watch for. Eddie had an alibi; he was returning to shore after a fishing trip, and while fishing, the motor conked out and would not start. Now they were headed home very late. They had two fish and about 9 million dollars in gemstones for the night.

Joaquin had no such alibi; all he had was a stranded Van Zant 240 feet above the Bay, a long stretch of water to cross to safety and no plan for the Van. Originally, the plan was, the gang would both enter the backside of the estuary, tie-up at a private dock and disembark. Frenchy would pick up the criminals in Alameda by car.

Up at Yerba Buena Island, the Coast Guard base came alive with activity. Blue lights and navigation lights were turned on and the docked vessels began to peel off into the open water. If they had had attack helicopters, they would have been in the air already too. Ever since 911 the phrase *terrorist activity* was like a dog whistle that the military could not resist. Words like *Islam-0-Nazi* were spoken as if they were real things, when in fact they were fabrications designed to justify pallets of cash for the military and their supply chain. For decades of post WWII years, the Coast Guard mission had been Search and Rescue. Now they were part of Homeland Security and benefitting from all that 911 cash. Commanders were anxious to use all of it tonight, much to the dismay of the common criminal element trying to work. Everything would have been cool if things would have gone according to plan and the gang would have would have gotten out of there earlier, but Joaquin and Van were behind the 8-ball now and the Coasties were on full alert. Joaquin pulled his cell phone out of his pocket and hit the speed dial for Eddie and waited for him to pick up.

"Yo bro, howze it go? Got the Van? Gimme a *roger*, man!" Eddie sounded happy and sing-song.

"I got shit and shoved in it, that's what I got. Van's ass is still up there, the power is out, the Coasties are on the move, I can see all the flashing blue lights from here and I don't like that. Where are you, Eddie?" Joaquin said.

"Well, let's see-right now we are... we cool, the Estuary. You be careful out there, man. In about 10 minutes we'll be tying up to the dock. Frenchy's waiting there already." Eddie reported.

"Well, I'm still here; I'm still waiting for Van Zant." Joaquin answered.

"Don't get caught bro, that'd be bad." Eddie said.

"Right, really bad, you fool." Joaquin answered, pissed off at his very high accomplice, Eddie. He clicked off the cell phone without another word.

The Coast Guard boats were scrambling and anything out in the open water of the Bay was fair game. He couldn't risk being out in the open too much longer, but Van Zant was still up in the crane.

"Van: where the hell are you? The Coasties are on the move; it looks like World War Three up there." Joaquin spoke into the radio

The Coast Guard at YBI and the .50 caliber Zodiacs were at a dead run toward the South Bay. The big cutter was away, flanked by two 40 footers. Lots of bad scenarios played themselves out in Joaquin's imagination, he was in *deep doo-doo* here. Worst case, he might just have to make a run for it without Van. The only thing for sure was he would soon be in the soup in the moments ahead. The next move he made better not be a false one; indecision or half-measure would not serve. It all came down to a moment; a chance or an accident could tip over his little cart. It was a 50/50 chance in those brief moments when you put all your chips on red and waited for the little bouncing ball to fatefully drop. It was either a sickening feeling in the pit of your hollow stomach or a sense of relief. There was no joy here; only the relief that you didn't lose this time, all you got was another turn; you got to play again. It had been a long time since he last felt this way, crouched in a rice paddy with bullets pocking the water around him, soaking with mud, sweat and fear. If he lived today, all he got was a chance to do it again tomorrow.

"Crime has a dark side too, Zilm, you never thought about that." Joaquin mumbled in the night.

"Van, where are you? All the lights are out over there now!" He repeated into the two-radio. He could no longer wait; he needed to be acting one way or the other and do it now.

"I'm still up here! The power is out, and the winch is dead! The hook is still hanging down and won't come up. The place below me is filling up with flashing red lights. Don't leave me here Joaquin!" Van Zant said.

Joaquin motored into the rip-rap. His cell phone rang. It was Eddie again.

"Hey man, what's happening out there? We got time to swing by Dunkin Donuts and grab a box of dog-nuts, we got the munchies." Eddie sounded positively cheerful. And stoned. It occurred to Joaquin that God watches over children and fools and Eddie fit *both* definitions.

"Get a box of chocolate with sprinkles and bring them to us-*in jail* you fool! We're in the soup here Eddie, Van is still up in the crane!" He spoke.

"Roger, Cap! What's he doin' up there, anyway?" Eddie said with oblivious enthusiasm, unaware that the dark rider was galloping toward Joaquin and Van and closing fast.

CHAPTER 15

This Ain't No Foolin' Around

"What about me?" Van Zant asked his question into the little radio.

Zilm heard Van Zant on his radio, but he did not want to be the one to tell Van that he was a dead duck up there. Total power failure occurred in the electrical room and he was on borrowed time after all the lights in the Towers began to flicker, signifying that the happy frog was doing his job and an explosion was imminent. Zilm spoke via radio to Van.

"The power is out for good, Van. Save yourself any way you can." Zilm spoke into the radio.

"I'm 200 feet above the ground! What I'm gonna do; fly away?" Van Zant asked over the two-way radio.

A conversation broke out among the occupants of the Wong Way boat.

"Down the ladder." Eddie.

"Eddie, get real. Think about it, he can't do that, the cops are there." Zilm blurted back.

"He be in a hard place." Cash.

"He's kinda screwed, isn't he?" Rick.

"Well, you got that part right; he be screwed, glued and tattooed." Cash commented. Everyone got silent in the boat until Rick broke it.

"We can't just leave him, can we?" Rick spoke.

Leaving Van Zant behind had crossed everyone's mind, Rick was just the first one who said it.

Over at the Tower shoreline, Joaquin started to think out loud to himself.

There was no sound on the quiet Bay other than the approaching sirens. Joaquin broke the silence when he keyed the mic on the radio and his voice crackled over the 2 inch speaker like water droplets on a hot grill.

"Van, I'm gonna take this boat right over against those rocks like we planned. You got to jump into the Bay; get your ass off that crane. You're a dead man up there."

Eddie, Cash, Rick and Zilm all looked back and forth at each other as they sat in the Wong Way listening to Joaquin on the radio to Van.

"Jump?" Rick asked and Cash answered.

"The man's right. There's no other way, it's the right thing to do and if Van gets caught alive, we all go down with him. But if he be dead, he can't say a thing. Course, he might survive the jump, you don't know." Cash stated as a matter of factual explanation.

"Roger." said Zilm.

"I say go for it and good luck." Eddie said aloud and had an afterthought.

"Hey, there ain't no Chinese gangs in San Quentin are there?" Eddie asked the group in the little boat.

"You be a charter member, Eddie." Cash said. "They'll bugger you until your almond eyes get round."

"Say, just how come there aren't Chinese gangs in prison, anyway?" Rick wondered.

"Because all the dumb Chi-nee are still in China. Breakin' rocks. The smart Chi-nee came to the US- they be doctors and engineers now, not jail-birds." Cash sized it up the way he saw it.

"What happened to Eddie?" Rick asked.

"He smokes too dang much dope." Cash said.

*   *   *

Time had run out up in the crane tower and Van Zant knew he was a sitting duck. He had to act now. A sketchy plan formed in his mind-and jumping was not in it. He'd rather eat glass than jump into the Bay water from 200 feet at night.

"I'm gonna slide down this cable-OSHA style. But before I drop, make sure you're underneath me, 'cause I can't swim!" He spoke to Joaquin into the two-way radio.

"Don't worry, I got ya." Joaquin answered back.

Van Zant lashed a few turns off his rope around the dormant cable. He had practiced this before in OSHA training, but he never thought he would have to use it for real. He took one last look around at the shimmering lights of the Bay before he stepped off the end of the crane and began his descent. He slid down the cable and found it to be greasy and accelerated until he came to the end of it, twenty feet above the water.

"I'm gonna let go, don't let me drown." He let go and Van Zant promptly dropped into the water.

"Save me Joaquin!" Van Zant thrashed about, head and shoulders struggling against the chilly water.

"Shh! The cops will hear you." Joaquin grabbed Van Zant and rolled him aboard.

"Thanks for reminding me." Van Zant panted a sarcastic reply as he shook the wet off his head. "Let us get the flock outta here."

"Big *roger* on that." Joaquin agreed.

After they were out a way, Joaquin lost no time unspooling 40 mil plastic film from large spools into the dark bay from his little boat as he sped off into the dark water toward the back entrance to the Oakland Estuary. The Uzi went into the water too.

"Planning on a shoot-out, were you??" Van Zant asked when he saw the machine pistol go over the side.

"No, I was planning on staying alive, orders from Mandy." Joaquin replied.

"Well, that's funny Cuz, I had the same thought." Van Zant said. He pulled out a sidearm and dropped it over the side as well.

"Oh, by the way Joaquin," Van Zant turned toward Joaquin at the stern, "Thanks for not leaving without me."

"I thought about it." Joaquin said. Truth was that Joaquin was the guy who *would not* leave you behind, Boy Scouts honor.

The rest of the gang was safe and warm in the car with Frenchy. This was the first time they had ever worried about Joaquin. They did not have to worry too long before his voice came over the two-way radio.

"I got Van; plan A; we got this now." And that was his last transmission before the little radio went over the side into the water.

"You da man." Rick said into his radio.

*   *   *

Right Rear Admiral Daniel C. Pettibone was on the phone to Homeland Security HQ in San Francisco. He was used to getting calls in the middle of the night and he *hoped* it always meant one thing: terrorist activity. San Francisco, as far as he and the agency was concerned, was always in a state of Orange Alert, all in the agency knew it to be a very unstable area. It was common knowledge that subversives of every type congregated within the Bay Area. It had a very high foreign-born population, very suspect. The Universities of the Bay Area were magnets for intellectuals and, as he well knew, intellectuals asked too many smart-ass questions of the wrong stripe for his liking. And as far as he was concerned the Navy had done the right thing to close all Bay Area facilities years ago and move to Republican and military-friendly turf in San Diego.

"Just what the hell is going on out there now at this un-godly hour?" He sat up in his PJ's and barked into the phone.

Colonel Lewis of Operations SF was a wiry, high-and-tight and detail oriented individual. He strictly observed protocol and the chain of command. He always let a superior make the decision, never offered opinions unless solicited, and he offended no one above him. He did feel free to offend many below him, however. He knew to have certain facts and details in place before he picked up the phone to a superior officer or his ass would be grilled. Rightly so, as he saw it.

"Admiral, we have a potential situation developing in the South Bay. We have an explosion. Primary explosion appears to have gutted electrical control room of a high rise, causing complete power failure in what appears to be an act of sabotage."

"Good lord, we're under attack!" The admiral interjected, thinking to himself, *"At last! The terrorist appears!"*

"Yes sir, it appears so, sir." Lewis continued, "We have no hostage situations at this time, we have no attackers located or seen, no hostile communications of any kind, no civilian casualties. We have dispatched all personnel by land and sea. Local and county police are on scene and we are in communication. Land forces are expected to set up a perimeter within 4 minutes, patrol boats are speeding and expected to be on scene in ten. I expect a preliminary report from our personnel no later than 0310 hours."

"Good, good report Lewis. Go Code Red immediately." Admiral Pettibone said.

"Very good sir, will do. And sir? Lewis asked.

"What is it, Lewis?" Admiral replied into his phone.

"First responders report one person in the vicinity of the primary explosion. A security guard apparently was there at the exact time of the explosion and received minor injury from the explosion." Lewis added.

"How did it happen that he was there at the exact time of explosion?" Admiral asked.

"Don't know yet sir. We have yet to interrogate." Lewis said.

"Now I do not want to hear that it's another corn-fed, Christian gun-nut-homeboy like Timothy McVeigh, Lewis. All we ever get is white domestic terrorists or kids with guns killing kids, the newspapers are full of that crap and I'm sick and tired of it. Please tell me he's foreign born. Please. I don't have to tell you we need a win; domestic terrorists are way ahead in the terrorist category." The Admiral was begging.

"Oh, it's good sir. He's here on a work visa, family in Iran, name of Ahkmoud Azzerzin." Lewis reported.

"Oh, that is good Lewis, his name flows off the tongue. He's guilty as sin. I know it. Hold him, interrogate him, the elusive Islam-o-Nazi." The Admiral replied. "We'll get to the bottom of this."

"Yes sir." Lewis responded.

*   *   *

As it was turning out, the main problem for Lt. J G Jones with this assignment was that he didn't drink coffee. He was a gunner on the Homeland Security Patrol boat in San Francisco. His job was to operate the .50 caliber machine gun on the bow of the speedy little rubber boat. No one had ever fired the guns before, all to say that nothing had ever happened to fire the 50 cal *at*, as they travelled at 40 knots from one Starbucks to another in the picturesque landscape of SF Bay, drinking lattes. At first, it was just a joke amongst some of those assigned the duty. The assignment was looked upon as a plum assignment, but after two years of travelling the Starbucks Triangle, the novelty was wearing off. Sausalito Starbucks to Marina Green Starbucks, to Jack London Square Starbucks constituted the route they followed night after night. Jones was bored to tears with this assignment. On the other hand, some of the crews of the Terrorist Strike Force saw the situation as much more than a government gravy-job. To this gung-ho group, it was the constant vigilance and the presence of the Coast Guard gunships that held the Muslim horde of Al Queda and their ilk at bay. It was hard to say if they were right because not much had happened. To the thinking of his chief officer, Master

Chief MacDowell, there was little argument to be found. He was convinced that it was the vigilance of his gunboats that kept terror in check.

"The Hajis are everywhere." Master Chief MacDowell instructed the crew." You think not? Go over to Berkeley. Go to Fremont and San Leandro- don't even talk to me about Oakland. Our presence here lets them know that we are ready for them. It is a fundamental law of physics son; wherever there is an action there is an equal or greater reaction-that is what we are-the greater reaction. And we stand ready. We will meet and react to *any and all* subversive activity on the waters of San Francisco Bay."

"I hang out on Piedmont Ave when I'm on leave-no terrorists in Oakland there, sir!" Rejoined Lt J G Jones.

"No terrorists? What's the matter with you Lieutenant Jones? You got eyes? Where you from boy?" Chief MacDowell asked.

"Nebraska, sir. I'm a corn-fed Husker." J G answered.

"Well, you got that part right anyway, farm boy. You play ball there?" MacDowell asked.

"Yes sir, tight end, sir." Lt J G Jones reported.

"Good, good. Well let me tell you something son: you ain't gonna *see* or *hear* terrorist activity until it happens. Our presence is a deterrent to that; we are a strike force should we be called upon. We *are* and will *continue* to be vigilant. Now what are you doing up on Piedmont Ave, for Christ sakes, JG. You a homosexual?" MacDowell asked.

"No sir, the best rated singles pick-up spot in the Bay Area is located there, sir. It is where the college girls go. They like to party, sir." J G reported.

"Well, that's okay J G. You had me worried there for a minute. Hanging out in the East Bay can be dangerous, but it's okay for chasing tail." Master Chief MacDowell knew what he was talking about from experience.

"He goes to a gay bar, sir." Another patrolman informed, nudging his fellow crewman and giggling.

"Don't ask and don't tell! Remember that! The Armed forces welcomes all!" MacDowell barked and added, "This conversation is over. Now get up on the bow and wipe down that fifty, Jones."

"Yes, sir. They're lying sir, I'm not gay." Lt Jones reported as he left the small enclosure that was the cabin of their boat.

When he was on the bow, Chief MacDowell turned to the remaining crewman in the cabin and said,

"Is he really gay?" MacDowell asked.

"Don't know sir; I don't ask, I don't tell, sir."

"Of course, of course. Carry on." Chief MacDowell knew where all the gay bars were in the East Bay.

The assignment of Terror Patrol may have been boring, but it was a cushy assignment. It was impossible to prove a negative, and the papers were full of Middle East terrorists in the Middle East. Fear was an easy sell. Funding for the patrol would never end even if nothing ever happened, and the fact that nothing had happened in 6 years, proved the value of the patrols in the eyes of the funders. Fabulous sums went into Federal, State and local enforcement agencies, allowing them to purchase tactical vehicles, weapons, patrol boats and militarize all local enforcement agencies who wanted the gear, and of course they all did. Homeland Security was more of a concept than a deterrent. A concept that had a never-ending revenue stream to back it up. It could disappear tomorrow, and the public wouldn't even know it.

The radio in the patrol boat came alive with an alert.

"All boats proceed to the shores of South San Francisco at maximum speed!" Blasted the radio.

Chief MacDowell pegged the throttles of the Zodiac forward till they touched the glass windows and the boats responded by jumping to their maximum 55 knots and the boats travelled in tandem toward the south bay at great speed. Lt JG readied the magazine feed on the .50 caliber machine gun and was joined by an assistant. They were ready for action within the minute, trigger finger itching. The .50 cal could do major damage, chop targets to pieces at great range. They hurled themselves into the fray at breakneck speed. Soon they would be in South San Francisco and on scene. They would not make it as it turned out.

Everything was fine until the speeding boats hit the Visqueen that Joaquin had deployed from the stern of the Zodiac, the plastic sheeting was invisible in the water. It had the intended effect of stopping the propellers of the patrol boats; wrapped up horribly in a plastic wad around the props and the two at the bow gun fell overboard with the sudden stop; first one boat hit it, then quickly the other. Luckily for Lt J G and his assistant on the bow, they were wearing their crash helmets and float jackets. Unfortunately, Master Chief MacDowell chose to ignore regulations regarding a safety harness. He bounced his head off the plate glass windows and now lay sprawled and unconscious on the floor, unable to answer the radio call from his partner boat, similarly disabled alongside of him. Everybody aboard was rattled and unable to answer the radio, especially the un-harnessed unfortunates who were now floundering in the water or on the deck unconscious after the speeding boats came to an abrupt halt. They had gone ass-over-teakettle. Code Red ain't no foolin' around, it ain't no party, and it did not always go as planned.

*   *   *

Joaquin and Van were entering the Estuary back entrance after their crossing of the bay, they were starting to feel safe.

"We made it man, we pulled it off." Van Zant said

"Yeah, so far, so good. Eddie's got the goods in the Wong Way, and we got a clear shot home. It's up to Cash now. Wow, we did do it." Joaquin was starting to realize the magnitude of the caper.

They joined the Wong Way, tied up at the courtesy dock. The rest of the gang was just up the walkway waiting in the car.

"Let's sink these dang boats." Thus said, they pulled the plug on the Wong Way and cut holes in the Zodiac bladders. They watched from the courtesy float as both boats filled with water and a half an hour later, both had sunk to the bottom of the muddy Estuary, invisible.

"We be just like regular people now. Man, we pulled it off." Cash said.

"Hard to believe looking back at it. It's a lifetime pop." Joaquin answered.

"Yeah; a lifetime pop." Van answered and they walked up the ramp to the awaiting car.

CHAPTER 16

The Tool Bag

"Frenchy; girl, get that cat out of this car!" Joaquin said as he and Van Zant slid into the back seat of the car. Frenchy had scooped up a wandering stray cat while she waited.

"He was just walking around the parking lot, lost. It's cash on all fours, like a walking $500 bill!" She defended.

"I don't care if he was handing out tickets to the A's game, he goes out!" Joaquin stated.

"Let the cat go Frenchy, stay focused." Said Zilm quietly. She opened the door, and the kitty ran out on the pavement.

"Just like throwing a $500 bill away, whatever you say." She mused wistfully as the cat wobbled away.

"Get on with it, downtown, my place, backdoor." Cash instructed.

"Can I burn one in here?" Eddie asked the group.

"No." Came the reply from a chorus of the occupants.

Frenchy cut over to High St, up to 13 and then down through Piedmont to Broadway. The carload pulled into the alley behind the pawn shop and they disembarked. There were 6 of them, they crowded the space. Cash sat down at his desk.

"Can I burn one now... please?" Eddie repeated his question.

"You go out in the alley if you wanna get high." Cash answered.

"I guess I can wait. I wanna see these things, Joaquin." Eddie said.

"Yeah." Said Reeger. "I don't even know what they look like yet and I just stole 'em." Joaquin opened the little box and placed it on the table for all to see. The huddled group looked down at the little box on the table like the wise men looked down at the baby Jesus in the manger. Reeger broke the silence. "I thought they were bigger than that."

"Well, they not, Einstein." Cash commented.

"So, what happens know Cash, you keep the stones and find a buyer?" Eddie said.

"That be about it. Man, I don't know how long it be 'til I find the right one, if that be your next question." Cash replied.

"Matter of fact it was." Eddie answered. "You all down with Cash keeping the stones?" He looked at the faces around the Jesus box.

"I'm good." Said Reeger.

"Me too." Zilm chimed in.

"No tricks, Cash, you know what I mean." Van Zant said.

"Let Cash do his thing, that's what he does. He'll do the best he can to get rid of these things. It's in our interest and his. We got out of there clean, we are way ahead of it and nobody's going to screw it up now." Joaquin spoke.

"Okay, but you know the rules here." Van replied.

"There is a severe penalty for any misdeed. I will personally see to that." Joaquin said. He took a handful of stones and let them run through his fingers to their place in the box. "This is our ticket, remember that."

"You don't worry 'bout me." Cash defended.

* * *

The gang fell into their routine the next day; Eddie opened the garage, Joaquin went to work, Reeger drove a couple of loads to the dump, Cash opened the hockshop and Zilm went to the Krystal Towers. All was not routine at the Towers, however, as Zilm soon found out upon arrival.

"This is a crime scene, no entry." The police were all over the place. There was every type of enforcement vehicle; Homeland Security, ICE, police, Highway Patrol, fire trucks, EMT's. At the center of it all was Coast Guard Rear Admiral Pettibone.

"We have a suspect, a foreign borne. We will interrogate." Pettibone was on his best game with the other enforcement types watching him.

"Good. This looks bad-possible sabotage and robbery. They hit the safe at Global Investment for a ton, diamonds worth a fortune." Said Inspector Davis who was now heading the investigation for the South City police.

Zilm was turned away at the gate, but he could not help but snoop around. He was mostly interested in the electrical control room and the frog; he liked the frog. He spoke to the guard.

"Can I go in? Maybe get my tools? I work here." Zilm spoke.

"Who are you? Why you want in? You stay where you are, I'll call Inspector Davis." The guard said.

"Well, forget the whole thing, okay? I don't have to get my tools anyway; I can get them tomorrow." Zilm had poked a stick in a hard dog turd now and it started to stink.

"You stay there, that's an order." The officer had a little mic clipped to his epaulet and he now spoke into it. "We got a suspicious character at the fence, he wants in, claims to want his tool bag."

"I'm not a suspicious character!" Zilm protested. "I just wanted to pick up my tools!"

The reply came over the two-way to the officer. "He stays at the fence and I will be right down." Said Davis.

Davis was about to retire, and he had a mind to go out on an elevated pay scale. There might be a promotion and a raise for him in this, especially if he could wrap it up quickly. He didn't particularly care about accuracy either, just needed a plausible suspect and fortunately, he had one being held and potentially another at the gate. He walked down and confronted Zilm.

"What's your name son? I hear you want in. Do you know anything about what happened here last night?" Davis asked.

Zilm looked as guilty as sin, starting to sweat like a whore in church. "My name is Robert Zilm officer. I just wanted my tools. I work here."

"And what manner of tools might those be?" Davis was narrowing his focus. He as a pro.

An image of his tool belt flashed through his mind, big bold letters that spelled out 'ZILM' and the contents were all electrical tools. There was no way out. "I'm an electrician and they are electrical tools." Zilm replied.

"Is that so?" Like the spider to the fly, Davis was feeling as if a closer examination was warranted. "Well Robert, why don't you step inside for a few routine questions? You can get your tools while you're here. How would that be?"

Zilm had a bad habit; his eyes moved in a rapid side to side movement when he was nervous. His thoughts raced, *"Oh shit. How did this happen so fast? Did I take that tool bag with me last night? I hope I didn't leave it anywhere stupid, like in the control room or at Global."*

If his tool bag was found at the crime scene, it was a dead bust. That would be good for twenty years in the joint. They escorted Zilm to a little room with a table and three chairs. Ahkmoud Azzerzin was already there. Zilm and Ahkmoud were friends but right now being his friend might not be wise.

"Hello Mr. Zilm." Ahkmoud greeted him, glad to be with a friend in this little room.

"You two know each other?" Inspector Davis.

"I know lots of people I work with." Zilm feared he better get on his game, or this conversation was about to go sideways. "Ahkmoud is the front man, everyone knows him."

"Everyone you say?" Davis replied.

"Yes sir." Zilm was gaining altitude from an imminent crash.

"Have a seat." Davis said.

"Ahkmoud: you ever hear of Halvah?" Davis asked.

"Oh yes sir, particularly good, sir. It comes from my country; I have Halvah ever since I was child." Ahkmoud was a completely honest man and, as far as Zilm saw it, a complete fool. He could see where this was going to go.

"Did you have Halvah last night?" Davis asked. He knew about the Halvah wrappers; in the trash behind Ahkmoud's desk and at the base of the crane.

"Oh yes sir I did! Incredibly good energy food!" Ahkmoud answered.

"Well, can you tell me why there happens to be Halvah wrappers on the ground underneath the crane?" The 64,000-dollar question from Davis dropped like a hammer.

"Oh no sir." Ahkmoud was catching on, they thought he did it! Little perspiration beads began to form on his forehead and Zilm was filled with sangfroid, relieved to be out of the spotlight. Too bad for Ahkmoud.

"Halvah is a known terrorist snack food. Did you know that?" Davis pointedly asked.

"No sir, not terrorist snack food! Halvah is candy from Persia! A thousand years, before your country was born, we eat Halvah! You racist profile me! That's what you do!" Ahkmoud caught on.

"Take it easy Mr. Ahkmoud." Inspector Davis said calmly.

"I am Ahkmoud Azzerzin! Son of Abdoulah Azzerzin! American citizen like you!" Ahkmoud was hot, Mr. Davis turned his attention to Zilm.

"Mr. Zilm. You are an electrician by trade, you stated. Are you not?" Davis came out with a big fat softball question that Zilm took a swing at.

"Yes sir, I am."

"Are you aware that there was an electrical problem here last night?"

"No sir, I was not. I showed up for work this morning as usual and found the area sealed off. That was the first sign of trouble I saw."

"The first sign of trouble. To whom, Mr. Zilm?"

"To me, of course, Inspector." Zilm was caught a little off guard.

"And what time is your usual time to show up for work?" Davis was leading somewhere, Zilm did not know where and the ground beneath his feet now started to feel squidgy.

"Oh, about 9AM." Said Zilm glancing for a clock, none in sight.

"Are you always on time at 9AM?" Davis.

"Yes sir." Zilm.

Inspector Davis made a note in his notepad. "I think that will be all for now, Mr. Zilm. Oh, by the way, where are your tools?"

Thoughts raced through Zilm's head; *"Oh shit; It's like a bad dream, it never ends. Where did I leave those God damn tools last night? How long will it take me to get to the border after this nightmare is over? If I left them at Global, I would be in handcuffs already, yes? Last thing I remember, I was grabbing a pair of side cutters from the bag for re-wiring 110V for 220V at Global Investments."*

Zilm punted. "They were stolen sir, I hoped to find them on the jobsite somewhere this morning." Zilm answered without missing a beat, a trait gained from years of avoiding a playground beating.

"Stolen, you say?" Davis

"Yes sir, stolen." Zilm.

"A lot of electrical work went on last night, Mr. Zilm. The entire control room was shorted out. You know that's smart: I mean really. I see a lot of crime and a lot of dumb criminals, but these guys are smart; they know about metals and electricity, cranes. I gotta admire them in a way."

"Really?" Zilm lapped up flattery like a dog.

"Yes, really. You know what I'm talking about, you are an electrician, Mr. Zilm." Said Davis.

"I'm no criminal, I'm just a worker here. If you think that I knew anything about this, you're nuts!" Zilm was saying all the wrong things.

"Calm down Mr. Zilm. Nobody is accusing anybody. I'm just gathering the facts, putting the puzzle together and admiring a well-thought out plan. Smart guys, that's all I'm saying." Davis was dumb like a fox. There was a silence in the room that seemed to last ever-so-long. Zilm was not going to talk anymore.

"These are all just puzzle pieces, that's all. The picture is not clear without the pieces in their place. It is my job to try and put them in place, you understand." Davis was everybody's best friend, the congenial detective trying to be helpful.

"You two can go now, you have been very helpful, thank you. We may need to get a hold of you in the future. Please leave your contact information, your Social Security number and Driver's License. Thanks again for all your help, Mr. Zilm and you too Mr. Azzerzin." Davis said and added.

"It may be best if you stay in town for a while. Don't go on vacation or out of state, eh?" Said Inspector Davis.

"What kind of mess am I in now?" Zilm thought as he shuffled toward the door. *"And how was I so very, very helpful to this gumshoe dick? How did I end up a person-of-interest in the Krystal Towers heist? Van Zant will kill me, I got to think and fast.*

"No sir, I'll be right here when you want me." Zilm spoke as he headed for the door.

"Mr. Zilm!" Davis shouted at the retreating figure.

"Yessir." Zilm answered.

"Your tools. Wanna go inside and have a look around for them?" Davis let the question fall like the door on a Hav-A-Hart animal trap, now Zilm knew how the helpless kitties felt. This Davis was smarter than he let on.

"Oh yeah, I almost forgot. I can come back and look around after you all are done." Zilm replied. He knew he had mis-played his hand, he wanted out before he folded like the morning paper.

"Whatever you say Mr. Zilm." Zilm knew he had stepped on a dog turd. If he was not a person-of-interest before, he sure as hell was now.

*   *   *

"Frenchy: what am I gonna do? They had me in this little room, it was the third degree treatment! I was lumped together with that Iranian, Ahkmoud. They think he's a terrorist, probably got me pegged for an accomplice, for Christ sakes! This Davis-guy set me up like a bowling pin. I played right into it." Zilm was distraught and he was walking rapidly back and forth in the room, waving his arms like he was trying to fly. Frenchy sat on the couch doing her nails, listening and being calm.

"Oh, stop flopping around like a fish, Bobby. You're okay. He was just fishing." She spoke as she applied color to her nails.

"Fish? Yeah right! I'm the catch of the day!" Zilm replied.

"Oh stuff; he doesn't know anything." Frenchy showed extraordinary aplomb considering Zilm's distress.

"I tell ya; this guy was just like Columbo; dumb like a fox." Zilm continued to be worried, Frenchy continued to show disinterest.

"Don't worry Bobby-if things get bad, we can always go to Mexico-take it on the lam like that Fugitive guy-that show on TV. We can live in the sun, drink by the pool, swim-maybe I can get a suntan-you know I want a suntan, Bobby!" Frenchy was talking as if living in Mexico was the opportunity of a lifetime, then she had an afterthought. "I thought Columbo discovered America?"

"I can't even afford a *bus ticket* to Tijuana, Frenchy. Besides, Mexican food is too spicy-it gives me gas. I am in the soup here, French. Van Zant or Joaquin is gonna execute anyone who messes up, I know it. I got it come'n both ways-from the cops and the from the robbers! Both are gonna be on my ass! What am I gonna do?" Zilm was whining.

"Well, nobody's on your ass yet. Maybe you should just tell Joaquin that they hauled you in for questioning, come clean like nothing serious happened." Frenchy offered.

"I'm worried about my tool bag." Zilm stated.

"Oh that. Well, you can always get another one, just go down to Home Depot-they have lots of them there-I saw them." Frenchy thought she had stumbled on the solution.

"You don't understand. Maybe I did leave *my* tool bag with *my* name on it in the building we robbed! Maybe even it's at the crime scene itself-I can't remember." Zilm confided.

"Oh, well that is bad-I see what you mean. But wouldn't they have arrested you already? Isn't that a dead-bust? I mean leaving your bag with your name on it at the crime scene should be good for a one way ticket to Sing Sing, no? Maybe we should get outta town now. Hey! We already speak Canadian, and the food isn't spicey-we could hide out there!" The second solution from Frenchy was offered with the equal enthusiasm as the first.

"I'm not going anywhere just yet; I told the cops the bag was stolen, they told me don't leave town. I'm just gonna call a meeting and tell the guys what happened. It's all I can do right now." Zilm was resigned and down-hearted.

"You're right Bobby-come clean. Be upfront-nothing bad happened yet. It's all in your head. They just wanna sweat you out, they're grasping at straws. They'll pinch that rag-head before they arrest you." Frenchy didn't know much about PC, but she knew all about how racism worked.

"Maybe. But Ahkmoud's clean, he's a smart guy and he's nobody's fool. Once they decide it isn't about terrorism and it's just a robbery, he's off the hook." Zilm was thinking out loud.

"Well okay. Call your meeting and come clean and if it *does* go south? Can I have the convertible? Pleeease? You know I love that car." Frenchy remained oblivious to most things beyond her nails and nose this morning.

* * *

Zilm got to Tony's first and went to the back table without a word to anyone he passed by. He had a hangdog look on his face like a man on the way to the gallows. Tony noticed the look right off from his place behind the bar.

"Somebody run over your dog Bobby-me-boy?" Tony said.

"Worse, Tony." Zilm answered.

Next, Reeger, Van Zant, Cash and Joaquin all came in at once, laughing and joking. The gang all settled in around the back table.

"Okay Zilm, you little fairy, got your undies in a bunch or what? It's your show, what's this all about?" Van Zant was in a good mood.

Zilm began slowly. "Well yesterday I went to work at the Towers and the cops were all over the place. It was fenced off as a crime scene, so I asked the guard if I could go in and get my tool bag. The next thing I know, they got me in a little room for questioning."

"Ho-lee-shit Zilm; You ever hear of returning to the scene of the crime?" Van Zant asked the question.

"But you said just go to work and stuff. That's all I was doin?" Zilm immediately started to whine.

"But not at the place we robbed-that's the one place you can't go to." Van said.

"What did they ask you, Zilm" Joaquin piped up.

"Well, you know, what time I usually show for work, was I aware of this and that, where did I leave my tool bag." Zilm was a bit sheepish.

"Tool bag? Where *did* you leave your tool bag, Zilm, 'cause I'll kill you right now if you say it was at Global." Van Zant said.

"I told them it was stolen." Zilm.

"Where is your tool bag, Zilm" Cash.

"I'm not sure." Zilm said. "I might have left it somewhere."

"Holy cow, Bob; don't tell us it's at Global…" Reeger joined in.

"Of course not! I'm not *that* stupid." Zilm.

"Well just how stupid you be?" Cash.

"Now we have to kill ya before you rat us all out. And don't tell me you wouldn't because you would if it would save your own skinny ass. The hard-cold facts of life here now, Zilm. We'll be quick about it, we'll be gentle." Van Zant had boundary issues.

"Slow down Van, hear him out." Joaquin stated. "What did you tell them Bob?"

"Well, when I realized I couldn't remember exactly where my tool bag was, I just told them it was stolen. I got afraid. This detective was cagey. I couldn't tell if he had it already or what. What if they found it at Global?"

"We'd be done for, that's what. That's why we have to kill you right away." Van Zant stated as a matter of fact.

"I told them it was stolen, so we're covered, right Joaquin? Nobody has to die; I wouldn't rat you guys out." Zilm looked at the silent faces looking at him.

"Honest, they were just on a fishing expedition. Honest guys, it was not a big deal, you gotta believe me." Zilm finished with a plaintive statement of innocence.

"This is serious shit right here, Zilm." Cash said.

"Cash is right Zilm. What if they do have the bag? This could be bigger than you make it out to be." Reeger said.

"Okay. Let's not jump the gun here. Let's put these pieces together; intelligent-like. You don't remember where you left it and you told them the bag was stolen. If it's in Tower #1? We're okay. If it's in Tower #2 or Global? It's stolen." Joaquin stopped to think, then he spoke.

"You might be okay. You need an alibi now-get Frenchy to cook something up, swear that you were with her." Joaquin said.

"Truth is, there be a crack in the ice now and we be on it; we don't know where it gonna go now." Cash weighed in.

"Get your story straight with Frenchy, Zilm. Stick to your story. So far, the bag was stolen, you were with French all night and you're on the record for that. Anything else?" Joaquin asked.

"I told them I show up at 9AM for work every day." Zilm answered.

"What time was it they had you in the room?" Joaquin asked.

"I can't remember, I don't have a watch." Zilm was afraid he was at the gate way before 9AM, but he was not about to say that now.

"You can't remember when they nabbed you and… you can't remember where you left the tool bag. That don' t sound too good." Van Zant had that deadeye look as he looked from face to face at the table.

"Honest guys, I showed up when I always show up in the morning for work, I just don't know exactly when that was yesterday!" Zilm pleaded.

"Bob, if your timeline is all wrong-why are you there early? What if this is the only day you are *ever* at work early?" Joaquin asked.

"Hey; I'm your lifelong friend! I'm not gonna rat you out. You know that don't you?" Zilm was feeling cornered.

Silence at the table, broken by an animated figure coming into the back room. "Sorry I'm late guys, my favorite show on TV-these English guys get a car every week and test drive it. These guys crack me up-they usually wreck the car too! What did I miss?" Eddie reeked of pot, as usual, stoned and oblivious to the somber faces.

His question was met with silence. "Did somebody die? What's goin' on?" Eddie asked.

Reeger spoke, "Zilm got questioned by the police."

Joaquin added, "He thinks he left his tool bag at the crime scene."

"The fool went back to the scene of the crime yesterday morning." Cash said.

"We're all scared shitless." Reeger said.

"We ain't scared shitless. We just gonna kill the mo-fo." Van Zant.

Eddie began to laugh. "This ain't no joke Eddie, get-a-grip." Joaquin was calm.

"That's where you're wrong Joaquin, it *is* a joke-on the old Zilmo. I told him last night to just throw the tool bag in the Bay. He said it's valuable, so, he stashed it under the seat of the of the Wong Way. If he doesn't have it, it's under about ten feet of water right now. You guys crack me up- ya'll be like Tony Soprano or something." Eddie said.

"Thank you, Eddie." Zilm said with relief.

"No problem, Z-man." Eddie.

"Good enough." Reeger said. "You really had us going there Zilm."

"Not good enough for me." Van Zant said.

"Whaddya mean? What's your deal Steve?" Joaquin.

"It's evidence at the scene of the crime *or* in the Bay. I think he better retrieve it." Van Zant.

"Man, who's gonna find it ten feet under water?" Zilm protested.

"Anybody that comes snoopin' around-on purpose or by accident." Van Zant was not to be placated.

"The man's right; we got a lot rid'in on this. Just go down and fish it out Zilm. Then, we be sure." Cash said.

"Oh man. Everything happens to me," Zilm sighed

*   *   *

Low tide occurred at 3AM, so Zilm was up early. He was having coffee in the little kitchen when the knock came at the front door. He walked across the living room and opened the door and there was Rick in his frogman suit, mask and snorkel. He had talked Reeger into the job of retrieving the tool bag from the muddy waters of the Estuary, knowing he had a wetsuit.

"You can take the flippers off Rick, at least until we get there. It'll be easier to walk that way. C'mon in." Reeger flapped his way to the couch and took off the flippers.

"I was just doing it for effect, what do you think?" Reeger said.

"It's great Rick, it's all working for ya, it's real *Sea Hunt*." Zilm said.

"What's *Sea Hunt*?" Reeger asked.

"Didn't you ever watch that old TV show when you were a kid? You know, Mike Nelson? Lloyd Bridges? Sharks? Goggles? Mask?" Zilm asked.

"Are there sharks in the Estuary?" Reeger had a slight quaver in his voice.

"No." Zilm responded.

"I guess we didn't get that *Sea Hunt* channel." Reeger offered.

"Guess not. Let's have coffee, I made a pot" Zilm suggested.

"Cool." Reeger said.

After coffee, they drove down the freeway to Alameda. It was deserted outside; there were two hours every day when no one was active, 3AM and 4AM. The people were either in bed waiting for the work-alarm, sleeping it off or humping. No one was out on the freeway except Zilm and Reeger.

"Now when we get there, Rick, you just walk down the dock and jump in. I'll carry your gear. My tool bag is under the seat of Eddie's boat. Get it and let's get out of here." Zilm instructed.

"Yeah, okay Zilm. If it's there I'll get it." Reeger answered.

"It better be there." Zilm had a flash in his mind of Eddie with a fat reefer, talking shit about things he imagined.

They pulled off the freeway at Fruitvale Ave and went to the empty parking lot at the ramp. Rick flopped down the ramp and rolled into the water headfirst. Much to his surprise, he buried his head in the mud shortly after breaking the surface of the water-the water was only four feet deep at low tide. He flipped over and stood up on the muddy bottom. He wiped the mud off his face mask and the top of his head.

"It's shallow!" Reeger shouted, surprised.

"Well okay, get on with it and don't wake up the neighborhood, for God's sake." Zilm answered.

Reeger disappeared under the surface and soon returned with what looked like a bag. It was covered in silt and crud from the bottom. "I think I got it." Reeger said.

"Good. Now come on out and let's get outta here. I got a mind to throw this thing on top of Van's car hood." Zilm said.

"No. That would be a bad idea." Reeger offered.

"Not really, but I should." Zilm retracted.

Reeger hoisted himself onto the ramp like a marine mammal, belly first. He took off his flippers and they wasted no time getting out of there, Zilm at the wheel and Rick all wet and muddy in the back seat.

"Well, that's the end of that. I hope they're happy now." Zilm stated.

"It's best this way, now, you're sure; so is the gang." Reeger replied.

"Such a trusting lot of fellows, that gang of ours." Zilm answered with overt sarcasm.

CHAPTER 17

Box O' Rocks

Beto and Berto Chacon were twins. They were also partners in Global Investments. Berto resided in Panama City and Beto resided in Los Gatos, California. Beto was also the operating manager of their partnership, which dealt in art, gems, antiques and all manner of valuables. He was a slick front man for the corporation; perfect English, smooth manners, impeccably dressed, perfect hair and swarthy complexion. Berto was the mirror opposite; unshaven, uncombed hair and usually attired in his bathrobe. His main interest was laundering drug money through the corporation and discovering entertaining ways of torturing his enemies and rivals in the drug trade. On this morning, Berto was waiting for a delivery from Amazon. He had come across a catalog from Northern Tool and Energy, and he was happy with his first purchase, a 1000 volt electric fence. It worked shockingly well. The brush grinder he purchased from them didn't work out, it was a frightening implement that now sat in the corner of his playroom. His disappointment with the brush grinder came unexpectedly and as a messy surprise when the victim's torso got stuck at the shoulders in the feed tube and the human body, at 98% water, splattered the room with a red and pulpy mess. The mistake stained the whole room and even 409 could not remove it. He had to re-paint the entire room. Currently, he was awaiting a 2000V cattle prod from Amazon. The phone rang before the doorbell, and he shuffled over in his slippers to answer it. It was his brother on the end of the line, calling from California on the SAT phone.

"Berto, we been robbed." Beto was straightforward.

"What you mean little brother?" Berto referred to Beto as *little brother* because he was older by a half hour.

"Last night they blew the safe in the office."

"What they get? The diamonds?"

"That's the good part; nothing. I had the diamonds in the safe at home and they got the fakes."

"Stupid gringos. What about Arabs now?"

"The deals off for now, maybe later for them. Berto, the insurance company doesn't know they were the fake rocks in the safe. They were insured for almost 10 million."

"Dio de madre. The stupid gringos do us favor, yes?"

"We might come out good if we can get the insurance money *and* keep the stones. We can sell the real rocks to the rag heads later."

"You de man little brother. I gotta go, the doorbell rings. Amazon here now." Berto said.

"I'll call you later." Beto hung up the phone and returned to his bathroom mirror to finish his morning grooming ritual.

* * *

Cash had to call Joaquin right away. The appraiser had just left the office.

"Joaquin: we got a problem. The rocks were appraised at ten dollars. The woman she laughed at me; said we had a box of acrylic costume jewelry, fakes. And she be right; she not jerking me around. The god-damned things look just like the one's on Amazon. It obvious they not real! Did Zilm even *look* at them?" Cash was distraught with good reason.

"That god-damned moron Rick had the box."

"What we thought be 9 mil in diamonds ain't worth twenty dollars! What those Global bastards trying to pull? They screwed us." Cash was dejected.

"This is bad on so many levels. Van is gonna think it's you who tricked us." Joaquin said.

"Me?" Cash said incredulously.

"Yeah you. The old switcheroo." Joaquin was straightforward.

"Wait a minute man, you know I'm good, there be no switcheroo about it-we stole fake diamonds! I tell you true Daddy-O." Cash was pleading his case.

"I know, but that's just me." Joaquin was non-committal regarding Van Zant. He continued with a meager offering of alliance. "Maybe he'll buy it? Get the appraisal in writing."

"Yeah, that don't be the end of it with that dude, I know that. What am I gonna do about him? This be bad enough without his action. I don't know what I do 'bout that, but right now I *do know* what I'm gonna do; I'm gonna get high as a Georgia Pine and drunk as a mo-fo-monkey. I see you later brother."

"Let's have a sit-down at Tony's tomorrow, I'll call the guys. Not a word until then." Joaquin said.

"I don't go bragging 'bout how I be stealing a box of worthless rocks, don't be worry'n on that." Cash said sarcastically and clicked off the call on his cell phone.

*   *   *

Joaquin arrived first at the bar. He nodded at Tony as he entered and went right to the back. It was a hard business ahead of him and his head was filled with conflicting thoughts. Part of him wanted to just walk away from this whole business. Zilm's bright idea was fading fast and he and the whole gang had been dragged through it.. He was convinced that Cash hadn't pulled a fast one. Joaquin was pissed that he had been duped by this slick dandy at this Global Investment joint. What were they up to? Were they going to rip off the Arabs and risk getting chopped in pieces and stuffed in a suitcase?

They would certainly rip off the insurance company if they could by staging a robbery Well, I guess we did *them* a solid.

Cash rolled into the Topper next and took a seat next to Joaquin at the back table. "Whatch you thinkin' bro?"

"I think we're short about 9 mil." Joaquin said flatly.

"We dat." Cash didn't have a lot to say, he had a bad hangover from a night out with his homies from the hood.

Van Zant, Frenchy and Zilm were next to arrive. They seemed in good spirits, but Van Zant immediately sized up something when he looked at Joaquin. He knew something was wrong.

"What's up Joaquin." Van said.

"Sit down, there's news. The diamonds are fake." Joaquin said.

"Be true. Appraiser laughed in my face. Look at these." Cash opened the box and revealed a layer of colored acrylic stones to Van Zant. Van Zant looked at the open box and then addressed Joaquin and Cash.

"No bullshit Joaquin? You are dead if you lie, you know that. Same goes for you Cash." Van Zant was into his dead-eye criminal mode.

"It's true Van. I don't know what's going on for sure. I do know Cash-and he's playin' it straight. I think Chacon was up to something sneaky, that's my guess." Joaquin didn't have a lot to add beyond that.

"I know what Beto is up to; he's a snake; he was gonna fake a robbery! I bet the real ones are still at his house in the safe. He's got the gems and now he's goin' after the insurance money. All he has to do is sit tight." Frenchy said.

"This doesn't have to be over, necessarily, does it?" Zilm added in.

"What you mean Tightey-Whitey?" Cash said.

"We and Beto are the only ones that know the stones are fake, right? And we know that Beto has the real ones, somewhere." Zilm deduced.

"And so?" Van said.

"So, we just blackmail the double-crossers…." Zilm began.

Voices could be heard approaching the table. It was Eddie and Rick. Eddie was in the middle of an explanation to Rick.

"They got this alien in the desert and they froze the little prick, yeah, it's true. They don't want you to know about it, but it's out there. They got all kinds of shit out in that desert-secret stuff you'll never know about. This alien had a ray gun too and they got that 'cept they don't want that to get out-the technology could fall into the hands of the Russians-make our nuclear shit obsolete, make a megaton look like a popcorn fart. But a lot of people know now, it's all over the internet. Facebook news had a whole page on it and now the FBI is in their shit; oh yeah! *This* is a national secret that we're not supposed to know about, but everybody does. People are disappearing, you go poking around and you are gone, Jack-history in the desert. There's a whole government unit that we don't know about-all they do is track down unusual things like this and people that know about it."

"You know about it and you're still here." Rick's innocent honesty was disarming.

"You can't keep shit like this secret for long! Cats out of the bag, Jack! There are people that pay big money for this information-I could sell what I know right now. I even know where the warehouse is! They be following my ass now maybe." Eddie was wound up. And, as usual, more than a little high. They walked through the door and headed straight back while Eddie continued his alien conspiracy monologue.

"What's the matter? You are one sorry looking group of cats." Eddie remarked as he assessed the long, silent faces sitting at the table.

"Sit down Eddie, shut up. We got trouble." Van Zant said quietly.

Rick and Eddie took seats and the silence continued. Rick looked from face to face.

"Rick: did you look in the box that came out of the safe?" Joaquin broke the silence.

"Of course, I did, I even ran my fingers through the diamonds. I wanted to feel what 9 million felt like." Rick replied.

"What did they feel like, son?" Joaquin asked.

"Well, to tell you the truth, I thought they would be bigger than that. It was dark, so I had to make sure they were in there. They felt like the rocks in my turtle bowl when I change the water. I have to change the water every week and I wash the rocks. The get all slimy and mossy if I don't, turtles can get fungus rash from the rocks, you have to be careful, you have to check their little legs and the shell. If the shell feels soft, he's sick. I'm really careful about that." Rick said.

"We don't give two shits about your turtle bowl you moron!" Van Zant exploded.

"We stole a box of rocks Rick! They were not real! He tricked us, Rick!" Zilm piled on.

Eddie jumped in, "I'll kill the mo-fo; I'll walk in and go postal, I'll unload on his ass, I'll cut his heart out and eat it, I'll find out where he lives, I'll kill his family, I'll kill his dog, I'll burn him out."

"Take it easy killer." Joaquin said with a degree of calm.

"What are we gonna do?" Frenchy fretted.

"We gonna stay cool, whatever we do. Whatever his game is, the game ain't over with this Chacon dude, but cool is the rule." Cash said.

"Cash is right. We gonna make a plan to get those stones-Chacon has got 'em squirrelled away somewhere." Joaquin said.

"We can quit, can't we? Is that an option?" Frenchy was unsure.

"Oh no; that is not an option, that mother's gonna pay and we're gonna get those stones! He's got 'em and we're gonna get 'em- case closed." Eddie jumped into the conversation.

"We do have the *dirt* on *him*." Frenchy said. "He's a dirty-dog-dirt-bag."

"I feel bad, I feel stupid. I'm sorry guys, I guess I was excited." Rick said.

"Would have been the same even if you *did* see they were phony, Rick." Joaquin said.

"True dat." Cash offered.

"Frenchie's right, we do have dirt on him, he's got something to hide from the insurance dicks and we know the real stones were not stolen." Zilm was interrupted by Eddie.

"We know where they are *not*." Eddie interjected.

"Okay ladies don't get your undies in a bunch. Let's think about this. We may not be done here. Let's put the screws to this Chacon-guy. Let's see if we can make a deal with him." Van Zant was cool.

"What kinda deal?" Eddie asked.

"Let's say we don't rat him out to the insurance dicks. That's what we have to offer him. In return, he gives us the real stones, he gets the insurance money." Van Zant made it sound simple.

"You sure about this Van? This is big-time shit here. He's not gonna just hand out 9 million in diamonds like we be goin' through the drive-thru window at In-N-Out." Cash questioned.

"Well, if you got a better idea, I'm all ears bro." Van said back.

"I think it's a great idea! Blackmail, old school style!" Eddie exclaimed.

"Think it through, Eddie, it may be riskier than you think." Joaquin cautioned an exuberant and high Eddie.

"You want out Joaquin? Just say so. We got this bastard by the short and curlies the way I see it and I'm not letting him loose." Van Zant was blunt. "This is my chance and I'm taking it."

"Man, you think we got the goods on him, but he's got the goods on us too; we're criminals now." Joaquin looked around the table at the faces as he spoke. All eyes were on him now.

"It's tricky, I'll give you that." Van Zant said.

"Let's just rob the mother and then kill him!" Eddie had his own back-up plan.

"It might come to that Eddie." Said the Van.

"He's got a bad-ass twin brother in Panama too." Said Frenchy with a degree of trepidation.

"Well, that makes it even, cause I'm a bad-ass too." Said the Van.

"And I'm a bad-ass!" Eddie added with glee and exuberance.

"I'm in. I was afraid it might come to this." Joaquin relented.

"The less people know about this the better, Joaquin." Zilm said and added, "Why isn't anything ever easy? It seems like we're always shoveling shit against the tide. Just once I want things to go my way. God, what have I got myself into now?" Zilm said.

"Man-up and shut up." Cash said with a little disgust.

"Then we are agreed? We blackmail this Chacon bastard. Zilm-you case the house. Get a Google Earth shot. Frenchy-see if you can get a feel for what the cops know. Rick- you hang on to that box of fakes. Eddie-keep your powder dry, get with Joaquin and I to figure out something for a blackmail note." Van Zant said. The ball was rolling, and the group grew silent in thought as they contemplated yet *more* criminal activity.

"Gee, it's not working out the way we thought, is it?" Rick pondered.

CHAPTER 18

Plan B

Frenchy looked around the Global office with hooded eyes. It was crowded with official types investigating the robbery. Detective Davis was there of course, but also insurance investigators had arrived as well. Beto Chacon was also there, watching the proceedings from the window behind the closed door of his office. His worst fears were that it would take a long time to process this crime and declare it an official robbery. The presence of so many insurance snoops was not at all a welcome development, even though he knew his story was golden and beyond reproach. There was no way they could disprove it, save to discover the diamonds in his possession. All the same, they made him nervous with all their pointed questions. The longer they were around the longer he had to hold the stones in his safe at home and act like they were stolen. He didn't like to hold them there, he had to move them ASAP-anywhere but in his possession. He had had little choice in the matter, he was to bring them into the office that day of the robbery. They were his one-way ticket to Leavenworth while they were in his possession now. He didn't even know where else to stash them and he didn't want to be caught transporting them. It was a tricky business; the heat was watching; he could not afford a false move. He thought about running to Panama but that would blow his chances and cover; fleeing the country was a dead bust, an omission of guilt, a very bad idea and it would result in a lifetime of company with his psycho brother in Panama. The best idea he could come up with was to do nothing for the time being, leave the stones where they were until he figured it out. He had to sit tight like he was innocent. Just field the questions and stay cool.

* * *

Detective Davis walked about the office at the Global Investment Corporation, observing the break-in scene. He jotted down a few notes before he settled upon questioning the employees first, and then the owner.

"Do you like it here, Ms. Gigot. It sure looks a like a nice office. Just how long have you worked for Global Ms. Gigot?" Detective Davis casually asked Frenchy.

"Oh, about two years I guess." She replied.

"And before that?" Davis pressed.

"Oh, this and that. I'm a domestic counselor by trade actually."

"I see. And just what is a domestic counselor?"

"I assess a home and arrange it to increase the harmony within its walls."

"Like Feng Shui, huh? Well, that's really interesting, an Eastern philosophy-kinda-thing."

"Like that sort of thing." Frenchy replied.

"Are you also involved in the pet industry as well? I read that somewhere. You kinda do a lot of things, a Jill-of-all-trades, so to speak." Davis probed.

"At times. I have found pets and returned them to their owners." Frenchy was getting a little nervous. This detective? How did he know this stuff?

"Kind of an entrepreneur. If opportunity knocks-there you are!" Davis joked. Unconvinced of the humor of this line of questioning, Frenchy remained like a stone at her desk.

"Ms. Gigot, did you know that a transaction was to take place the day after the robbery?" Davis returned to his business-like composure.

"I did not." Frenchy lied.

"Ms. Gigot, may I ask you a personal question?" Davis asked.

"I suppose." Frenchy said with apprehension.

"Ms. Gigot, are you romantically involved with Mr. Chacon?"

"Certainly not!" Frenchy said.

"Have you ever been romantically involved with Mr. Chacon?"

"I don't see what business it is of yours who I fuck!" Frenchy lost her composure.

"I'm sorry, Ms. Gigot, I didn't mean to pry too deeply, but people talk and there is a lot at stake here, you understand my position. I'm untangling a mess is all. I'm not too concerned about your personal details." Davis.

"We dated a long time ago." Frenchy said.

"Does Mr. Chacon share information with you? Information, say, about sales transactions?"

"I already told you-NO!" Frenchy sensed it was a trap.

Davis fumbled through the pages of his notebook. Some confusion passed across his brow. "Did you tell me that already? I'm sorry, I neglected to record it and I don't remember it that way." Davis.

"Well, I did. My duties here are strictly secretarial and executive level information never comes my way." Frenchy stated.

"That's all for now miss Gigot. Please stay in town until this matter settles, it won't be long, I'm sure. You've been very helpful." Detective Davis made a few notes in his pad and walked to the back of the office.

"What the heck was that?" Frenchy muttered inaudibly after he left. She was slightly rattled but didn't show it.

* * *

Detective Davis knocked on Beto Chacon's door. The congenial Beto snapped to attention and answered it. "Come in, come in Detective." Beto was all smiles, ear to ear congeniality.

"This won't take long, Mr. Chacon. Seems straightforward to me. Close to an open-and-shut robbery it seems." Davis

"And so it *does* seem, Mr. Davis." Smoothly said with a toothy smile

"So, Mr. Chacon. Where were you on the night of the robbery?" Davis.

"I was home. I had dined out and returned home." Chacon was fairly dripping with sweetness. The charm machine was on ten.

"Oh really? Where do you like to eat Mr. Chacon? I go to Sizzler and order the surf and turf. Where did you eat this night?"

"Well, I went to Chevy's actually-alone. I ate and went home." Chacon answered warily this time.

"I love Chevy's. I always have the chimichangas there. I order them with that green sauce on the side. What do they call that stuff? I call it 'green sauce." Davis said.

"Tomatillo." Beto offered.

"That's it, tomatillo sauce. What did you have?" Davis asked.

Beto was becoming increasingly wary with every question of this off-topic chit-chat. He knew Davis did not care about his culinary interests, so he was a little stiff in his reply.

"Two chicken tacos, black beans, flour tortillas, diet coke." Chacon replied.

"I see. When did you first become aware of the robbery?" Davis.

"I was awakened that night by security." Beto had decided it was wise to keep it short; do not make conversation and do not volunteer anything with this detective.

"Did you come down to the office then? Immediately or later?" Davis.

"I had a cup of coffee, slipped my overcoat over my pajamas and got in my car. I arrived about 4 AM." Beto answered curtly.

"You got one of those Kuerig things? They're quick." Davis said.

"Yes; very fast." Chacon said

"Weren't you cold in just your PJ's? I get cold so easy, it seems." Davis asked.

"My overcoat is long and warm detective. Is there a question related to the robbery, detective?" Chacon was clearly irritated by the inanity of this questioning.

"Yes, yes, of course. What did you find at the office? After the break-in I mean." Davis asked.

"Well, the vault door was cut open, there was a hole where the lockset used to be. Inside the vault it was the same; the safe was cut open in the same way." Chacon answered.

"Do you always keep the jewels in the office safe?" Davis asked with feigned disinterest, looking around the room.

Beto had to say 'yes', there was no other answer that would do. It was only then that it dawned on him that he had been in a chess game and this loaded question was 'check' and it was 'checkmate' if he answered 'no'. He now knew for sure he was being played like a fiddle.

"Yes, it is very secure, it is the *only* place for a thing of this value." Chacon answered.

"And what value would you say that is, Mr. Chacon." Davis asked.

"The collection of colored diamonds has been appraised at 9.2 million." Chacon answered.

"Dollars?" Davis said.

"Yes, 9.2 million dollars." Chacon was curt.

Davis gave a low whistle. "That's a lot of money, Mr. Chacon."

"Yes, it is. But compared to some, not so much. I deal with very wealthy people, detective. In our world, we spend 30,000 dollars for an automobile and that is a lot of money. Wealthy people spend 500,000 dollars for an automobile, drive it a few times, and put it in the garage in a stable of similarly valued cars. It is not a lot of money for them to spend. Ever been to Dubai, detective?"

"No, I have not." Davis.

Chacon chose this moment to establish his superiority over his interrogator, he began a lecture aimed at a lower class in which this annoying, gumshoe hick resided.

"In Dubai, detective, homes are sold for 50 million dollars and the owners do not even live there, merely visit it once a year. They are built upon man-made jungle islands, and they are named after countries. Imagine, detective, a 50 million dollar home called 'Sweden'? 40 years ago, Dubai was all sand in the desert. Now? Dubai is a gleaming city with the tallest buildings, the most expensive homes, cars, hotels and restaurants; all that you can imagine. These are very religious people, detective. For two hours every day they pray to Allah on their knees. For the other twenty-two hours of a day, they worship wealth, because they know that wealth not only represents power, but wealth *is* power; wealth is the power that transforms the desert, nations, people." Chacon obviously had *worship-issues* himself. Davis made a few notes in his book.

"Well, I guess that about covers it, Mr. Chacon, thank you. I'm gonna have to see this Dubai place. Have you ever been Mr. Chacon?"

"Oh yes, many times." Chacon said with a small amount of condescension.

"I gotta see this place. Mr. Chacon, we may have more questions, but really, it looks simple to me; a jewel heist by a professional gang with bonus points for ingenuity. That crane part was genius." Davis.

"I have to agree." Chacon still had his nose up in the air.

Detective Davis again made notes in his pad and paused on his way to the door and turned back toward Beto Chacon.

"One more thing Mr. Chacon. Who owns these stones? I mean, who holds the insurance policy? You know what I mean." Davis.

"The collection belongs to the Global Investment Corporation." Chacon stated.

"That's what I figured, Mr. Chacon, I just had to make sure." Davis jotted notes in his pad again and left the office, once again regained to the high ground in this brief exchange. Chacon watched his retreat, not sure how much this gumshoe suspected.

* * *

Frenchy sat at her desk; the investigation in the office whirled about her. Fingerprints, photographs, detectives, cops, insurance investigators and a maintenance crew. She had taken an extra half hour to dress this morning. She was ready to flirt, and it looked like the game was on. One of the insurance inspectors was giving her the eye when he thought she wasn't looking-but she was, she had radar for this sort of thing. Before long he came over to her desk and flirted ineptly. He wore a cheap suit, had a bad haircut to match his breath and scuffed up shoes. His chin receded below thin lips and his sharp nose may have saved his face, but alas, God had given him a set of beady little pig eyes, close set, black and furtive. Of course, he thought himself suave and smooth.

"Hey gorgeous, tell me; who was the last person you saw handle the jewels?" Charles Napier leaned in with one arm planted on her desk like he was a film noir detective in a B movie.

"I beg your pardon. You may address me as Ms. Gigot, please." Frenchy had this guy's number right away. By and large, men like he were stupid and predictable-a stereotypical man-splainer, clueless to the needs, wants and worldview of women. He had all the symptoms; it was written all over his pasty face. Frenchy continued.

"Well, let's see… I think Mr. Chacon had them, but I can't be sure, I'd have to think about it for a bit." Frenchy answered.

"I tell you what; let me buy you lunch sometime, and you can think about it then. How about that?" Napier moved right in.

"Well, I don't know, would that be proper, considering?" Frenchy was coy.

"Sure, we do it all the time, just a matter of routine!" Said the little man. He had never taken a client out to lunch ever and most especially never a good-looking one, but that didn't stop Napier from trying. He believed that the law of averages was part of a romantic pursuit; eventually even a blind pig finds an acorn.

"Well, I have a date with my girlfriend for lunch, but dinner is open." Frenchy was obvious, weaving her web, Napier was too full of himself to get it.

"Let's make it dinner then; a working dinner-always my first choice." Mr. Insurance-guy was enthusiastic, he could hardly believe his good fortune on securing a dinner date with the alluring Ms. Gigot on the first try.

"Okay, tonight at seven say?" Frenchy had this chump; this was easier than petnapping and actually, it was a lot similar; just dangle a treat and they beg for it.

*   *   *

Zilm sat at a table at a wi-fi coffee house and zoomed in on the property at 103511 Stratford Street in Los Gatos on his laptop, it was the residence of Beto Chacon that he was staring at, gathering intelligence for Plan B. It was a nice property; gated, manicured landscaping, outbuildings, pool. Zilm was fascinated with this Google Earth app, such great detail and the whole world was at his fingertips, he didn't even have to leave his house to case the house. Still, he would see if he could glean a few details the old-fashioned way on foot; security, housemates, exposure, ingress-egress, all the factors the gang needed to know for a break-in. He was also fascinated with the neighborhood surrounding it, fascinated with what wealth could get you. Stately homes, fine cars, sidewalks of brick with trees and restaurants and shops arranged like a Disneyland scene. Zilm had his own wealth-issues, and they now demanded his curiosity as to how the other half lived. Were they having more fun? Were they happier? Did they have less to worry about? In his upbringing, money was always the thing in short supply, poverty was like a low-grade fever, money; that was the thing that it came down to, was argued about and anguished over. It was as if money was the vaccine the family needed to be cured of what ailed it. Little Bob was smart-and he got smarter with age but could never quite figure out an expression filled with contradiction;

"money can't buy you happiness." That was just plain confusing. Certainly, the expression was not coined by anyone who *had* money. He was gonna test that theory out. Maybe money could buy happiness? Maybe a rich guy invented that saying just to keep him happy and *in* poverty? At least money might take the edge off until *real* happiness came along. In his opinion, he suspected people like Beto Chacon had it all going on. He closed his laptop and glanced around the room before he got up and left. It was a good-looking group; young, well dressed, staring at their ever-present lap-top or phone.

Out on the sidewalk he went and paused in front of a parked Lamborghini Vedanta. He had never seen one up close but here it was in a parking space on the street like it was crummy old Honda. A young woman and her seven year old daughter were inside in the deep black and yellow leather bucket seats. She was dressed in Armani, the little girl in a soccer uniform. Zilm could not resist a comment.

"I bet you are the coolest mom at soccer practice." He joked through the open passenger side window. He was bent over double to access the low slung vehicle. The young woman behind the wheel laughed.

"It's just for fun." She admitted exactly what Zilm suspected. Dollar figures went through his mind in estimation of its cost. These Lamborghini's started at $489,000.

"I know, I love my McLaren." Zilm lied convincingly, hoping to join her car club someday.

Their tribe had it all going on and he wanted to be in it! No one was broken down, fringy or ragged and there was not an urban camper or blue tarp for miles. Zilm was in an enclave of the well-to-do and he liked it here, in fact, this is exactly what he had in mind for himself. He got in his shabby Chevy and drove to Stratford Street to continue his task. 103511 was surrounded by a stone wall and a black metal grate fence. He parked and got out on the sidewalk. He immediately noticed the obvious way in; climb a large tree and hike out on an overhanging branch and drop into the yard of 103511. It was just a nice single-story house with a big yard and no high-tech security. He took a picture and then another with his iPhone and put them in a separate file for review later, but it was not all peaches and cream. A guard and a dog were seen over on the other side of the yard. The guard had a large Glock sidearm. Zilm strolled down the sidewalk toward them. He didn't get to far before the dog started to make an unholy racket with barking and straining. Every time he took a run at the fence, WHAM! He ran out of chain. The stupid pooch was an intimidating force and drooled danger. The guard spoke.

"Don't worry about him. He gets excited but he's on a chain and really, he's harmless." He was a middle-age grandfatherly type.

"The dog doesn't look harmless; he looks more like *vicious*." Zilm answered back, safely on the other side of the fence.

"He got trained to be that way. Get him away from his professional duties, he's just a lazy old house-dog." The guard was friendly and cheerful. He patted the dog on the head for emphasis.

"See?" He stroked his head. Zilm was not convinced.

"That's nice." Zilm hated dogs, this one especially. They were always barking or begging or pooping in public. They stank, they shed, they guilt-tripped all day long. They jumped on the furniture; basically, they tried to take over the house in any possible way they could. Every time he saw a pair of big brown eyes staring up at him, he wanted to kick the little furry fucker. They licked their pee-pee, they smelled strange poop in the street, they were disgusting. Cats he could tolerate, but dogs were just wrong in every way. He kept going down the sidewalk and noticed that the fence went all the way to the end of the block. Getting in the yard might be easy but getting in the house might present problems, especially with that canine poop machine and Grandpa Glock on the job.

Zilm sat in his car and thumbed through the picture gallery on his phone. He expanded the shot of the front door until the page he displayed was one huge keypad-the lock mechanism for the door. He wanted to order one online and practice jimmying it open. Just as much as Zilm hated dogs, he loved the internet. What a boon to criminals, what new horizons it opened to nefarious forms of income and information! Crime was now a growth industry, fueled by the online information age. The whole world was now accessible to criminals right from the comfort of their living room sofa or desktop, a whole world of sheep just lining up to be shorn and just a false click away. Truly an age of miracles and wonders.

*   *   *

Joaquin and Van Zant sat in the diner and had coffee. Van Zant stared at the cup in front of him and spoke. Joaquin stared out the window.

"We got this guy cornered." Van Zant sounded assured.

"Yeah, I know. How so?" Joaquin continued to look outside.

"Well, think about it. He can't go to the cops-he can't cry to the insurance people. He has to deal with us. He's screwed." Van Zant.

"I get your meaning. He's trapped like a rat." Joaquin said.

"Exactly. He might be a flight risk though, that's our only problem. That's what I would do; I'd be off to South America with a shitload of diamonds." Van Zant fantasized.

"The sooner we get him the note the better then. Let him know we are on to him-and watching his ass." Joaquin said.

"Right." Van Zant continued.

"I promised Mandy I would not die." Joaquin explained.

"Nobody is gonna die. Don't you be worryin' about that." Van Zant.

The Krystal Towers robbery had propelled them into the ranks of the most notorious safecrackers. Whether they realized it or not, they were pros now. But they were not killers.

*   *   *

Cash sat around with homies from the hood in the back office of the pawn shop. Cash had been tight all through high school with the leader, Moreese Brown, both of them excelling on sports teams together. After graduation though, Cash went to Cal Berkeley and Moreese went to the street and there, their separate educations resumed. And their destinies were forged.

Cash liked his clothes and today he wore a lavender shirt and black tie under a tan suit and two-tone shoes. His homies, in contrast, wore all manner of saggy, baggy and casual T shirts emblazoned with scenes of money, whores and guns. Gold chains and oversized watches accessorized their outfits, and the tennis shoes were colorful and unlaced. All the men were in their thirties and affected menacing faces. They were bad ass.

"Got buzzed pretty good the other night." Moreese said.

"Yeah, how high the moon. Like old times." Cash replied.

"Those white boys you hang with? How you know this shit turn out right? The way I see it, they fuck it all up already." Spoke the man Moreese. He had a gold grill with a rhinestone set in the front tooth.

"I told you 'bout that shit?" Cash was surprised.

"Yeah." Moreese replied.

"We on it; don't worry 'bout that." Cash replied assuredly.

"How 'bout we help you out, Cash?" Moreese said.

"I told you-we got this-we on it!" Cash told the gangster.

"We finish it right with this Cha-con dude. You get your action the same way, but now you be with us. We cut you in-you get it from both ends. You a smart guy, you went to school." Moreese explained.

"Smart enough." Cash said.

Moreese was a stone criminal and Cash fenced his stolen goods. The young Moreese grew up in the 'hood and raised himself without much benefit of a family. He got knocked around from the big kids, as most grade schoolers do, but one day he fought back, hit a fourteen-year-old antagonizer with a bat, then hit him a few more times, rendering him unconscious. He was charged with assault. He got sent to Youth Authority after high school, then an adult penitentiary when he was 18. His face had been hardened to a stony stare whose eyes you did not want to meet. He was not afraid of dyin'; it was even odds that hell or heaven might be better than this earthly existence he had seen so far. He stood up in front of his gang and laid it out plain for Cash.

"We just rob this dude, that be all to it. You get double cut-one for stealin' and one for sellin.'" A general laughter and approval broke out in the assembled homies.

"Look Mo; I'm tight with these guys, they be my home-boys now. We in it to win it. This ain't for you." Cash said.

"Okay, okay. We cool." Moreese reassured Cash.

"Good." Cash said.

"Maybe we talk later." Moreese said as the group of his gangsters went out the back door into the alley, and alone with his boys in the alley, Moreese took a conspiratorial tone and addressed the group.

"That boy confused. He forgot who his peoples be."

"That negro got himself gen-tree-fied."

"He been colonized like a country-fried penguin."

"That boy be an Oreo."

"He like a little white bitch."

"We don' forget who our peoples be."

"We tight, no worry 'bout dat, Homes." Came the reply.

*   *   *

Detective Davis shut the door in the briefing room and the gathered men took chairs. "What do we got here Detective Davis?" The captain of the unit had the floor and the attention of the assembled men in the room.

"So far it looks like a sophisticated robbery of a very expensive collection of jewels. It's a B&E like we haven't ever seen or heard of before. They used a plasma torch to open the safe and the adjacent crane to enter and escape. They knocked out the power grid with water and-get a load of this-a smiling frog spit water all over the control room and shorted it out; cute huh? The part that bothers me is that it occurred the night before the jewels were to be sold."

"Your meaning being?" The captain spoke.

"Meaning the coincidence was suspicious." Davis continued.

"I don't get it." Said a lieutenant.

"Well, just one more night and the robbers get nothing, the jewels are gone-sold off to the new owners. Did they know that? Was it just a coincidence that they got so lucky? In the nick of time, these men pulled off one of the cleverest robberies, a robbery with many moving parts, a robbery with much planning, forethought, surveillance and whatever. Did they go through all that to a crack open an empty safe? The answer bothers me; I don't think so." Davis explained.

"I see your point." Said the lieutenant.

"Somebody on the inside? Is that what you're suggesting?" The captain spoke again.

"Maybe way inside. These guys knew what and when. These guys are thorough and do not leave a lot to chance, these guys are not some dudes from the hood, these guys are pros. I figure four guys-minimum, more if somebody was on the inside-to pull this off the way they did. Organization and discipline are what I see here." Davis explained.

"It makes sense. Got any ideas about the inside identity?" The captain spoke.

"There's 9 mil in insurance on those stones and Global Investments and Beto Chacon are the beneficiaries. Investigators are on the look-out for fraud. But that's routine-they always do that with large sums of insurance money at stake." Davis replied and added, "Knowledge of the sale; the workers at Global maybe? There are others on the buyers end as well."

"How many people we talking about? Five, ten? What?" The lieutenant asked.

"Well, Beto Chacon, that's one. There are 2 employees in the office, so that's three. But then there is an unknown number of suspects in the security detail of the buyers who could just steal the gems or sell the info to pros." Davis said.

"I see the problem, it's one of those many-faceted clusters. Stay in touch with Lloyds, see if they turn up anything of a suspicious nature. Question the witnesses again, look into the background of this Global Investments and Chacon." The captain instructed. "You never know, you could catch a break."

"Roger skipper, I'll keep you informed of any developments." Davis replied.

"Good. Anything else? Anyone?" The captain looked from face to face.

"Okay, that'll be all. Let's get on it. Catch these birds."

*   *   *

The insurance Dick was on a date with Frenchy and Frenchy was on a fact-finding mission with the Dick, literally. Zilm had instructed her as to what she needed to ask and what not to say. Frenchy knew what she might have to do.

"So; how is the investigation going?" Frenchy knew right away that this was too obvious.

"Oh, you know, just routine stuff. I do this every week." The Dick said.

"I bet you do have some stories though. Criminals and such, crime investigations?' Frenchy pressed.

"Well yeah, people, you know; they are tempted to take advantage when monetary gain is a possibility. Lots of stolen car frauds, household robbery frauds, homeowner small stuff. We just pay those off." Dick went on.

"I hear those stolen jewels were no small potatoes though. You don't just pay those off, do you?" Frenchy edged a little closer to the Dick.

"No small potatoes indeed. In fact, we bring in a special unit for this type of thing." The Dick was clamming up a bit.

"Oh, like they do the SWAT team on NCIS?" Frenchy asked with a little nervous laugh. Dick chuckled because Frenchy did.

"Well, it's not that severe. But we do take it seriously. We deal with the big money claims accordingly, there's a lot at stake. We look for irregularities."

"Is there anything irregular at Global? It's got to be big; I mean it's a world-famous collection."

"It appears to be a straight up heist. So far, anyway." Answered the Dick.

Frenchy sat quietly picking at her salad, but her mind was racing in circles wondering what her next tack should be. Being obvious would arouse suspicion. She hadn't gotten much so far. She broke the silence with a different approach-flattery.

"So, tell me; what are you doing when you're not looking for criminals?" She kept her eyes on the salad.

"I collect stamps and coins. I read books on the Civil War, I'm a big fan. I participate in the re-enactments. It's a lot of fun, really." Dick showed modest enthusiasm.

Oh boy, this guy's a real fireball of excitement, Frenchy thought. I bet those stamps are a hoot-how exciting is that? And coins? Let's spend the weekend together-just you, me and the stamp book. WE can watch the paint dry too. Her mind was filling with sarcastic remarks she couldn't speak out loud.

"Tell me more about his re-enactment?" Frenchy said, dreading the coming explanation.

"Oh, it is something to see. I like to sport the union uniform in the first charge at Gettysburg, that's my specialty." Dick was busting buttons now, so excited to tell his specialty to this beautiful woman.

"Didn't they all die or something?" said the French-Fry.

"Oh yes. thousands died in the first ten minutes it is estimated." Said the Dick.

"I see." Frenchy paused and began again. "How does one die properly-in the re-enactment I mean?"

"Well, that's actually what I am noted for. Getting shot can be quite dramatic. Not really shot, of course, but fake-shot. I'm very good at it and then I just lie there like I'm dead." Said the Dick.

"Wow, that does sound like fun!" Frenchy checked herself before she said, "And then you just lie there, you say?"

"Very still and quiet for however long it takes."

"Does it take long; I mean the lying there."

"I have died in the first charge and lay on the ground for two hours, that's my personal record."

"What is the world record then?"

"Tom Peters lay dead on the ground for four days in 1998."

Frenchy's head was swimming with boredom now. The unimaginable *nothingness* of that world-record shattering achievement. She may have stumbled upon a sub-species of homo sapiens here; homo re-enactamus.

"Oh yes. We all get together afterwards and talk about it, you know, who died well, charged well, changes for next year, that sort of stuff." Dick volunteered.

"This sounds like more fun than… stamps in a book!" Frenchy just had to say it, hoping the Dick could not detect obvious sarcasm.

"Oh yes, we prepare all year for the day of the battle. There's a Facebook page and everything." The Dick shifted gears to stamp collecting.

"I've got a 1918 Air Mail."

"Oh really? I'd like to see that." Frenchy said. The line of conversation was not going the way she wanted, and her mind struggled with schemes to put on the brakes She knew she was on the verge of the inevitable. The edge of the cliff was dead ahead. The inevitable arrived.

"I'd love to show it to you. We could get out the coin collection too. I have some very nice pieces there as well." The Dick leaned across the table just enough to show intimacy. "We could see it any time you like. Tonight even."

Frenchy was cornered by a greasy-haired toad in a cheap suit. Pretending you were dead was suddenly becoming a reasonable alternative for her tonight.

"Oh, I'd love that, it sounds exciting. Really!" Let's get this over with; she could not bear another dinner and conversation with this fool, better to just screw him and get it over with.

"Excuse me, I have to powder my nose." Frenchy added. Which was the truth-but it was the inside of her nose that was going to get powdered. She was off to the lady's room.

"I lost this battle, but the war isn't over yet." Frenchy murmured in front of the lady's restroom mirror just before she took a big snort off her little gold spoon. Gettysburg, here I come!

She returned to the table, fortified. "Shall we go? I just can't wait to see that air mail stamp."

"Absolutely my dear, right this way." The Dick made a dramatic swooping gesture with his arm, just like in a Hollywood movie he had seen, inviting Ms. Gigot to lead out the door. Frenchy obliged, she was doing her part; it was an intelligence gathering mission and she was in her own different movie. They took his cheesy car, and the ride was punctuated with awkward small talk about the insurance business.

"So, are we done at Global or is there more?" Frenchy was casual, like she didn't care much for the topic.

"Well, I'm done. That is my part of it. It's in the hands of my seniors and Detective Davis." The Dick answered.

"You're all done? Oh no. I won't be seeing you around again?"

"'Fraid not. I filed my report and turned it in-finito!" The Dick was feeling Continental, using the only Italian word he knew.

"Looked like a pretty straightforward robbery to me; they blew the safe and took the jewels." Frenchy said to the windshield.

"Right. But these things are never over right away-unless the criminals are captured, or the goods are discovered. My part is over and that's all I care about. In fact, I am starting a new case Monday-a carjack. High-end stolen car and I have been assigned to lead the investigation." Chales Napier said proudly. Frenchy was unimpressed of course.

"You were never in the lead of the Global investigation?" Frenchy feigned stupidity, dreading the answer she knew was coming.

"No. That was an important case, involving millions in compensation and for this we assign 5 or 6 investigators." ID said.

Frenchy groaned silently inside. This charade Zilm had put her up to was not going to be repeated 5 or 6 times; she was *not* gonna screw 5 or 6 nitwits. In fact, she was already wondering how she could get out of this, now that she knew this Dick was a dead-end. Frenchy had to think fast-what was her next move going to be.

"Oh no! My cell phone! I left it in the lady's room at the restaurant, we have to go back!" Frenchy exclaimed, thinking fast.

"Are you sure?"

"Yes, I'm sure. I've got a lot of my contact info and pictures of my nieces and nephews and pets." All of which was a lie, she had no pictures of beloveds, especially pets. She hated pets and children.

They arrived back at the restaurant, and she dashed in while Napier waited in the car. She ran right through the seating area and into the kitchen and called an Uber. Her driver, Mahmoud, would be there in three minutes in his white Prius. Three minutes seemed like three hours, standing amidst the pots, pans and Honduran kitchen crew who were completely baffled by the presence of the crazy white lady. Frenchy stepped out the back door. She had instructed the driver, Mahmoud, to come around to the rear of the restaurant. The insurance Dick was waiting patiently in the car in the front, motor running, expecting the best piece of tail he ever had, soon to return through the front door.

The Uber arrived and Frenchy took a backseat and began talking to herself.

"That was closer than a Brazilian wax but twice as painful. Stamps and coins, just imagine. What a blight on the gene pool of the species *he* is."

She had a private laugh out loud, and Mahmoud looked in the rearview mirror, at the crazy lady, longing for a return to his homeland where the orange trees were in bloom and the old, retired men strolled underneath their boughs discussing politicians and the price of coffee.

*　*　*

Eddie was pissed that the rocks were fake. He was grousing to Rick as they knocked back a few beers at Tony's. Eddie always seemed to be on the verge of being pissed off at something, it was his go-to emotion.

"The one time I want to make a score and I get the double-cross from some slick taco-bender." Said the little Chinese man with the Prince Valiant haircut.

"It's not fair." Chimed Rick."

"Damn right it's not fair. And I tell you what; I don't have to sit back and take it up the butt."

"Hell no. You got standards. You wouldn't do *that* kinda sneaky stuff." Rick was calm.

"I say burn him out-just fry his ass. A few bottles of gasoline, rags and-poof! No big deal."

"Better run that one by Joaquin. We got a plan already." Rick cautioned the little impetuous man.

"Yeah, well Eddie Wong has his own plan if that don't work out, I tell you that!" Eddie declared. Talking tough was the thing he enjoyed most.

*   *   *

Van Zant sat at the kitchen table at Joaquin's. The little pug dog stared up at him from the floor, Joaquin fixed a drink at the sink. They were alone in the house.

"We tell this guy we got the goods on him and we're gona rat him out. Send him a picture of the fakes or something, like a ransom note kinda-thing. *Do this or else*' we say." Van's plan was simple.

"In so many words." Joaquin amended it.

"Right. What can he say? We got him by the short and curlies, case closed." Van laid it out plain.

"You would think so. What about that Panamanian brother-dude Frenchy told us about?" Joaquin asked.

"What? Is he so big and heavy he doesn't gotta pay his dues too? What would you do if you were him? Can you spell *In-car-ceration*?" Van said.

"Frenchy says his brother is a smuggler and Global launders his money. Those are bad hombres." Joaquin noted.

"We were in Nam; we were bad hombres." Van said.

"I was a stupid 19 year old kid with an M-14 back then. And I had an army behind me." Joaquin.

"You still got the same balls." Van.

"And I want them to stay right where they are; not nailed to a Panamanian wall." Joaquin.

"It's gonna work I tell ya; this slick is gonna fold like the Sunday paper when he gets the ransom note and the brother is gonna stay put in Panama." Van Zant spoke with assurance.

*   *   *

Nigel Leeds was in charge Lloyds of London's top investigators. He had seen quite a bit in his time in the way of fraud and this Global thing stunk like rotten fish. It bothered him. It was obvious that there had been a break-in, but what got taken? He was talking to his under assistant investigator, one of the several on this Global case.

"I say Tommy, I'd feel a whole lot better about this Global bit if there was something more solid than the word of the beneficiary, something's just not tickety-boo over there. Too many questions remain unanswered-what if Chacon stole them, in the first instance? What if the Arabians were in on it? What if the jewels weren't in the safe at all? What if they were stashed away? This is a 9 million dollar policy we are dealing with. That would tempt the devil to do right." Nigel Leeds was casting about in troubling waters.

"All we can do is surveil Chacon. It seems we don't have many options other than that. All the horses are out of the gate and if the Saudis are behind this, bloody hell, they'll cut you into pieces if you don't look right. That little sandbox down there is full of vipers. You can't even go poking around in it and keep your head attached to your shoulders." Mr. Tommy Burke answered.

"You're right about that, I wouldn't go there. Bloody savages, I hear they eat snake meat." Said Leeds.

"That's probably not the worst of it, sir." Mr. Burke answered.

"Probably not, the bloody wogs. The American police have been helpful, it seems they have something on the ball over there, they're watching Chacon closely. I don't see a quick payout on this business, Tommy, not on your life, not indeed." Nigel Leeds stated forthrightly in typical British fashion.

"No sir. The stones may turn up yet, sir. We must wait is all. Maybe all will be satisfactorily settled, yet." Burke said.

"Hmmm, maybe. That would be nice. In the meantime, this Chacon fellow seems to be sailing close to the wind, if you get my meaning." Nigel Leeds had his doubts and had a professional suspicion about everything.

"Indeed, sir." Came the answer back.

*   *   *

V an Zant had been elected to write the note and make the first contact with Global. There had been a big discussion over this.

"The phones are tapped, you just gotta assume that. I saw the stakeout cars; they're watching the house." Zilm said to the assembled group.

"Yeah, even going to deliver the note-they'll see your ass. You gotta mail it-and I don't mean email. That's all hacked up like a cane field by now, worse than Hillary and Ben-Ghazi." Eddie added.

"Okay, so we mail a note. What do we say?" Van asked the group.

"Say this: How would you like to get butt-buggered in the shower for twenty years?" Eddie chuckled and then added, "Or… you can get 9 mil and go live with your brother in Panama for twenty years?"

"Frenchy said the brother is not that nice." Rick said.

"That's not the point moron." Eddie said. "It's got to sound like we're bad-ass."

"We need something that is slick and professional." Joaquin threw in his 2 cents.

"How about this; a picture of the box of rocks and a note that says he can have the picture and the box, collect the insurance money and nobody knows the difference." Van said.

"I want the rocks we stole, I like 'em." Rick commented.

"Well, you can't have 'em." Van replied.

"I like your idea, Van. It says it all with an economy of words." Joaquin said.

"I like 'an economy of words', that sounds intelligent." Rick said to no one, and no one responded.

"The picture is the key. Whatever the note says, the picture says it all." Zilm liked it.

"How about just the picture?" Frenchy said with enthusiasm.

"Then how's he gonna know the deal? Think about it Frenchy for Christ sakes." Eddie shot back.

"Oh yeah, there is that. You're right." Frenchy conceded.

"I still like the shower-thing. Can you imagine? It makes my butt hurt to think about it." Eddie asked.

"Okay; so, we got a letter and a picture, that's settled." Van stated.

"Do we just send the picture first? Alone, by itself, as a kind of warning? Then later send the note stating the terms?" Frenchy posited.

"I like that too." Rick said.

"How about the picture and the butt-bugger warning?" Eddie piped up.

"I think Eddie's coming out of the closet." Zilm said and Eddie flipped him off.

"Okay look: we send the picture and the terms. All professional…" Van began.

"With bullet points!" Frenchy interrupted.

"With bullet points and an economy of words-and no graphic stuff." Van continued.

"That'll work, if it doesn't then Eddie can write his shower note." Van smiled at the inference.

"Eddie would like that." Zilm added.

"I like that!" Rick said with enthusiasm.

"Is there anything you don't like?" Zilm asked.

"And if all that doesn't work, we'll firebomb that mofo!" Eddie stated with his usual bravado.

"Right! He's gonna fold like a cheap suit!" Rick exhorted, and then he paused in thought before he spoke again.

"Why does a cheap suit fold better than an expensive suit?" Rick wondered aloud. All eyes were on him, but no one spoke.

*   *   *

It was a beautiful fall day that Beto stepped out into, full of promise, birds that sang into the warm air surrounding his beautiful home in a neighborhood of privilege. Could it get much better than this? In the driveway stood his cobalt blue Maserati, at the ready to give him a luxurious ride in brown leather seats to his office overlooking the Bay. *Money* was the key in all this and there was great promise today of 9 million more. More was always better than less, everyone knew that. In his worldview, everyone revered people like him. But he didn't have one thing-enough money. The price of admission to his world began with a fine house, cars, a summer house, expensive schools, a club, charities, dinners, golf, rich friends, etc. It was an expensive lifestyle.

"It's great to be me." Thought Chacon as he walked to the mailbox.

Junk mail, bills, real estate flyers and a little blue envelope with real handwritten addressing. Wow, that's different, he thought. Beto loved getting letters and most likely this one was from his little niece in Panama. But here it was-like a red flag-a single 43 cent stamp, local postage with no return address. Everyone he knew used email nowadays. He sorted it out from the rest and sat down on the stone wall and opened the envelope. He read the letter inside:

"We have the box of fake rocks, we stole them. Here's the deal; you get the insurance money, and we get the real diamonds- we don't rat you out, nobody is the wiser. We'll be in touch."

A swirl of thoughts raced through his head. Trouble-just when he thought he had the world by the tail, just when he thought it was all going so well. Run to Panama? That was his first thought. No, that's no good, he might end up murdered for his diamonds by his brother. Do I want to take this deal? Questions without answers swirled through his head.

"I have to call my brother in Panama. He'll know what to do, he's badass. They don't know it yet, but these criminals have stepped in dog-doo-doo." Chacon spoke to the birds.

The walk back to the house was ridden of the warm air, singing birds and promise that Beto had felt and heard moments ago. The shadow of trouble, loss and his brother Umberto were now a cloud that hung in the air over his head. His beautiful grounds and neighborhood failed to give him any comfort at all as it had before. He knew that the time had come to call Berto, much like one would summon an evil genie from the bottle, enter Berto. Once he was out, the world of Umberto Chacon consumed much of the air. But what choice did he have? He must call him-on the Sat-Phone at once.

*   *   *

Umberto sensed trouble the minute the Sat-Phone rang. This was his secure encrypted line only used for emergencies. He figured it was probably some of his cartel guerillas in the jungle in some turf war with the Federales or crying about the food again. Why couldn't they leave him out of their troubles and figure shit out for themselves? But it was Beto.

"Berto, we got trouble with the gringos. They want to extort the insurance money or else." Beto gushed.

Umberto thought about it and asked calmly, "Or else *what?*"

"Or else they will rat us out to the cops." Beto said.

"I don't think so, I will not allow that." Umberto replied.

"Well, you better do something then if you think you can stop them." Beto was on the verge of whining.

"Me? Why me? This your mess little brother. You make it, now you clean it up, yes?" Berto said. Sometimes his little brother was worse than the rebels in the jungle.

Beto didn't *clean up messes,* he was an art dealer, a broker of valuable objects. There was a pause in the line. Beto was in thought, he was without words until the deal formed in his mind.

"Half of my share to you-if you help." Beto said.

Berto was a businessman and he sensed opportunity. "Half? How much the insurance pay?" He asked.

Beto was silent; he considered lying. Berto was always conning and swindling family and friends. Even when he was a kid he always had to come out on top.

"9 million. You get half of my half, plus your half." Beto finally said.

"Okay. I wave my magic wand; it all goes away. You don't worry." Berto said.

"Deal." Beto relented.

✳   ✳   ✳

Umberto Chacon stepped on the plane to San Jose, and he was not alone. He was bringing along his posse, although posse didn't adequately describe his associates; 'mercenaries' was the word that accurately described them. Central America was a place where life was not valued as much as the Estados Unidos, and these men were used to that standard. They were briefed on the job at hand and laughed at the naivete of such a simple task, gringos thought they were so special; they did not realize the simple solution to the problems they had created for Beto. They kissed their family's good-bye at the airport and promised to bring them something from Disneyland, vowing to be back next week. It was more like going on a vacation to Florida than a serious business trip.

✳   ✳   ✳

Under blue skies and a balmy and arid seventy two degrees, Beto drove to the San Jose airport with a troubled mind. His notorious brother would soon step out of the airport gate. Beto was quite used to the refinements of wealth and educated friends here in California, but he knew what brutish life was like in Berto's Panama and his life would soon be transformed. There was no turning back now that Umberto was involved. He pulled up to the rental car agency and got a large van and then proceeded to the parking structure and walked to the gate. He waited and fidgeted with his laptop. His instructions from Berto were simple; find a gun show, get a van. Berto strolled out of the gate corridor, followed by his associates and nobody was smiling.

"Berto! Welcome to California!" Beto went to give him a hug and it was rebuffed.

"Beto-brother: we do not hug, we not women. You got car for us?"

"Right this way." They walked in silence. They stopped at the baggage carousel and struck up a conversation as they waited.

"We're going to the Cow Palace, there's a show there." Beto said.

"A palace for cows? Is joke? Not funny." Berto replied.

"No, no. It's just a name. It's an exhibition hall, a name is all. I think they used to have rodeos there.

"I like rodeos." Berto saw his bag and positioned himself to make the grab. His associates did the same in turn. All the men proceeded to the van.

They drove up the Peninsula. "It's clean here, me likie that. Houses; they nice." Berto observed out the window in the drive to the Cow Palace. They parked in the enormous lot that was barely one quarter full, Berto looked around.

"Where the people? Nobody come?"

"Don't worry, they're inside." They walked through the turnstiles at the gate and the cavernous wooden hall opened up before them. The empty seats rose to near the rafters. The main floor was set-up with exhibitors selling guns. The entourage grunted approval.

"This better, look at this; beautiful!" Berto exclaimed as they all walked down along the long tables and booths displaying all manner of weaponry. The Berto entourage was in a paradise of guns of all caliber and design, and they responded with gleeful approval as they chattered amongst themselves like children in a toy store. Berto seized a weapon, a lethally long and black .50 caliber rifle with rounds as long as your hand. It was like a small artillery piece.

"Now this! This for me!" Berto exclaimed as he held the gun up for examination. A paunchy exhibitor stepped over and addressed Umberto. His most striking feature was his baseball cap, emblazoned with a large American flag in the background with a diving eagle in the fore across it, claws outstretched and holding a rolled copy of the Constitution. His T shirt stated, *"I kneel before only one man-and he died on the cross."* A cute little kneeling cartoon figure knelt before a cross. The exhibitor had a nametag, Willy Wilson the Third. Willy now addressed Umberto.

"The man does know his weapons, yesiree! What you got there my friend is the finest weapon of its kind-lethal! That baby will shoot through a concrete wall, bring down a helicopter, take out a Humvee, vaporize a man. There are *NO* wounded after this baby is done. You got range, you got punch, you got a weapon that you can transport. When you're ready to fire just unfold the legs, take a position, aim and let the fun begin!" Mr. Wilson extolled the virtues of a BMG rifle, a salesman through and through. He continued.

"The name is Willy Wilson, but all my friends call me Woody. That scope you got your peepers on can sight in a target at 1000 meters and it ain't cheap, but a worthy accessory to the BMG." Woody-Willy Wilson extended his hand for a shake, and it was ignored by all. His NRA shirt was also emblazoned with "2A" and his name tag, "WWIII", was above the pocket. He sported a goatee and had numerous turquoise accessories such as a big belt buckle, bolo tie clasp, bracelets, rings and a turquoise-studded watchband that added about five pounds to his paunchy and eager self.

"I take this one. I take a hundred rounds." Berto said.

"Whoa pardner, that there is about $100 a round, that's a whole ammo box." Woody-Willy informed Berto.

Berto motioned to his mercenary associate, and he stepped forward with a briefcase. He took out a stack of $100 bills and put it in front of the man. "How much the gun?"

"That's a $5,000 gun my friend." Woody-Willy said with pride. "But today only and for you-$4500."

The associate took out another stack, counted out $4500, and put it on the table.

"You got yourself a deal my friend, I'll throw in the fiberglass airline case and that ammo box goes with the whole shit-a-ree." Woody-Willy Wilson was pleased, Umberto was pleased, and all his new toys went into the shopping cart pushed along by the posse.

Good fortune smiled on WWIII the day Berto stepped in front of his booth at the gun show. Before he left, Berto bought AK's, AR15's, handguns, fragmentation grenade launchers (and black market grenades under the table), 2 Uzis and all the necessary kits to convert them to fully automatic. There was practically nothing left in the booth after they left, their shopping cart was stuffed with barrels sticking out of it like a porcupine on wheels. A second cart and third cart strained under the weight of the ammo. They were ready for anything, or so they thought. As they made their way out to the van, Berto turned to his brother Beto and stated:

"I love this country Beto. Is there a Target store here too?" Berto asked. They went straight away to Target and bought sunglasses, shirts, pants, shoes, toys, a TV, laptops, Nintendo's, cosmetics, food and a Starbucks coffee on the way out. Each man had a cart full of consumer goods.

"We only got so much room for this stuff, Berto. Slow down." Beto was worried that it wouldn't fit in the van.

"We make it fit." Berto was adamant. After trying several different configurations, they stuffed it in and climbed all over the merchandise for a seat. They had to sit on this crap on the drive to Los Gatos with the toys and stuffed animals on their laps. They were family guys with presents for the children as well as hired killers.. Driving through Los Gatos inspired awe, the ostentatious wealth displayed by the fine homes set the men to drooling. The bodyguards stared out the windows at the occasional mansion as it went by. In Panama, Berto's house was the only mansion they had ever seen and now here, everybody had one. They had not said a word up until now until the big thug asked the question:

"No gatos in Los Gatos?" The thug said with a tone of disappointment. It was greeted with silence as the scenery went by.

"Does the president live here?" Berto asked.

"No, this is Silicon Valley. Google, Apple, Twitter, HP, Dupont; all the high-tech giants-it's better than the President." Beto answered.

"It's very nice. No Mexicans? Porque? … the border walls?" Berto asked.

"They live somewhere else, in San Jose." Beto answered.

"We go there?" Berto asked.

"We go there too." Beto answered.

"Then some got over the wall, si?' Berto said.

"Si." Came the answer.

∗   ∗   ∗

Detective Davis walked into the captain's office with news.

"I think we got some kind of development in the Global case."

"Like what?" The captain asked.

"Well, surveillance reports that a vanload of thugs arrived in Los Gatos. It pulled into the gate and 6 men got out. I think the Chacon brother showed up, the twin. That's all we know." Davis stated.

"Why would the brother show up?" said the captain.

"Why would a posse show up? That's the question." Davis said.

"Indeed. Looks suspicious. Looks like trouble. Notify Lloyds." Captain said.

"I did. They don't like it; they smell a rat." Davis said and continued, "I think it's time to talk to Chacon again, maybe nose around Global."

"Do that." The captain said.

Davis took the elevator to the 26th floor of the Krystal Tower #1. He had an appointment with Chacon later that afternoon. He walked into the office and all eyes fixed on him as he walked into the room. Frenchy got up from her desk and greeted him.

"Detective, you're early. I'll notify Mr. Chacon." She offered.

"Ms. Gigot, how nice to see you again. Before Mr. Chacon, I would like to speak to the security detail. Are they available?" Davis said, noting that Ms. Gigot always smelled of cigarettes and perfume, he smelled it as soon as he walked up to her desk.

"Well, I don't know. Their office is on the first floor, I will call them for you." Frenchy Gigot sang.

Within moments Davis reentered the elevator and was on his way down to the lobby to see the security people. He was thinking about Gigot and how she seemed awfully nice. Was she flirting? Was she attracted to him? He liked her perfume smell and her tight fitting clothes. He wanted to jump her bones. His train of thought was interrupted when the elevator doors opened to a sterile, marble and glass lobby. There was not a single accessory visible that indicated human life. The man behind the desk got up and led him to a little door and opened it. Inside sat a few men in front of TV monitors and control boards with much detritus strewn about that indicated slovenly human life. A man in a suit got up and greeted him.

"How can I help you?"

"I am Detective Davis, South City Police. It's about the Global robbery. Any chance of speaking with the security team that first arrived on scene?"

A man at the monitor board spoke up, "That would be me and then Lewis arrived. We responded when we got the call."

"Excellent. Mind if I ask you a few questions?" Davis asked.

"Fire away." Said monitor-man.

"Well first, state your full name." Davis said.

"Cedro Ordonez."

"How long have you worked at the Krystal Towers?"

"Since the beginning, two years maybe?"

"And when did you first realize there had been a burglary?"

"It was shortly after the power went back on."

"The time please, if you could."

"Well, that would be about 3 AM I think. We were all running around assisting in the re-power, then we saw the damage on the monitor when the screens came back up." Replied Ordonez.

"What did you do first? Did you go up to the 26th floor to Global?"

"Right away. As soon as the elevators started working, we all started canvassing the floors from the top to the bottom floor. It was all hands on deck when we discovered the Global incident."

"Were any of the criminals detected by any security cameras?"

"No, nothing. All we saw was the cut in the glass entry, the jagged cut on the metal safe door. And it was wide open, it was obvious we had a big problem."

"Did you notify Mr. Chacon?"

"No, I notified my superior, I assume he notified the tenant."

"Thank you, Mr. Ordonez, I would like to speak to your supervisor." Ordonez dialed a number and after a brief wait, Supervisor Dean arrived.

"I am Robert Dean, chief of security." A lean man in a trim suit introduced himself.

"Mr. Dean, I'm Detective Davis of the South City PD. I am investigating the Global robbery. On the night of the Global break-in, you notified the tenant Beto Chacon, is that correct?"

"I did. After I saw the damage, I knew right away what had happened and I called him at his home."

"And what time would that have been, Mr. Dean."

"A little after 3AM, maybe 3:30 AM at the latest." Dean said and Davis noted that in his pad.

"You stayed until Mr. Chacon arrived, I assume?"

"Yes; I, Lewis, Ordonez, we all waited."

"How long?"

"About 45 minutes we waited until Mr. Chacon arrived."

"Was he alone?"

"Of course, yes."

"What was he wearing?"

"I can't remember exactly."

"I remember he had on fancy leather shoes and a nice jacket. The shoes were two-tone wing tips." Ordonez chimed into the conversation. Davis thumbed through his note pad and studied a few of the pages before he spoke again.

"Mr. Ordonez, what else do you remember?" Davis turned toward the guard.

Ordonez thought for a moment before he spoke. "I am afraid there isn't much else. We were all very excited at the time. I remember that Mr. Chacon went right to the safe and looked inside. After that, I went out on the balcony."

"How about you Mr. Lewis? Do you recall anything further?"

"Pretty much the same. I stayed behind with Mr. Dean and looked around in the office."

"Anything else Mr. Lewis?"

"No, but for a moment, I thought I heard Mr. Chacon in the vault, and he laughed."

*   *   *

"Now what?" Frenchy thumbed through a self-help magazine as she sat across from the table from Robert Zilm.

"Just wait I guess." Zilm responded without conviction.

"Might take a while." Frenchy said without looking up from the pages.

"I know that French. Don't think it doesn't aggravate to know that, okay?" Zilm was a little touchy.

"Okay, okay. Just saying." Frenchy continued to stare at the pages.

"We all gotta just be cool; do our jobs, continue like nothing happened." Zilm explained with pained calmness.

"Might not be that *eee-zee.*" Frenchy sang and continued to thumb through the pages.

"I know that French! What do you want me to do? What else *can I* do? Just go up and knock on his door? Ask for a look around the house maybe?" Zilm had reached his limit of tolerance on the subject.

"No, nothing you can do, I guess. It's a fairly good bet 9 mil in diamonds is just laying around like a lost pet right now. Tempting to just go and snatch it. He's got a safe in his bedroom, I saw it. I bet that's where they are."

"What were you doing in his bedroom?"

"Call it a job interview."

"I thought he was gay?"

"He's gender-fluid, non-binary."

"What's that?"

"Don't be a dinosaur, Bobby."

"Well, I wanna know; who does a gender-fluid person have sex with and most importantly, did *you* have sex with this gender-bender?"

"Gender-fluid is an identity. Non-binary is an identity. They're not about sex."

"Don't try and sell me that LGBTQ identity business; everything is about sex. Or money." As far as Zilm was concerned it was a settled issue.

"Not everything." Frenchy said. Then as an afterthought.

"Dinosaur." Frenchy had the last word.

* * *

"Van Zant has Joaquin under his thumb, he's starting to run the show." Eddie was grousing to Rick at the Topper Club bar.

"I noticed. What are we going to do? Duck-luck if this works now, really." Rick said. "We gotta sit here and wait."

"Yeah, well, what if the insurance pays off and they snap the trap shut-on us!?" Eddie was thinking aloud.

"Yeah, I saw that in a movie once." Rick said.

"Have you ever seen anything that *wasn't* in a movie?" Eddie asked.

"Now that you mention it, no." Rick replied.

"I thought so. We gotta do something Rick. This scheme of Van Zant's is liable to fall apart more sooner than later. And the later we wait the better the chances it has of falling apart! We gotta go talk to Joaquin." Eddie said.

"We gotta go talk to Joaquin, yeah, that's what we gotta do." Rick agreed and added, "What's the statue of limitations on a crime like this?"

"Statue of Limitations? You mean *statute,* moron." Eddie imagined a big statue in the middle of New York harbor holding a jailcell key.

*   *   *

Joaquin was sitting on his front stoop drinking coffee when Eddie and Rick arrived. He had just confessed the whole story to Mandy. There was still a red mark on his cheek from the slap she tagged him with. There had been a shouting match and then a departure to her sister's house. Her words rattled through his brain as he thought back on the ugly scene.

"You fool! You are now a common criminal and like criminals-you got nothing! You should just walk away with your life-but *noooooo*-you persist like a degenerate gambler chasing his losses! Joaquin: this is risky business and getting riskier. It's dangerous, don't you see? You know it is. Let it go. You had your chance and now that chance is gone. It only gets harder from here on out, can't you see that? I cannot watch this if you follow through with it, I just can't. It's like a bad dream, it's a slow motion crash. I will be there for you when you hit bottom, but don't make me a part of this." Mandy was adamant.

Now all Joaquin had was a nice morning on the front steps, alone. Even the little dog went when Mandy left. He knew there was truth in every word she said, and it hurt. That's how she saw it and who could fault her? But there were different versions of the truth and he held one of those; his truth was focused on winning, not losing. He wanted to come away with something and he thought there might still be a way. Eddie and Rick drove up and exited a little MG.

"'Morning Joaquin, nice day." Eddie spoke.

"It's nice somewhere, I guess. Mandy just left for her sister's house. She knows what we're up to." Joaquin said.

"Well, that was bound to happen. It might be for the best, dude. The less she knows, the better. If we get caught, that is." Eddie responded with reason.

"Oh great, Mandy leaves me, and you think it's a good thing." Joaquin said with sarcasm, down in the mouth.

"I don't mean it that way, you know what I mean." Eddie explained.

"She even took the dog!" Joaquin spoke.

"Well, that's definitely a good thing." Rick said, the memory of the little beast that chewed his dental plate was still fresh in his mind.

"Joaquin, Rick and I were talkin'. We were thinking maybe this was not the smart way to play it. The ransom note and all." Eddie approached the subject tentatively and continued with his idea.

"We could try another way; let Frenchy try and locate the stones." Eddie said.

"And why would we do that, Eddie?" Joaquin asked.

"She could see if they were in his house and then we could just try and take the friggin' things." Eddie blurted his very simple idea.

"What? Just shoot our way in and shoot our way out afterwards? Like Butch Cassidy and the Sundance Kid?" Joaquin asked.

"I liked that movie." Risk said.

"It sounds like a good way to get *killed*. Or *kill* somebody; you want that? You wanna be a killer tough guy?" Joaquin questioned.

"Nobody has to die." Eddied defended meekly.

"It could work. Maybe?" Rick added tentatively.

"This is real life, people die doing this, Rick." Joaquin explained.

"But what about the extortion plan? We could all end up doing twenty years, that sounds like danger to me." Eddie explained.

"Damned right, it's dangerous too! It's a mess! There could be a trap, or worse, a shootout!" Joaquin answered.

"It all be dangerous, my man, any way you slices it. You got to control the next level. You got to be the man in control." Eddie swaggered, now in his gangster persona.

"The man in *control*." Rick echoed.

"Eddie, we're a lot of things and killers ain't one of them. Give the plan a chance, for Christ sakes. Let the note tell him we got him cornered. Let's see if he folds. Don't do anything stupid, please?" Joaquin said.

"Actually, it's more like a jewel robbery movie I saw once where the house with the jewels was sold and empty when the robbers got there. It's not Butch Cassidy and the Sundance Kid, it's a different movie." Rick explained to Eddie.

"Please, spare me the details." Eddie said with disgust.

*   *   *

It was football season and football, everywhere but America, was soccer. The similarity in the fan base was the same, however, if not more rabidly enthusiastic. Umberto's big bad men were sprawled about the couches and easy chairs, potato chips spilled off the coffee table and onto the floor, the empty beer cans fell off the coffee table in solidarity with the potato chips. The magnificence of a 65 inch plasma TV held the men in rapt attention as they cheered and jeered the players. Beto Chacon looked on to his living room from the dining room table. It was once a tidy set-piece of fashion, now it was a rowdy rumpus room, replete with the detritus of football fans. Over in the corner Berto oiled his new toy, marveling at the beauty of his BMG .50 caliber. He was anxious to try it out.

"Hey brother, we go shooting, huh?"

"Sure thing Umberto, any time you want." Beto replied.

"We go now, you and me; leave these stupidos here to watch their TV."

"Sure thing Berto, we'll go now." Beto always walked on eggshells around his brother because the guy was dangerous, like a hand grenade that could go off any time. Agreement with Berto was always the smart choice.

"We'll take my car." Beto said.

"Is nice car. Maserati, real leather seats, surround sound." Certain things impressed Umberto. They piled a few of the weapons in the car, unobserved in the garage. The surveillance teams were across the street in the car among junk food wrappers and spent coffee cups, occasionally putting the binoculars towards Beto's house. The brothers departure was an event in the cops otherwise boring day when the garage door opened, and the Maserati rolled out the gate.

"What's goin on over there." Said cop one to cop two.

"I dunno, nuthin?"

"Should we follow them?"

"Naw. Call it in, let them decide. Want another donut?"

"Those things will make you fat."

"I'm already fat."

"They'll make you fatter then."

"What's the difference?"

"Your pecker will disappear under your belly. You want that?"

"I want you to stop talking about my pecker, that's what I want." Said cop two and stuck his hand into the greasy white bag and pulled out a chocolate raised donut with coconut sprinkles.

*   *   *

Beto drove out into the mountains toward Santa Cruz. There was a dirt side road by the reservoir, and he pulled off the highway and drove a few miles into the woods until he came to the ruin of an old farm, at which point they stopped. Umberto rushed to the trunk of the car like a child rushes to the Christmas tree on the holiday morning. He was anxious and he flung open the trunk and reached for the big black weapon.

"Niiiice." Berto cooed.

Beto walked around the abandoned farm. It was a relic from an era before silicon chips replaced the acres of fruit trees in the valley below. It was quiet; birds chirping, crickets, a buzz from some insect in the warm grassy field. Behind him came the metallic clacking sounds that Berto and his weapon made as he prepared it with ammo. It suddenly occurred to Beto that maybe it had been a mistake to get his brother tangled up in this, but what other options did he have? It was like his childhood revisited, except now his brother was kind of edgy, dangerous and had thugs. Things weren't always like this. Umberto suffered fevers when they were little, and he had emerged somewhat different, and that difference manifested itself in dark ways. Pets disappeared, fires started, toys were broken. Their sister came home terrified one day, screaming that Berto was in the church eating the sacred bread, drinking the holy wine and breaking votive candles. That was the end of home life with Berto, father sent him off to the military academy and told him to beg for the forgiveness of God on his knees. That didn't happen. Thereafter he would come home for the holidays angry and violent, telling stories of how he hated it there, how they beat and sodomized him. The family was happy to send him back-just get rid of him because Berto was the one who had gone bad, and the priests were beyond reproach. An exorcist was brought in. Today, it was just a memory for Beto. So was the military academy that Berto burned to the ground.

"I am ready brother, loaded and locked, as you say in your gringo movies." Berto was smiling an evil grin.

"Locked and loaded brother, that's what we say." Beto started walking back towards Umberto. Suddenly the gun erupted, and dust flew from the foundation of the farmhouse as the bullets came out the other side of the concrete wall. A heinous laugh of glee came from Umberto.

"It goes through the wall! *Eeeeeeeeeeeeeeeeeee* lookee there!" He cried in joy. Sure enough, .50 caliber rounds went through the foundation wall. It did not bring joy to Beto, however. More like dread of things that may come.

"Is good little brother, yes? Very powerful. Me *likee* this gun!" Berto was a little more than pleased. He put the BMG back in the trunk and took out the AK. He fired on fully automatic, and 30 rounds were off in an instant, a hail of ejected brass casings flew through the air and littered the ground with shiny brass cylinders at his feet.

"Oh brother, this! I don't have these yet at home. We have M-14's, pistolas and the RPG's." Berto set the AK back in the trunk and took out the fragmentation grenade launcher. He shouldered the stubby little rifle and aimed at the barn.

"Don't do that Umberto! The Federales will hear, and they will come and arrest us!" Beto was waving his hands as he ran towards his brother. Umberto had a supreme look of disappointment.

"Federales? Let's go, not happy now." Berto put down the weapon and closed the trunk, got in the car and sulked. Beto got in after him and down the road they went in silence. Berto spoke when they were almost back in Los Gatos.

"When the gringos they come?"

"After we get the insurance money." Beto answered.

"We tell them to come now."

"They'd know it was a trick, it's too soon." Beto answered.

"How long we wait?"

"Maybe a month?" Beto replied.

"Not possible; *Im-po-see-blay*. Gringos make trouble, we show them trouble."

"Too soon is not good brother, I tell you this Umberto. You have to listen to me. This is Estados Unidas, not Panama. It's different here." Beto was pleading.

"I like it here little brother, I do your way. But too many gringo-laws. At home I free, Federales reasonable men. Here, they like the men at military school, they want to push you around with their rules, beat you. I can push back now; I can beat them until they *beg* me to die." Berto had a settled worldview. Beto was unsettled and apprehensive; those were the words that described him.

*   *   *

Detective Davis was on the phone to Nigel Leeds of the Lloyd's of London insurance corporation.

"Good afternoon detective, you got something over on that side of the pond, hmmm?"

"Well, actually there are a few troubling developments."

"Such as detective?"

"Mr. Chacon received house guests the other day, five men are now in residence in his Los Gatos home."

"I see, anything else?"

"It's a little thing, a discrepancy. Mr. Chacon stated that he threw on a robe and went down to the break-in sight right away. However, a member of the security detail stated that Mr. Chacon arrived in a nice pair of shoes and a snazzy jacket."

I see. It is an odd thing. What do you make of it?'

"The thing that bothers me most is that one of the arrivals is identical in features to Mr. Chacon and Beto Chacon has a twin. Umberto Chacon of Panama City appears to be visiting his brother."

"And what do we know of this Umberto chap?"

"He is a known smuggler and a social deviate."

"How unsavory." Nigel Leeds commented.

'Yes, unsavory. He is not traveling alone, that's troubling too."

"Sticky-wicket, perhaps?"

"It could be. My fear right now is that Chacon has the diamonds and the muscle from Panama has arrived."

"Oh dear, insurance fraud? You are alleging that, then? Will you get a search warrant? What are your intentions?"

"Not yet. The one thing I don't want is a shooting war in Los Gatos. If those men in that house are bodyguards, entering won't be easy. I think I have to bring in the Feds before we get a warrant to search."

"I think so too, it is rather growing at an alarming rate if all seems as you say. Keep me posted Mr. Davis, but I tell you this; the minute you find evidence that the stones are in his possession, I call Scotland Yard." Nigel Leeds said his good-byes and went on to the other cases piled on his desk. His assistant walked into the office.

"Trouble with the Americans sir?"

"Possibly. We may have a fraud on our hands. A rather substantial sum is at stake."

"Oh dear."

* * *

Van Zant and Joaquin sat across from Cash. They were at the pawn shop, in the back office. This waiting business was bothering more people than Berto. It had been two weeks since the heist and everyone was getting edgy.

"So, what we doin' here? We waitin' for Chacon to get insurance money, that the play?" Cash asked, knowing the answer.

"Right, we are waiting." Van Zant answered.

"You are still good with that Joaquin?" Cash said.

"I guess so, what else? We could demand the real diamonds now, I guess. There are cops nosing around now, Zilm seen 'em. That's an added risk to us if we got the stones." Joaquin said.

"Damn right it's a risk. It's all risky shit now. We really stepped in it this time." Cash replied.

"You guys' better stay cool." Van Zant said.

"Rick and Eddie are getting nervous." Joaquin said.

"Well, you better talk those boys down if they be on the ledge. Eddie-he be seeing flying saucers and aliens and Rick does everything Eddie tells him to." Cash said.

"It's not that bad, Cash. Eddie just likes to talk tough; he thinks he's a rapper-gangster." Joaquin defended.

"Okay, well, it's on you then; keep you eye on those boys." Cash cautioned.

"What concerns me is our next move. I'm starting to feel like my ass is out in the open. Do we got this figured out right? Chacon is on the hook for fraud and we're on the hook for grand theft. It's like one of those Mexican stand-off things." Joaquin said.

"The circular firing squad." Cash said.

"'Zactly." Joaquin answered.

"Man's right, Van. If Chacon go south; what do we get? We get the jail." Cash took them further down the road of doubt.

"Then what do we do?" Joaquin posed a question.

"Could demand the stones." Cash repeated the alternative.

"You gotta be prepared to back your play up." Van Zant observed.

"Man's right." Cash said and silence descended like overcast skies.

"If he gets out with the goods and he gets out of the country, it looks bad for the good guys." Joaquin said.

"Meaning us." Van said.

"Meaning FUBAR." Joaquin answered.

"Tango Uniform-toes up." Van said.

"The question still be out there; *now what*? We got to go to war now?" Cash posed.

Well, here it was, Mandy was right; the gambler chasing his losses. The caper was off the chain now that armed thugs were involved. The three of them hadn't fired a weapon since the 1968 Tet Offensive forty years ago-and that didn't go so well either. Now here they were, forced to contemplate a shoot-out.

"Maybe it's time to re-think this cluster." Cash said.

CHAPTER 19

The OK Corral

Men in the dark of the night crept along the stone wall in a residential neighborhood of Los Gatos, ahead of them stood the oak tree they would use to access the yard of Beto Chacon. The men were armed and carried glass bottles of gasoline. They're objective was to get the stones, they assumed they were in the house. It was a chancy gambit; there was no guarantee that the stones *were* in this house, but the chances were good that they were.

There was a four-way Nintendo game going on inside the house and the Panamanian gun thugs shouted and shot at zombies walking down narrow corridors, popping up around blind corners and all the rest of those annoying things that zombies are known to do. Berto had purchased some goldfish that day and he was amusing himself in the kitchen adding toxic ingredients to their water bowl to see the effect. Beto was on his laptop looking at porn. Outside, the security guard and the doggie slept on the front porch in the quiet neighborhood. The intruders entered the compound by an overhanging tree branch. Their first objective was to take out the guard and dog on the porch.

"You sure we gots' the right house, fool?" One intruder said to his associate criminal.

"Yeah, I be sure. I did that Zillow-thing they gots' now. These computers be crazy man. I Google this, I Zillow that, I Link-in, I Link-out and I *know* shit. They even got satellite pictures." Replied the associate criminal.

"Cool." The group crept along the side of the house to the front door where the dog and the guard were sound asleep.

"Bow-wow, you dead." Moreese smiled a big toothy grin, revealing his grill and diamond tooth before he pulled the trigger on his Glock 32 with a silencer. The dog and guard immediately slumped where they were without a sound after receiving shots at close range. Moreese Brown signaled the rest of his group and they let go the firebombs against the walls and roof of the house. They waited quietly in ambush for the occupants to flee. In the house, the breaking bottles against the walls did not go unnoticed after they exploded.

"Berto!" Beto shouted in alarm.

"Get guns!" Berto responded. Four men in the living room dropped the Nintendo controls and reached for the weapons. Berto was right there with them, grabbing the big .50 cal and the ammo box. Beto ran for the safe in the bedroom and proceeded to grab the ornate little wooden box that contained 9 million dollars in diamonds. He ran into the living room and spoke to his brother.

"Berto! Into the garage, into the Maserati! I got the stones." Beto informed in a panic.

"You two go out the front, you two go out the back." Berto instructed his posse.

The front door of the burning house flung open, and the Panamanian guard made it about three steps before he was hit; a hail of bullets knocked him back and his Uzi sprayed wildly over the yard, killing the homey standing in front of him. The other gun thug stepped back into the house and dropped down and proceeded to fire from the cover of the doorway. The backdoor was covered by the homies as well and the two big Panamanians got their final reward in America when they exited. The brothers, covered by an enclosed hallway to the garage, went unnoticed in their escape. However, Moreese was right there lying in wait by the door of the Maserati. Berto immediately dropped to the garage floor behind the car when Moreese opened fire, pulling his brother down with him. He opened up with the .50 caliber and holes began to appear in the Maserati, glass shattered, holes appeared in the walls of the garage. There wasn't much that could withstand Berto's fusillade at close range and he slapped clip after clip in the chattering rifle that spit spent cartridges out the side faster than you could pull a trigger. Moreese clung to the floor for cover but there was no shelter there. Several rounds removed his head and several more reduced his torso to a bloody stump, piece by fleshy piece.

Cop One and Cop Two were still across the street in their car, both asleep. But not for long.

"What the fuck is going on over there?" Cop Two reached for the shotgun, cop one reached for the microphone.

"Unit 55, we got gunfire at 10535 Stratford, Chacon residence. Multiple shots." He spoke.

Cop Two flung open the door. "Let's go-you go around the back. I'll cover the front."

"Wait a minute cowboy- put on your vest first!" Said Cop One.

The Shotgun Cop charged across the street after donning his vest and slid behind a little tree, looking for the shooter. Bullets started hitting the dirt all around him and chipping wood chunks from the tree. The shooter was one of the homies left in the yard outside the front door. He was in the shrubbery somewhere, not too far away. Shotgun Cop opened up with the shotgun on automatic, smoke and noise came from the little cannon and six shots roared from the stubby little barrel. The shrubbery served as no cover and the homey dropped to the ground, full of 00 buckshot balls the size of little marbles. Cop One ran up behind Shotgun Cop.

"There's still a bad guy or two in the backyard." He spoke.

No sooner had he said that then more shots pocked the turf around them. The homey had emerged from the backyard and now he was here in front of them, standing straight up, arm outstretched, holding his weapon sideways, just like he had seen in his favorite black gangsta movie (black gangsters shoot like that as a courtesy to the opposing shooter, they make for a better target that way). Shots also came from the gun thug crouched in the front door. Suddenly the cops were in a deadly crossfire behind the little tree. Shotgun Cop reloaded and while he got ready for the next go-round, his partner took three hits in the torso. The bullets were lodged in his vest, and he was knocked back and stunned. He returned fire blindly toward the side yard where the shots came from. One of his hollow point rounds found its mark, the bullet expanded as it entered the body of the target and tore tissue and broke bone. The homey collapsed where he stood.

Shotgun Cop was reloaded with six shots of 00 buck. He sighted the remaining Panamanian shooter, now running from the burning house with his oily hair and his silk shirt on fire. Shotgun cop unloaded all the rounds in the direction of the flaming man. It was like a cannon broadside; nine balls to the cartridge can make a lot of big holes at close range. In fact, the Panamanian guy was hit 27 times by little balls, and they almost cut him in half. His upper torso continued to burn.

"I think you got 'um." Said Cop One from his place on the ground.

In the garage, Moreese lay on the floor, his head was gone, removed by rounds from Berto's killing machine.

"Stop Berto, he's dead already! Out the back, let's go!" Beto shouted. The brothers crawled toward the door and snuck out into the backyard.

Red and blue lit cars and fire engines were arriving out in the street now, doors flung open, weapons were leveled toward the garage. Four more policeman chased the two fleeing brothers into the backyard. The moment Berto had waited for arrived; he turned and fired his grenade rifle. Umberto put tear gas and fragmentation grenades amongst the pursuing cops, and they began to drop. Shotgun Cop and Cop One gave chase into the backyard. They saw Umberto's eyes just before they took a direct hit at close range from a frag grenade. The bodies exploded in pieces. Berto squealed with glee.

"Oh brother, *lookee* me!!" Berto shouldered the weapon and fired another grenade before they both took off running.

After the explosions stopped, the cops at the cars poked up their heads and saw that it was their turn to give pursuit. Four of them ran through the smoke, cautiously, and continued down the side of the garage. The newly arrived SWAT team sent four men around the other side of the house. The frag grenades were a caution, so both groups approached the backyard slowly and stealthily and the fleeing brothers put some distance between their pursuers. Overhead, a helicopter searched with bright lights and tracked the fleeing assailants. As the policemen and SWAT team emerged into the backyard, *they* were assaulted by a barrage of frag grenades. They dropped to the ground for cover. More police cars showed up.

"Keep going brother, don't stop." Berto was breathless but determined, now fleeing at a dead run through the yards, straddling fences.

"I'm with ya." Beto said from his position behind Berto. "Chopper overhead somewhere?" He heard one before he saw it.

"Is problem." Berto answered.

The SWAT team members opened up with their M-14's at the fleeing assailants, who were hopping fences, getting farther away. Beto let out a cry.

"Berto! Berto! I dropped the box! It's on the other side of the fence!" Beto was frantically trying to reach the box through the chain link fence. The cops were getting closer.

Plants and trees lost branches in the hail of bullets; the bullets shredded everything in their trajectory. 200 rounds were fired in less than a minute. The SWAT team reloaded and continued to give chase. Beto left the box where it lay and ran to join his brother. The helicopter had spotted the brothers and was giving radio reports of their position.

Beto and Berto were underneath a car, temporarily out of sight from the chopper. They were catching their breath.

"What are we gonna do now brother? We give up yet?" Beto was wheezing.

"No, we don't give up. They shoot us now-we die here in street like dogs. We cop-killers now." Berto answered. Surrender was out of the question; that ship sailed after they killed the first cop.

"Are we gonna die here Berto?" Beto was trembling.

"We all die someday mi hermano pequeno, I no wanna die today. We steal car; una primero, el helicopter tiene que morir!" Berto instructed. He leaned out from beneath the car and located the chopper overhead.

Berto took a bead on the chopper with the .50 caliber and fired three rounds and they all hit the flimsy aluminum fuselage. The rounds passed clear through it, severing hydraulic lines and electrical wires along the way before they came out the other side and went heavenward. The helicopter went sideways and then it went down into an adjacent back yard with a terrible explosion and fireball. Berto immediately got up and ran.

"Berto! Berto! Come back!" Beto was frantic and was left under the car, hollering.

"We split up, steal a car, save yourself!" Berto hollered at the ground ahead of him; never looking back at his brother. Beto wanted to quit, just give up, he had nothing now. He watched Berto disappear.

There came a burst of gunfire from over in the distant yard. Beto was alone, left behind under the car. All the commotion was now travelling away from him and toward the fleeing brother. It was getting quiet in his vicinity. Beto did have his life, but the little wooden box was lost in the chase. No way was he going back and look for it or he would surely die. He began to creep out of the neighborhood with all the stealth he could muster.

*   *   *

What is better than being a grandparent? Being a grandchild off course! Mrs. Patterson: age 74, dowdy, white hair, spectacles with a grand-motherly and pleasant demeanor, had just concluded a visit at her daughter's house and the two little curly haired cherubs in matching pink dresses stood in the doorway saying good-bye to Grandma.

"Good-bye my little sweeties, see you next week." She said to the little girls.

"Will you bring donuts grandma?" Said the taller girl.

"Of course, I'll bring donuts." She replied.

"With sprinkles grandma?" Said the short one. Actually, both girls were short.

"With sprinkles dear." Grandma replied.

"Thanks Mom, drive safe." Her daughter had the last word as she ushered her two little girls back inside the house and shut the door. Mrs. Patterson, self-satisfied, full of love and warm thoughts on the state of mankind, God, and all his good works, departed after her weekly Sunday dinner. She turned for her car parked in the driveway. She liked her car, kept it clean and the red color was always cheerful and bright. The grandchildren loved to go for a drive and Mrs. Patterson kept two car seats in the back just for them.

Backing out of the driveway, she looked both ways down quiet suburban streets, empty of pedestrians and cars. It was late, it was dark, the weekly dinner prepared by her daughter was over. She had heard the sirens a while ago, but they were long gone now. The fire a few blocks away was now extinguished. She pulled her little red car up to the first stop sign, reflecting pleasantly on her blessed life.

Berto emerged from behind the shrubbery of the corner house, his eyes wild with desperation, his five o'clock shadow now at midnight, hair sticking out in all directions. This was it for him-it was all on the line; die like a dog in the streets or escape to Panama. He dashed toward the red car stopped at the corner and grabbed the door handle. Mrs. Patterson looked at the wild hair and eyes of Berto and screamed. She froze; screaming at the rear-view mirror and unable to look out her window at the desperate man again. Berto did not hesitate; he slammed the butt of his rifle into the window, smashed it, and flung open the door.

"Move over abuela! I kill you!" Beto threatened her and Mrs. Patterson screamed louder, still frozen stiff. Berto pushed her over. Grandma Patterson was now sobbing and wheezing uncontrollably in the passenger seat. Berto was now behind the wheel, and he drove off to the sounds of the weeping old lady.

"Shut up!" He slapped her and slammed her head against the window. She screamed. She began to cry harder. Berto wanted no part of her, but he kept his head. She was going with him for now as a hostage. She couldn't talk to the cops if she was in the car. The time would come to push her out and he imagined what it would look like; the old lady out the door of a fast moving car, tumbling ass-over-teakettle down the freeway. It arrived in his head as a cheerful thought, and it brought a brief smile to his psychopathic face before he slapped her again. She shut up this time. He drove slowly through the sedate suburban streets, looking for the freeway entrance sign. He knew that a roadblock may soon impede his plan, but he had a hostage if it came to that. He must get to Los Angeles; he knew people there and it was close to the border. Berto had seen enough of this god-forsaken country.

Beto continued to hotfoot it through the backyards and alleys, making his way towards a bright yellow glare that he hoped was a Denny's where he might take refuge and wait for a convenient Uber.

*   *   *

Mahmoud could hardly stay awake behind the wheel of his Prius. Three jobs were pushing him to the limit. 10 years of study at the University and an engineering degree in Iran only qualified him as an Uber driver in America. Why was everything Middle Eastern so discounted in America? What kinda people were these? Being an Uber driver served to augment his other two jobs so that he and the family could eat and have a roof over their heads. America: he loved it, but all was not as it seemed, you could live in hope, but that might be all you lived in for a long while. Some immigrants who came from the old country now had stores, gas stations, donut shops, spas, dry cleaners, businesses of their own and he hoped for this. His Uber phone lit up with a request for a ride 5 blocks away. He signaled he was on his way. It was 1:30 AM, and the destination was a nearby Denny's.

Sitting in a booth at Denny's at 1:30 AM, Beto Chacon fit right in with the clientele around him. After emerging from the backyards and under a car, Beto's torn and dirty clothes raised no eyebrows amongst the late-night crowd at the counter and in the booths. He handled his cup of coffee and awaited the arrival of Mahmoud and the Uber Prius.

Outside, there were police cars patrolling and another helicopter overhead. Inside, Beto felt safe as he waited for the Uber getaway car. The white Prius arrived and Beto met it at the curb and climbed in.

"Airport."

"Arriving or departing?"

"Departing flights."

"No baggage?"

"No baggage."

Beto sat in the backseat for the short ride to the airport. It was a race, the cops would figure it out, but hopefully he would be at 10,000 feet above Mexico by then. He was on his way to Panama, wearing dirty rags. Better penniless in Panama than incarcerated in San Jose. What had become of Berto? Their shit was in the wind now and any way the wind blew, that is where the brothers would land. There were a lot more questions than answers. The main thing, the trick at hand, was to get through security and make it to the departing gate before it *hit* the fan.

Occasionally, Mahmoud would look in the rearview mirror at the fidgety and disheveled man with no baggage going to the airport. Something was a little off about this fare, but so was everything else about his new country. Mahmoud pulled into the parking structure and let Chacon out of the car and Chacon wasted not a second getting out. The place was empty, save for a lonely employee at the counter, staring at the screen of her phone. Chacon went to the ticket counter. He stared at the big flight board looking for a flight to Panama City. There was a flight tomorrow, ETD at 4PM. He'd be in jail by then if he stayed here. He went over to the person at the United counter. There was an alternative.

"I would like to purchase a ticket on the United flight # 172 to Mexico City." Chacon said.

"Let's see." She stared at the computer screen. "Sir, that flight leaves in less than an hour, you barely have time to board."

"That's okay, I need to join my sister on that particular flight." Chacon fibbed convincingly.

"I see. Will that be round trip or one way?" She asked.

"One-way please, we live in Mexico and are going home." Chacon fibbed again. The counter lady printed out his ticket and boarding pass, Chacon handed her the credit card and that was that. He breezed through security and hot footed it to Gate #92 and freedom from prison or death. He too, like Mahmoud, was now living in hope.

CHAPTER 20

Turtle Bowl

By morning, it was all in the news, the big shootout in Los Gatos; dead bodies, house fire, chopper down. All the networks were there, and the question arose over and over; who is this dandy Beto Chacon anyway? Detective Davis had been up for hours, and he finally got some sleep at 7AM. Within minutes of laying down, he woke up again to the alarm clock; the news of the shootout was coming over and over on his clock radio.

"Last night in Los Gatos, an apparent robbery attempt went terribly wrong and resulted in a shootout. The dead included gang members and police, and the loss of a police helicopter. The pilot of the helicopter is in critical condition with third degree burns. Witnesses described numerous gunshots fired in the quiet suburban neighborhood and a home was burned to the ground. The owner, Beto Chacon, is missing. 'Mr. Chacon is such a quiet man, so nice and polite, always so pleasant. I just don't understand how he could have been mixed up in this sort of thing.' Said neighbor Leonilda Hornsby."

"Oh shit, what a cluster." Davis spoke to himself as he stared at the ceiling from his comfortable bed. The phone began ringing and he knew right away that it was the captain.

"Davis-get your ass down here and give me your preliminary report-asap! We got dead cops. I don't like dead cops Davis and I don't care what all you know, make it sound like we have some idea, some notion of what the heck happened. You hear me? I don't want to hear some wishy-washy bullshit on the news tonight. I want suspects, I want arrests, I want to hear witness reports. I'm hearing about large caliber weaponry, frag grenades, tear gas and for God's sake, a police helicopter crashed! What the hell happened down there, WW III?" The captain was pissed, his chief was pissed, the mayor was pissed; everybody was all twisted up and they all wanted answers.

"Roger cap, I'm on it." Davis was so *not* on it. The only thing he was on was a Sealy mattress.

When Davis arrived back in Los Gatos an hour later, everybody was there. He pushed through a throng of cameras, reporters, first responders and gawkers. What was left of the Chacon residence was fenced off with yellow police tape and Davis lifted the barrier and entered the charred ruin. Forensic was there, the fire trucks still stood by, and the ambulances were long gone. Davis surveyed the wreckage with lieutenant Dean, drinking a large triple shot of Starbucks.

"Get any sleep?" Lieutenant Dean asked by way of polite conversation.

"No. And the captain is *up* my ass. What a mess this is." Davis said.

"There's more in the backyard, it gets worse." Lieutenant Dean said. "Who was this King-shit Chacon guy, anyway?"

"I suspect this will queer his insurance claim. He's a fugitive now." Davis stated.

"What insurance claim?" Dean asked.

"Chacon had a 9 million dollar claim with Lloyds for stolen diamonds. The Global Towers heist." Davis answered.

"So that's what this is all about then." Dean observed.

"No shit Sherlock. Dean: you're smarter than you look. The thing I can't understand is-why this carnage? It's a God damn suburban war zone! That's not Chacon's style, he's a finance guy; a dandy, an art dealer. This must be the work of the brother." Davis said.

"What brother?"

"Brother from Panama. Stakeout made him a couple of weeks ago, a twin at that." Davis informed.

"A 9 million dollar pile attracts a lot of flies." Dean observed.

"Apparently." They both stared at the charred rubble at their feet and kicked at the wreckage.

"Every department head and their dog wants answers. Everybody wants answers; what am I a magician? Like I can pull answers out of my butt like rabbits out of a hat?" Davis said.

"Like to see how many answers they can pull out of their butts." Dean had the last word before they split up.

Dean headed for the backyard. Davis walked through the ashes of the house. Everything flammable had burned and what was not burned, was melted. The brick chimney withstood the inferno, as did the toilets, tubs, sinks and one more thing, a little metal box over in another part of the wreckage. Davis walked toward it. As he got closer, he saw that it was a fireproof safe. The odd part of the scene was that the door of the safe was open.

"You forgot to close the safe door, Mr. Chacon. You *have to* close the door in order for the safe to work properly. Or…have you been a bad boy, Mr Chacon?" Davis mumbled quietly to himself. He took a few pictures. He motioned to Dean to check it out and Dean came over, kicking up ash and crunching charred wood.

"Check this out Dean." Davis motioned to the safe.

"Why is the safe door open? Whatever was in there, it's gone now." Dean went out on a very short limb.

"That's a real strong guess, Dean." Davis replied.

"Whoever or whatever, they were in a hurry." Dean said.

The two of them wandered into the backyard after snapping a million pictures of an open safe door. The evidence they found in the backyard showed that there had been a running gun battle. The ambulance cargo this morning confirmed that conclusively.

"Forensic got an ID on one of the victims, he had his wallet and passport in his back pocket. He was a Panamanian citizen who just entered the country two weeks ago, that's what we know for sure." Davis reported.

"Brother?" Dean asked.

"No; one of his pals. Umberto Chacon didn't travel alone." Davis was quick with that answer.

"So... the way it's adding up... a safe door is left open...somebody grabbed valuables from the open safe...then they ran out amidst a house fire... and into a gun battle?" Dean was slowly putting it together in his head.

"I'm nominating you for MENSA; Lieutenant Dean, that's genius police work." Davis said.

It didn't take long for the forensic team to add more clues to the puzzle. Davis and Dean learned that five of the bodies were local residents, black males, and all had minor criminal records from East Bay neighborhoods. Dean and Davis looked at each other upon learning that.

"Well, I'll be double-dipped in doo-doo, gangsters now? How do they fit into this?" Dean looked at Davis for answers as he spoke. The forensic guy hung up his cell phone and came over to the detectives. He told them of the information he had just received over the phone.

"Five bodies were locals; 4 bodies were of Panamanian origin and two of them were known to be mercenaries and wanted by the American consulate in Panama City for questioning in the murder of a judge."

"Shootout at the OK Corral?" Dean forwarded an opinion.

"All of that, but how do the East Bay guys fit into this?" Davis.

"Were they mixed up with the Global heist?" Dean asked.

"Global was the work of trained pros with precise knowledge of electronic security. They used a plasma torch and a construction crane for Christ sakes! That was not a rip-and-run robbery." Davis replied.

"Well, this sure was." Dean said.

"You surprise me sometimes, Dean. Astute." Davis said.

"Wait a minute; whoever... why then... if it was about jewels...why would they rob ...Chacon twice? Unless.........." Dean pondered.

"Chacon was in on it." Davis finished his thought.

*   *   *

Detective Dean went back to the office and Davis went home to type up his preliminary report and go to bed and sleep. Home was a two-bedroom apartment in South City. As a detective, Davis had an adequate career record, but as a homemaker he was a complete failure. There was no furniture; unpacked boxes and folding chairs served as furniture. He did buy a bed and a couch after the divorce but that had been the extent of his nest building phase. No sooner had he opened his apartment door, but the phone rang.

"Davis? What have you got so far? I got everybody and his brother on my ass with questions I don't have answers for." Captain Rogers was on the phone.

"Well chief, it looks like a robbery attempt and arson. We got 4 dead Panamanians and 5 dead guys from Oakland, and I can't put that together. Yet, that is. Beto Chacon is a fugitive charged with insurance fraud. He and his brother are missing, airport and border security are notified."

"That's great Davis, but what can we tell the cameras?" Captain Rogers asked.

"That Beto Chacon is missing, charged with insurance fraud and his house was burned to the ground in a robbery attempt by a local gang." Davis summed it up.

"If that's what we got, that's what we go with then. It might even be true. Good police work, Davis." Captain Rogers had his story.

"That's all I got for right now, Chief, I'll keep you posted." Davis rung off and that was the end of the conversation.

*   *   *

"Bobby; look at this!" Frenchy and Zilm were at the breakfast table. She slapped the front page of the newspaper with the back of her hand and held it up for Bobby to see. "*Gun Battle in Los Gatos*" it read in bold and big type.

"Lemme see that thing." Just one look and his stomach dropped three stories. Zilm reached for his cell phone. He called Joaquin.

"Joaquin; see the paper?"

"I saw it. The guys called; they saw it too."

"What do we do?"

"What can we do? Apparently, our play just went shithouse. Kiss those jewels good-bye."

"I'll think of something-it can't end like this, can it?" Zilm went into his whining mode.

"We're free and alive, Zilm. That's something, I guess." Joaquin.

"Yeah, but I can't spend that, now, can I?" Zilm.

"No." Joaquin.

"I'll call Cash, see what he thinks." Zilm was ready to grasp at anything; was there not any scrap of hope of him becoming a millionaire?

"Yeah, let's all go over there and cry." Joaquin said with unveiled sarcasm.

*   *   *

At Cash's place that morning, there were a lot of long faces.

"Cash; What do we do now?" Zilm was pleading.

"Question be, what we *don't* do now. Chacon on the run, so they know he dirty, we're good long as we stay quiet."

"Yeah, I guess." Zilm answered.

"Free and alive, Zilm; let's keep it that way." Joaquin said.

"Chacon was in line for the big insurance payoff. All he had to do is sit it out. His house burns down and if he had somethin' to see in there? And if they found diamonds in that burned up house? That be a different story, he'd be busted on the spot. I bet that boy grabbed somethin' and ran, I lay ten to one on that." Cash said and silence descended on the hapless group, some in pajamas, some fully dressed. Another arrival at the door and it was Eddie, late as usual.

"Did you see the news?" Eddie asked the group.

"We *is* the news fool-*we* is the bad news." Cash said.

"Yeah, Eddie; they shot guys, gangsters from the hood, cops too." Rick offered.

"What 'hood?" Eddie asked.

"One guy from Jingletown. They ID'ed one of the dead guys by his diamond studded grill, I remember that 'cause they say that was all that was left of his head." Rick was his usual unenthusiastic self when he gave his report. Joaquin looked over to see how Cash reacted to this news.

"Jingletown gangsters?" Van Zant asked, and silence once again visited the group.

"You know anything about this Cash?" Joaquin asked. "You know this black guy with the grill?" Joaquin asked.

"You think we all know each other, cracker? Like, we all be in the same tribe or somethin'? There's a million black folk in the East Bay, for Christ sakes! How am I gonna know *one* gangster-dude? That be some racist bullshit right there Joaquin." Cash said, playing the race card. He knew Moreese from Jingletown all right, but this was not the time to discuss *that*.

"How did gangsters get involved in this? While we're sitting around with our dick in our hand and some pansy-ass note, Chacon gets robbed by homies from the 'hood? How does that happen?" Eddie asked the question.

"Maybe they read about the Global diamonds in the papers?" Cash forwarded.

"That don't add up." Joaquin said.

"Maybe Chacon was working with these gangster guys?" Van Zant posed the question.

"That's a possibility." Joaquin mused.

"It's confusing to me." Rick joined in.

"Maybe the gangsters double-crossed Chacon and it went bad?" Eddie said.

"We'll never know now." Joaquin said.

"Dead men tell no tales." Rick added to the thought, "That was a good movie; an oldie but a goodie."

"That could have been you boy's dead in that yard, think on that." Frenchy said and added "You might have gotten lucky; lucky in an unlucky sort of way, I guess."

The assembled group was silent, Frenchy had gotten them to thinking on that unpleasant scenario. After the long silence, the soft voice of Rick broke it.

"This didn't go so well, did it? It was a lot bigger job than we thought." Rick said. Everyone turned his way and looked at him, slightly stunned by the naivete of the understatement and his worldview of things large and small.

"No Rick; it didn't go so well." Joaquin.

"Can I keep the box of rocks?" Rick asked the group.

"Rick, why would you want those worthless colored rocks?" Joaquin asked.

"I want them for my turtle bowl." Rick answered.

"Lord have mercy on that simple son-of-a-bitch." Cash said, standing in front of an old, framed picture of a high school athletic award presentation with Moreese Brown.

About the Author

Ernie Koepf resides in the East Bay with his wife Jan Moestue. They live with Elsie the dog and the 20 year old cat, Jenna. He is formerly a commercial fisherman out of Half Moon Bay, Ca. Please feel free to contact him at nearshoreguy@hotmail.com.